TRUE TERYN

THE LAST LUMENIAN SERIES

BOOK II

S.G. BLAISE

First paperback edition December 2021

Book cover design by Tim Barber from Dissect Designs
Edited by Julie Tibbott and William Drennan from NY Book Editors
Map Illustrated by Clif Chandler
Publisher: Lilac Grove Entertainment LLC

Paperback ISBN: 978-1-7347605-4-5
E-Book ISBN: 978-1-7347605-2-1

www.sgblaise.com

To Alex:
you were right; it did take less than six years to write the second book.

To Gabe:
who read this book as well (without any complaining).

To My Mom:
whose wonderful cooking fueled this book.

To all of you, Dear Readers, who came back for more.
Please know that it means the world to me!

PROLOGUE

In the beginning, the Omnipower created an archgod to govern the Seven Galaxies. It was an entity neither male nor female. Nameless, ruling over the twelve elements: A'ris and Dusky A'ris, A'qua and Murky A'qua, Fla'mma and Black Fla'mma, T'erra and Barren T'erra, A'nima and Diseased A'nima, Lume and Acerbus. It was power. A dark energy.

It took billions of years of worship to give it a form, gender, and names such as the Archgod of Chaos and Destruction, the Slayer of Souls, and the Dark Lord of Destruction. He ruled for many millennia, chaos and corruption reigning free, until She, a second archgod, Archgoddess of the Eternal Light and Order, was created. For the Balance.

Now the twelve elements were separated into six light elements: A'ris, A'qua, Fla'mma, T'erra, A'nima, and Lume; and six chaos elements: Dusky A'ris, Murky A'qua, Black Fla'mma, Barren T'erra, Diseased A'nima, and Acerbus. Each archgod ruling over their corresponding light or dark elements. For the Balance.

But the balance was not achieved. The Archgod of Chaos and Destruction wanted all the elements and the control back, creating a severe imbalance. Thus the first Era War broke out to restore the Balance.

The Archgod of Chaos and Destruction was too powerful, spreading corruption and creating His army of dark servants out of corrupted people, and dark fiends out of corrupted animals. Thus the Omnipower allowed the Archgoddess of the Eternal Light and Order to create Her army to fight back. For the Balance.

Hence a race of people called Lumenians was made from the six light elements, the very essence of the archgoddess and piece of Her soul. They were created to fight the corrupted and destroy them with their legendary Lume power—the one magical power that can disintegrate a fully corrupted dark servant or dark fiend. The Lumenians were so powerful they even defeated the last Ankhar, the general and beloved son-figure of the archgod.

The furious Archgod of Chaos and Destruction sought vengeance. He hunted the Lumenians to the brink of extinction. There was only one left to take up the mantel of sybil to become the general and right hand to the Archgoddess of the Eternal Light and Order: Lilla of the ruling House of Serrain of Uhna, the last Lumenian. Just in time to fight in the new, brewing Era War.

CHAPTER 1

"I'm not afraid," I mutter. My breath comes out in a puff of fog as I watch the tremendous black spaceship descend a hundred feet from me. It aims to land at the edge of the snow-covered Fye Island, where my friends and I wait.

The two setting suns paint the massive warship, the size of a small city, in a rosy light. I shiver as my gaze trails its jagged surface with cannons, missiles, and energy-shield piercing arrays. I've witnessed these world-erasing weapons in action.

"Good," Callum says. He tucks a long, dark violet strand of hair behind my ear. "Don't show fear and you'll be fine." His clear blue eyes glint with encouragement in his tanned face. The pale line of the scar that runs from his left eyebrow to his jaw crinkles as he gives me a smile. He looks younger than his twenty-five years, projecting a confident aura, dressed in his black, military-style uniform that emphasizes his muscular body.

I look away from Callum before he can detect worry in my dark violet eyes.

Muscles tremble in my belly. I press a hand over it, pretending to smooth my silver cape. I inhale the crisp winter air, which smells of the promise of snow.

I shouldn't be this scared! I am nineteen years old and not a child anymore!

I close my eyes for a second. The black spaceship and the desolate ruins of the Crystal Palace that was once my home disappear from my view. I can't imagine what Callum's father thinks of my "backwater" world of Uhna that he planned to conquer, not ally with. But his plans had to change once I claimed his son.

The powerful spacecraft lowers three clawlike black metal prongs that tear into the frozen ground. Chunks of rocks break off from the island's cliff-side and plunge into the Fyoon Ocean below. Gusts of hot air, smelling of brine and metal grease, whip dirt into our faces.

Ten feet away on my right, a pair of wooden double doors remain. Still intact, they survived the devastation the Archgod of Chaos and Destruction, aka DLD, wreaked on Uhna. They stand proudly, refusing to give in to reality. The hot air from the Teryn ship blasts the doors, shaking them in their frame. The wood creaks, resisting the pressure for a moment. Then the doors come crashing down to the ground. If they couldn't survive the arrival of the Teryn praelor, what chance do I have?

The back of the spaceship opens. A long metal ramp slams into the ground, reverberating under our feet. Black-clad Teryn warriors rush out, lining up like a living corridor in front of us.

Watching them, I realize I should have prepared better! I should have dressed more formally! Or I should have . . .

A hand touches my arm. I look down beside me at Glenna, my best friend and healer.

"You can do this," Glenna whispers, her dark crimson eyes full of compassion. "You've faced worse and come out stronger."

Nodding, I take a deep breath to release the tension.

A large but fit older man steps out of the ship. He wears a black uniform similar to Callum's but with a lot more colorful buttons on its lapel. There is no denying the familial resemblance between them. With a grimace, the man takes in the sad state of Fye Island. Then his piercing blue gaze lands on me.

I smile in welcome, not showing fear. I hope.

The older man's expression turns dark as he marches toward me. I can't help but wonder if he is upset about my Bride's Choice claim on Callum. We have never met, and he is already disappointed in me. Did he want someone else for his son?

I gulp down my rising anxiety.

The praelor wears an expression of confidence that borders on arrogance. He stops inches from me.

I refuse to step back and give in to intimidation.

Callum clears his throat and says, "Father, this is Ma'hana—"

I flinch at his use of my royal title. "Just Lilla," I interrupt him. I'm a princess in name only. There is a change happening to the Uhnan monarchy, and it may not last much longer.

4

"Sybil Lilla," Callum continues, "right hand of the Archgoddess of the Eternal Light and Order, general to Her armies in this Era War."

I cringe. This title sounds even worse. I have nothing to show for it—no army, only my seven friends who decided to join me, my only allies.

"General, is it?" the older man says with a snort.

Callum ignores his father and turns to me. "Lilla, meet Caderyn a'ruun, the Teryn praelor."

Caderyn crosses his thick muscular arms while glaring down at me. Even his short black beard, with a few gray hairs in it, looks furious.

What do you say to a warmongering emperor who has conquered many worlds and displaced thousands of refugees from their homes in the process? Refugees that sought asylum on Uhna. "It's uh . . ." I pause. I can't say it's an honor to meet him when he arrived at my world prepared to blast the corruption away with his armada, along with anyone who happened to be in his way.

I focus on his positive traits and say, "You have a nice beard! It looks well established. May I call you Caderyn?"

Caderyn scoffs. "No."

CHAPTER 2

Caderyn sure doesn't beat around the seaweed! A directness I have not experienced growing up in the Uhnan court.

Being a ma'hana in the royal court, the high society ma'hars and ma'haras, lords and ladies, kept a close eye on me, weighing my actions. They judged the unique looks I inherited from my mom, combined with my unwillingness to take part in their social machinations and found me lacking. The court voiced their opinions in vicious whispers behind my back, anonymously, yet ensuring they would get back to the ma'ha, making the king disheartened in me.

Then Callum a'ruun, second general of the Teryn army from Galaxy Six, came to Uhna because my father invited the Teryn praelium to diplomatic talks. Father had heard the news of other worlds getting conquered by the Teryn empire and wanted to avoid that very fate for Uhna, capital of the nineteen-planet-strong Pax Septum Coalition tucked away in Galaxy Five.

Caderyn returns my look with a scowl. Even Father couldn't hold a judgmental stare this long.

"You can't come with us," Caderyn says, prompting a gasp of outrage from my friends.

I open my mouth to argue, but Callum beats me to it. "Why not? I'm hers and she is mine!"

Blood rushes to my face, burning. I wish Fye Island would open up under my feet, and the Fyoon Ocean swallow me up.

Callum's best friend, Teague, who is a colonel in the Teryn army, winks at me with his dark brown eye. He drags a hand through his black hair that has streaks of scarlet, white, and blond. "What General Callum meant to say is that Sybil Lilla had invoked the Bride's Choice. As per our tradition, she has claimed Callum and she is entitled to—"

Caderyn laughs. "Son, no one is entitled here except me."

"What do you mean I can't come with you? I haven't even asked!" I say, finding my voice.

"First, those spaceships are mine, including the one Callum came here with, and not free to use as you wish," Caderyn says. "Second, you are not a Teryn, and as such I do not have to honor your Bride's Choice claim. We are done here."

"That won't do," the Archgoddess of the Eternal Light and Order—or The Lady, as I like to call her—says from next to me. With that one declaration, Caderyn destroyed any chance for love I had with Callum. I knew I was a fool to imagine that Callum and I could ever be together, fighting in the Era War.

Bitterness brings tears into my eyes, but I refuse to let those tears escape.

I look at Her and find myself in a perfect and beautiful meadow, with long grass stalks swaying in a balmy spring breeze, like ocean waves. Acolyte Aisla, the petite and blonde replica of the ethereally beautiful and golden-skin-toned archgoddess, raises her chin in my direction in an almost greeting while wearing a white wraparound dress just like the archgoddess.

"What won't do?" I ask The Lady with forced calm. She likes to transport me to this meadow that does not to exist in real life, whenever She feels like it. Usually when it's the most inconvenient for me, like now.

An explosion of happiness cascades down my spine from the Sybil talisman at the back of my neck, punishment for my insolence. The finger-length, oval, and transparent talisman that signals my Sybilhood amplifies the joyful emotions until they become an unbearable bombardment of pain, hovering at the boundaries of insanity. Attached to my spine with intricate gold filaments that extend from a pair of crab-like claws, the talisman is unremovable without the risk of dying in the process.

"Stop this!" I cry out and drop to my knees. Anger spreads through me, flaring up the magical silver marking on my back—a striking depiction of a tree with lush crown, wide trunk, and vines twining around it—covering from my neck to the middle of my back. My anger battles with the barrage of happiness but fails to neutralize its effects as it did before I was tricked into wearing the talisman.

"This will teach you to show your Archgoddess the respect She deserves," Aisla mocks.

"I . . . would . . . rather. . . die!" I say through clenched teeth.

The unbearable waves of love, happiness, and joy recede.

I get to my feet lest the archgoddess thinks I am prostrating for Her when it's the farthest from the truth. I'll never forgive Her for misleading me.

I rub my neck, and the despised talisman issues a strong electric zap that stings my fingers in response.

The Lady smiles at me, looking like benevolence personified with Her magnificent and divine beauty, but that kindness never reaches Her molten gold eyes. "I want you, my child, to go to the Teryn home world."

I did not expect Her to say that. "Did you not hear the praelor refusing to take me with him?"

"I want you, my child, to take over their army in my name."

"What . . . I mean, how? That's impossible!" I say. "I can't just announce that I am their new general and expect them to obey me! Why can't I start with another army first?"

"I need the Teryn army, and no other will do," The Lady says. "As to how you will acquire their army—you must figure it out on your own, my child. You seem to know the solution better than I do anyway."

"But—"

"Remember, my child, what is at stake—fail this mission and you will sacrifice trillions of innocent lives in the Seven Galaxies. The Archgod of Chaos and Destruction will kill them in His attempt to corrupt them for His army," The Lady says, and my face turns cold.

I will never forget the sight of those twisted, nightmarish, and corrupted *things*—the dark fiends and dark servants—that The Lady once showed me in a dream. I will never forget the scene on that red, rocky beach where I found a pile of dead bodies—people who died because the archgod tried to corrupt them—among them my beloved Deidre, the head chef. I made a promise to my mom, before she died, that I will always protect the innocents who cannot protect themselves. A promise I intend to keep, no matter what.

"Do not fail me, my child. You already botched defeating the archgod in His mortal form. It was our best chance to stop the Era War."

"I tried my best," I say. I know it's my fault. She doesn't have to remind me. I do that myself enough times, replaying the events of my battle with Him, wondering what went wrong. The battle that cost me dearly.

"Do not waste my time with excuses. They don't change the facts of your fiasco!" The Lady snaps. "I need the Teryn army and I need it now!"

I blink and the two divine women are gone.

CHAPTER 3

"What is wrong with her?" Caderyn asks, waving a hand in front of my face. "Why is she frozen like that?"

"Lilla," Callum asks, "can you hear me?"

"I, uh, yes," I say, and rub my forehead. "The Lady just ordered me to, uh, take over the Teryn army in Her name." There really is no better way, or better time to say it.

Caderyn throws back his head and laughs. "Never going to happen, little girl!"

Callum studies my face. "You are serious!"

I nod. "It's more important than anything else." More important than my Bride's Choice claim on Callum. I must keep my promise to my mom. I am responsible for trillions of lives in the Seven Galaxies. Even if it breaks my heart, I cannot put my own happiness in front of others.

I look away from Callum and his smug father.

The pulverized ruins of the once magnificent Crystal Palace face me, a sad reminder of the battle I had with DLD. The Lady is right. I failed. DLD escaped. Now the devastation that will happen in this Era War weighs heavily on my conscience.

I turn back to Caderyn and look him in the eyes. "Praelor, tell me what I must do for you to cooperate with the Archgoddess of the Eternal Light and Order and, by extension, with me," I say. "Even though you are supposed to be on Her side."

Caderyn laughs again. "The Teryn Senatus tried this tactic of appealing to my conscience. It did not work well for them. Just as it won't work for you, little girl. I know my duty and never needed others' input. There is nothing you can do to change my mind."

The praelor flicks his wrist in a circle. His warriors snap to attention, then make an about-face. All except for Callum.

Caderyn frowns at him. "What are you waiting for, son? We are leaving *now*."

Time stops. I look from Caderyn to Callum, knowing once an order was given by the praelor, Callum has no choice but to follow it. Disobedience results in a death sentence in the Teryn praelium.

"Wait!" I say, searching for a reason to change Caderyn's mind. "As sybil, I order you to stop!"

Caderyn chuckles. "The problem with titles, little girl, is that others have to recognize them or they have no power," he says and leans closer. "You could be the queen of the Seven Galaxies for all I care. As I said, you are not Teryn, and that is *all* that matters to me."

Callum steps in his father's way, a reddish-yellow light flashing across his blue irises. "I invoke the sixth rule!"

CHAPTER 4

Caderyn studies his son. After a long moment, he nods and snaps his fingers.

A Teryn warrior, with a mustache, dashes forward from the group.

The mustached warrior takes a round, red, and palm-size device out of his pocket. He throws the device in the air toward an open space on our left. Before the device can hit the ground, it bursts open into a twenty-foot-wide circle. A thin white line of light runs the circle's border, hovering at ankle height above the iridescent interior area.

Callum and Caderyn step over the line and move to the middle of the circle.

A loud chime sounds. The warriors surround the father and son with unveiled anticipation.

"What is going on?" I ask Teague, who had just finished eating a blue apple.

"Callum invoked the sixth Ground Rule," he says and hands me the apple core.

Holding it between two fingers, I ask, "What does that mean?"

I give the sticky core to Glenna, on my right. She makes a disgusted face and passes it to Elementalist Mage Ragnald on her right. The mage once served the royal house of Uhna. Now he is a magical mentor to me and a friend. The handsome two-hundred-year-old mage raises an eyebrow. He conjures a spark of Fla'mma and burns the apple core to ashes. The he pulls his long silver hair into a ponytail with a thin strip of leather and looks at me with storm-gray eyes as if to say, *You have magic too.*

I keep forgetting! It's still new to have the six light elements—A'ris for air; T'erra for soil; A'qua for water; Fla'mma for fire; A'nima for living things; and Lume for light—residing in a bright, white sphere somewhere in me, a specialty Lumenians have.

Teague places a hand on my elbow, guiding me to the edge of the strange circle, with my friends following. "They are about to start arguing," he says. "We shouldn't miss this."

The mustached warrior squats by the thin white line and touches the edge of the circle. A panel slides out with two circular buttons on it—a red and a green one. The warrior taps the red button. The white light that runs the border of the shimmering circle turns into knee-high flames.

Teague takes out a handful of purple boomberries from his pocket and shoves them in his mouth. "It's quite impressive technology, isn't it? Makes things so much easier." He wipes a splatter of purple juice from the corner of his mouth.

"Easier? How?" I ask.

Callum shakes his head. The warrior by the panel taps the red button again. The circle's border changes into three rows of daggers pointing inward.

Belthair gestures toward the circle with one of his six hands, his dark brown eyes glinting with interest. "How are the daggers better than the fire?" the ex-rebel captain—who once was my boyfriend and whom I thought dead until his shocking return to Uhna a few months ago—asks. "Wrong choice, in my opinion." He crosses his six arms over his muscular chest, clad in a black shirt that's tucked into gray pants. The cold winter wind rustles his short dark brown hair that frames a masculine and light-gray-toned face with sharp cheekbones.

Arrov stoops down from his nine-foot height behind us. "I agree. I'd prefer the fire if I were Callum." His weathered light blue face, framed with long light blue fur, shows interest. Ever since the battle with DLD, the once attractive prince and pilot has been stuck in an A'ice giant form due to a blast of corruption. Now he can't get out of this form.

The men around Arrov murmur, "Yes, much better."

Glenna asks, "Does anyone know what's going on?"

"We kind of figured it out," Isa says. She swipes short, black strands of hair, styled in a bob, off of her forehead. Her nearly identical twenty-year-old twin sister, Bella, nods. They are both dressed in a pink winter coat that doubles as a minidress. Their emerald-green eyes show unbanked excitement as they study the scene in front of them. Isa and Bella might have royal origins, but they are the best hackers in the Seven Galaxies, and my ex-rebel companions.

Caderyn shakes his head at the daggers. The mustached warrior taps the red button again. The border changes into three rows of laser lines reaching knee-high. Caderyn smiles, baring his white teeth. The warrior hits the green button and a loud horn blares.

Before the horn's sound can fade, Callum fakes a jab at Caderyn, following it up with a cross and a right hook combination.

"Are you telling me that they argue by *fistfighting*?!" I say. "How . . .? I mean, why . . .? I mean, stop this!"

I move to intervene when Teague's hand comes down my shoulder, hauling me back with unexpected force.

Teague squeezes my shoulder until it hurts, his expression livid. "Never, *ever*, cross a fight circle's boundary! You hear me? Never! Promise me right now!"

I blink at him. "Fine!" I shrug my shoulder, trying to dislodge it from his iron grip, but he won't let go. "I promise, okay?" What got into him?

Teague releases me and we turn back to the circle.

Caderyn avoids his son's hook by stepping out at an angle, then sucker-punches Callum.

"What you observe here, Lilla," Teague says, "is part of Teryn Ground Rules that the warriors follow strictly. Number six allows physical settling of disputes notwithstanding familiar ties between the *fightee*, who started the fight, and the *fighter*, who is challenged into a fight. The Ground Rules cover most types of fights, celebratory and contentious, stating that arguing must happen outside, on Teryn ground, never on a Teryn ship or in a Teryn building. If Teryn ground is not available, using a portable fight circle sanctions any ground. These rules cut down on brawls breaking out over the slightest issues, in the wrong places, causing unnecessary property damage."

Arrov nods in appreciation. "Sanctioned fisticuffs. How nice!" When I stare at him, he adds, "You have to admit, it is useful."

"How many of these rules do you have?" Isa and Bella ask before Glenna can say a word. They stick their tongue out at her, hoping to get a rise out of the healer. Sure enough, Glenna narrows her eyes back at them.

"There are ten of them," Teague says, watching Callum dodge a fury of punches from Caderyn while veering close to the laser lines, "but three hundred and fifty if you count the subrules, addenda, and clarifications."

Callum sidesteps at the last second, dancing away with quick feet to the other side of the circle.

"Why do you need so many?" I ask. I find this side of Teryn culture fascinating and peculiar at the same time.

Caderyn rushes at Callum, but Callum snaps his knee up and kicks out, right into his chest, propelling his father back a few steps.

Teague snorts. "The same question our Brainiacs ask. They desperately want to eradicate these rules!"

"Brainiacs?" I ask, but Teague doesn't hear my question as he shouts encouragement for Callum. His voice is one in the cacophony of shouts from other warriors.

Glenna tucks the white strand of hair behind her ear and looks at me. "I don't like this."

I nod. Me neither.

Ragnald rubs his chin. "I, for one, find it captivating how the Teryns are preoccupied with physical fights. I wonder if they encourage these fights to become better warriors. Or if they simply accept that their nature is too aggressive and that they cannot go long before channeling some of their anger into physical altercations."

Caderyn lunges at Callum, who snaps a hook kick across Caderyn's face. Caderyn's head snaps back, but he stays rooted to the spot.

He laughs and shakes his head. "That was a good point, son," he says and punches Callum with a hook in the face.

CHAPTER 5

I cover my eyes. "I can't watch this!"

Glenna puts a hand on my arm. "It will be fine," she says, "they are almost done. No, wait. One more kick . . . and three more punches . . . now they *are* done!"

I remove my hand. The fight circle is gone and most of the spectating warriors have dispersed.

Callum approaches me with a darkening bruise on his jawline.

"I really wish you wouldn't have done that," I say to him.

Callum cups my cheek. "This is a serious matter," he says. "I would do anything for you."

"What a mess," Caderyn says, looking at me and shaking his head. "I am stuck with this 'alliance' and this poor excuse for a legendary Lumenian. Not that she looks like one."

Caderyn is not wrong. I don't look like a typical Lumenian. They are strong, with a golden skin tone, long blond hair, and molten gold eyes, like The Lady and Her acolyte Aisla. No, I look like my mom, with my dark violet hair and eyes. I love that fact, although I've learned that she and I are exceptions to the rule.

Isa grins at Caderyn. "Have you met many Lumenians?" she asks and bats her eyelashes at him in a flirtatious way. Caderyn glowers down at her in response.

Meanwhile, Bella glides to Belthair behind the praelor's back. She touches Belthair's shoulders and whispers something into his ear. He nods and taps away on a worn, leather gauntlet on his right arm, activating an Umbrae, a six-foot tall and oval-shaped gateway that consists of swirling shadows. He and Bella step inside and disappear.

"It doesn't matter whether I met a Lumenian or not," Caderyn says. "I don't want her on my ship! It's best for us if she goes on her own way."

Except I can't do that. Not if I want to complete the mission The Lady gave me.

Callum snaps, "That *she* has a name and it's Lilla!"

"Praelor, why are you making such a big deal?" I ask. "Don't tell me you are afraid of me."

Caderyn grunts. "I am not afraid of anyone! It's simple—you are not a Teryn. What you are is a nuisance, and a stubborn one. You dabble in matters that are more complex than you can imagine. You'll just have to find another army for the Archgoddess of the Eternal Light and Order."

What's so special about being a Teryn? All they've done is bully other worlds under the pretense of cleaning up corruption. Displaced millions of people, making them refugees stuck on foreign worlds. They act haughtily and superior to others. Is that what I must become to be accepted by Caderyn? What if Caderyn represents the worst of what it means to be a Teryn?

"We've just argued over this," Callum says with a growl. "Why are you going back on your word? We need the Sybil and her magic to combat the fully corrupted!"

Callum stands his ground with his hands in fists. He is fighting for me, for the sybil, though in his eyes I can detect pain over the Bride's Choice claim his father won't honor. We both understand our duty, even if our hearts beg otherwise. But I cannot give into that pain. I have a promise to keep and a mission to complete. Then I'll deal with the Bride's Choice issue.

"It changes nothing, son! You should know better! I've spent enough time on this strange planet with too much water. Now it's time to get back to reality. We battled the Archgod of Chaos and Destruction's corruption without magic, and we were doing great. We do not need her kind."

"*I* fought fully corrupted dark servants," Callum says, "unlike you! No matter what Teague or I did, they kept regenerating. Without Lilla's Lume magic we wouldn't have survived!" He reaches for the triangular buttons over his heart that decorate his military-style jacket and grasps them. "You have no idea what's out there! To refuse the Sybil is to refuse the archgoddess! I cannot stand for that!"

"Don't you dare!" Caderyn shouts.

An Umbrae portal opens to my left. Bella and Belthair step out of the shadows, with Belthair holding a chunk of dripping metal equipment that has colorful wires dangling from it.

"Stop this foolishness, son! You know why we can't allow any outsiders to step foot on Teryn! We are leaving and that's the end—"

Isa sashays in front of Caderyn. "With what spaceship are you planning to do that?"

A loud clank sounds, coming from the Teryn spaceship.

We turn to watch the humongous craft listing to the side, creaking, and almost hitting the ground.

CHAPTER 6

"I command you to give it back!" Caderyn bellows and reaches for the purloined equipment.

Isa laughs. "Didn't you explain the peculiar situation with titles? Well, we don't recognize *yours*." Bella adds, "You could be the king of Seven Galaxies for all we care."

Belthair throws it to Ragnald before the praelor can reach him.

"Ragnald," I say, trying my best not to laugh at the purple-faced Caderyn, "please hand it to the praelor." Joke aside, this is not how I would like to influence his decision. He already has a low opinion of me.

Ragnald reaches out, pretending to hand it to Caderyn, but at the last second he whips his arm to the other side and Arrov snatches the equipment from the mage's hand. "Not so fast, Lilla," Ragnald says. "We'll give it back to him when he starts respecting you as the Sybil."

Caderyn lunges at Arrov.

Arrov throws the dripping metal chunk back to Belthair, who opens an Umbrae portal and steps back, disappearing.

"That's enough," I say to my friends, then turn to Caderyn. "I'm, uh, sorry for the behavior of my—"

"Do not apologize for a well-executed plan," Caderyn says. "A good general should always know how to strategically utilize their people's skills."

A muscle twitches under my left eye. Is there anything I can do right? "All I'm asking is a chance to prove myself as a Sybil. Tell me what I have to do!"

Caderyn looks first at Callum standing rigid, his hand still locked over the rank buttons, then turns to me. "I admire your tenacity. Tenacity is one of the cornerstones of honor." He pauses in thought then says, "I will consider allowing you to recruit my army *if* you earn my Guardian Goddess Laoise's blessing."

"That's a low blow!" Callum snaps. I glance at him in surprise.

"That's it?" I ask.

Caderyn chuckles with a knowing look. "That's it."

"I accept," I say. "Now you have to take me to Teryn."

"And us," Isa and Bella say.

"I'm coming, too," Arrov adds. Glenna and Ragnald nod in agreement.

An Umbrae portal opens next to me and Belthair steps out. "Me too," he says and drops the dripping metal piece into Caderyn's hand.

I look at each of my friends. I appreciate their support and loyalty. "Are you sure?" They all nod in confirmation.

"Looks like I'm taking you and your entourage," Caderyn says, grumbling, while looking us over. His gaze snags on Arrov. "Son, just what are you? A giant or a man?"

Arrov growls.

"Son, I hope your fur doesn't stink when it rains."

Suddenly the ground shakes under our feet as if a terraquake is approaching.

CHAPTER 7

The loud and rumbling sound draws closer, like hooves thundering on the ground. Or webbed claws.

Fearghas gallops out of the forest, through the palace ruins, heading straight for Caderyn.

"Fearghas, no!" I cry, stepping in front of the praelor, blocking him from my battle horse.

Callum shoves me out of the way, embracing me so I can't move. "Praelor, get out of the way!" he yells.

The warriors pull out their longswords, readying for an attack.

"Don't hurt him!" I say.

Caderyn glances at Callum, then at the warriors. They stand down, but he still doesn't move out of the way. He watches Fearghas calmly, heedless of the danger galloping toward him.

"Run!" I shout, but it's too late.

Fearghas rears in front of Caderyn. Thick muscles vibrate under his black hide as he rends the air with webbed claws. His neighing sounds like an ear-piecing scream. He drops his front legs to the ground, staring at Caderyn and baring his sharp fangs.

"I thought you found a new home for Fearghas in the village?" Glenna whispers.

"I thought so, too." It was heartbreaking to say good-bye to my horse, but the villagers on the other side of the island promised to let Fearghas roam freely. I just wasn't expecting the villagers to let him out so soon.

"Is that blood around Fearghas's mouth?" Belthair asks, pointing with his top left hand.

Maybe the villagers didn't *willingly* let my horse out.

Caderyn stares back at Fearghas, indifferent to my horse's dangerous temper.

They stare at each other, unblinking, for a few long minutes.

Fearghas is the one who breaks eye contact. Stepping closer to the large man, he nuzzles Caderyn's neck.

Glenna and I exchange a look of shock. Fearghas has never warmed up to anyone this fast!

Caderyn pats the horse's thick black neck. "You're a beaut, aren't you, Fearghas?" he murmurs.

The answering neigh is soft and almost embarrassed by the compliment. I can't decide to be upset with Fearghas for giving in so easily, or relieved that he didn't maul the praelor.

Maybe there is something good in Caderyn that Fearghas senses but isn't obvious to me.

The praelor glances at us. "Fearghas definitely comes with us."

"All right then," Callum says, and puts a hand on my back. We head toward his compact space vessel that waits at the other side of the island.

"Son, where do you think you're going?"

Callum points behind him. "To my spaceship—"

"We are taking *my* ship," Caderyn says. "You can have your old room back."

CHAPTER 8

My back hits the wall in Callum's living quarters aboard the Teryn spaceship the second the slanted metal door swooshes closed. We slipped away from the others at the first chance we had, while boarding was in process. No one paid us any mind.

"I have you where I want you," Callum says and leans closer, his gaze full of open desire.

I shiver from the unveiled heat in his eyes and thread my arms around his neck. "Is that so?" I kiss him, just a feather-light touch on his lips. "How do you know this wasn't *my* plan?"

Callum smiles and lifts his hands in a mock surrender. "Then I have no choice but to succumb to your master plan. Do with me as you wish."

Giggling, I glance around. His quarters are furnished with a bed by the wall, two low-back gray chairs, a similarly styled sofa, and a metal table. A floor-to-ceiling transparent wall slants inward and open to dark space peppered with white specks of stars. Also visible is the oceanic world of Uhna below. The tremendous spaceship finished its ascent but hasn't left Galaxy Five yet.

A surprising ache of pain jabs into my chest. It wasn't long ago that I wished I could be anywhere but on Uhna. Now that the wish has come true, sadness hits me. Unshed tears weigh heavy on my chest, constricting my breathing, pressing down.

Callum touches my face with a gentle hand. "What's wrong?"

"I'm happy to be here with you, but . . ." My voice buckles.

"You're homesick."

Nodding, I try to smile but my eyes well up.

Callum hugs me to him, his strong arms wrapping around me. "I understand."

We stay like that, quietly, for a long moment.

I shake off the shroud of sadness and pull away to look at Callum. I touch his face, tracing the jagged scar. I'm overtaken by a feeling of love

23

so powerful that my breath hitches. I never thought I could love someone so completely.

Callum runs his gaze over my face. "You, being here with me, feels right. I don't know what our future holds. I don't know how we'll ever have the Bride's Choice honored, but I am grateful for the time we have together." He slides his hands down my arms until our hands connect.

"About my father," he says with a grimace, "I should have prepared you for what to expect. I was a fool!"

"Don't apologize for him. After the destruction DLD left behind, you and I didn't spend any time together." We both got stuck in the middle of the monarchy collapsing while dealing with alliance matters. Gods know Father was of no help! He turned his back on Uhna, blaming his injuries for his lack of interest, and locked himself in his well-appointed apartment.

"No, we didn't have enough time together," Callum says. "I thought it would go better with the praelor." He looks like he wants to say more but doesn't.

"Better? I'm here, aren't I?" I say and put my hands on his chest.

A smile lifts the right corners of his lips. "That's right. Now what are you going to do?"

Heat rushes to my cheeks. I lean in but stop a hairbreadth from his lips. "Where to start?" I whisper.

"I have a few suggestions," Callum says and kisses me.

I return his kiss with passion that threatens to burn me up if I keep it locked in a second longer. I kiss him until our breath becomes one and—

Bangs sound on the door.

I jump, bumping my head against Callum's.

Callum curses. "Go away, Teague!" he snaps without taking his eyes off mine. "Now, where were we—"

More banging sounds, much louder. The metal door shakes from the force of the hits.

"Open up," says a male voice that's not Teague's, "or I'll break the door down!"

CHAPTER 9

"I have not honored your Bride's Choice," Caderyn says as I step outside Callum's room. He escorts me down a windowless corridor toward my own living quarters, on the other side of his spaceship.

"I thought the Bride's Choice was but a formality," I mutter. I recall Teague telling me that Teryn dating customs were not as strict as Uhna's. I don't understand why Caderyn wants to keep Callum and me from even spending time together. This feels personal, against me.

"It is not a formality when a non-Teryn invokes it," Caderyn says, confirming my suspicion. "I had a feeling that you might get . . . *lost* and end up in Callum's room."

Shame stings my face, but I keep my gaze in front of me, on the inclining corridor with inward-angled gray wall panels. I feel like I am sixteen years old again, forbidden to date without Father's permission.

"I wasn't lost," I say and lift my chin in defiance.

Caderyn laughs. "It takes k'stones to speak to me like that. I can appreciate that. Though not many dare it and survive long enough to brag about it."

"I guess I just have to consider myself lucky," I say, and Caderyn snorts. At least he finds me amusing. That must count for something.

The corridor narrows until my arm brushes against the angled panels. They have a hide-like texture, making them feel like living things. One of them closes on me, pressing down and robbing me of air.

Sweat breaks out on my forehead and hands. I try to focus on the soft light coming from around the seams of the rectangular panels, but to no avail.

Chills run through my spine in waves. I struggle to keep breathing, fighting the urge to flee, and stumble on one of the metal grates of the floor.

Hot-and-cold-and-hot-again feelings, intensified by the magical markings on my back, heat up. My skin glows golden. My magic bubbles to the surface, ready to burst out of me.

I can't lose control here!

25

"Slow down your breathing," Caderyn says in a calm voice as he continues to march forward without looking at me. "Inhale for the count of three, hold it for seven, and then exhale for seven."

I follow his instructions, inhaling the clean air with a hint of metallic scent and exhaling as I count to four.

The panic withdraws to the back of my head but is not gone. Never fully gone.

The corridor widens out, to my relief.

Staring at my boots, I try to shake a feeling of embarrassment. An old habit that still clings to me from when I had to hide this weakness from the court. Will Caderyn hold it against me now?

Under the metal grate floor, a green long-beaked salamander swims by in the gas fuel of the spaceship, cleaning it from space particles. How simple life is for that salamander! Not a worry in sight, like dealing with uncooperative allies who are supposed to be on your side in the Era War.

How much easier it would have been to think of Caderyn as a ruthless, cold, and uncaring bully. With this act of kindness, he ruined that image. Even Fearghas was taken with him.

We pass a couple of open doors.

On the right, Belthair leans with his back on the wall outside of his room. When he offered to join the fight against DLD, he probably didn't picture being at the mercy of the Teryns. He glares at the passing crew, including Caderyn and me, while six of his hands are busy whittling finger-long pieces of wood.

Across from Belthair, Arrov sits on the floor in his quarters by his cot with his furry knees pulled up. He joined my cause because he had nowhere else to go, being the seventh son of Queen Amra of A'ice. Now here he is, pulling long light-blue hairs on his forearm out of boredom or maybe hoping to revert to his old self.

Glenna pops her head out from the next open doorway, raising an eyebrow when she sees me with Caderyn. She refused to stay back on Uhna. She insisted that I will need healing and she didn't trust anyone to handle it besides her. Behind Glenna, Ragnald makes a bed on the floor. The mage follows her now, wherever she goes, to prevent the corruption that DLD left behind in

Glenna from spreading, evident in that white streak among her dark crimson hair. Though she barely tolerates the mage's presence.

Isa and Bella, grinning widely, wave to Caderyn from the next room. They're still running from that heist they pulled on their royal parents, "accessing their inheritance early," as they called it. They joined my cause, too, for fun.

My ragtag, practically worldless army of loyal friends. They may not look like much, but I wouldn't have it any other way. I'll just have to do my best not to let them down and do my best to complete my mission. All new beginnings are hard, but I need to start somewhere.

Caderyn stops at the last door in the corridor, next to the twins. I guess that room is going to be mine.

"Thank you," I say to the praelor.

He grunts in response, then leaves without a word.

CHAPTER 10

I know I am dreaming, but I can't wake up. I watch a beautiful green world turn black as the Archgod of Chaos and Destruction's corruption spreads on its surface like a horrible, unstoppable disease.

"Another world ravaged," booms The Lady's voice but She is not present otherwise. "I need that army now! I need to fight back!"

"I'm doing my best!" I try to shout, but my mouth feels stuffed with sticky boomberry jam, and no sound comes out.

The monotone hum of the powerful spaceship engines rouses me, and I take a moment to calm my beating heart.

While I only witnessed it in a dream, I know from previous experience that once The Lady shows up, it is real. Somewhere in the Seven Galaxies, a beautiful world had been devastated. All those innocent lives lost! While I am locked in a pointless struggle with Caderyn, who refuses The Lady's requisitioning of his army.

I open my eyes to stare at the low ceiling of my room on the Teryn spaceship. Dimmed light shows the edge of the paneled gray wall where my narrow bed is attached.

On my right, a floor-to-ceiling transparent wall shows dark space with stars flashing by. They appear as streaks from the speed the ship travels. My inner clock suggests it's still the middle of the night. I tap the smooth wall, and a galactic clock—used in the Seven Galaxies for unified timekeeping—flashes blue, validating my assumption.

My gaze takes in my cramped living quarters, with a table in front of a chair bolted to the gray-carpeted floor. They stimulate my claustrophobia and I take a few deep breaths to maintain my calm.

I untuck from a white blanket. Sitting at the edge of the bed, I pull my mom's journal from under the pillow. I trace my fingers over the journal's dark purple cover, which feels plush in places while charred and blackened in others. I turn the pages, reading passages, and studying the maps she drew of the smuggling tunnels under the Crystal Palace.

A soft knock sounds. "Lilla, are you awake?" Glenna asks from the other side of the door.

I put the journal down and let Glenna in. We both sit at the edge of my bed.

Glenna points at the journal and says, "I'm glad it found its way back to you."

"Me too. I am grateful that Beathag gave back this treasure. She thought this would be enough to reconcile what happened between us, but it was too late." Beathag was my friend, yet she betrayed.

I open the journal and page through it. "I've reread it so many times. The adventures my mom had! How brave and confident she was!" She left Lume, the mysterious home world of the Lumenians. She escaped from The Lady, who wanted to lock Her people there to protect them from DLD.

Glenna nods along with my words, her attention rapt on me.

"Did you know that she and Father met in an unconventional way?" I ask. Glenna shakes her head. "Mom never had to ask anyone's permission or approval to love him. She never had to earn any god or goddess's blessing before she could live her life the way she wanted. Unlike me. I miss her so much! I wish I could ask her advice. What would she think of Callum and Caderyn?"

Glenna pats my arm. "I've never met your mom, Lilla, but I think she would have approved of Callum, because you love him. As for Caderyn, she may have advised you to prove him wrong."

I smile. "You're right."

Glenna tries to smile back, but tears appear in her eyes. She places a hand on her flat stomach and says, "I, um, thought I was pregnant. But this morning I learned otherwise. Nic and I wanted to get married and start a family. Now I feel I lost him twice!"

"Oh, no!" I say and embrace her petite frame just as sobs rack her body. "I'm so sorry!" Glenna and my half brother, Nic, loved each other so much, but DLD happened. Nic was betrayed and killed in front of us. Because of me.

Glenna cries for a few moments, her body shaking, her wails muffled in my arms.

I coo nonsense words and rock her, fighting tears of sorrow on their behalf. They never had a chance at a happy life.

Glenna pulls back and wipes her face on the sleeve of her pink nightgown. "I'm sorry for bothering you," she says, "but I couldn't stay in my room. It hurt too much."

I rub her heated back. "I understand."

Glenna gets to her feet. "I knew you would," she says and hugs me. "It's time for me to get my next dose of magic medicine from that mage."

I squeeze her hand. With a wave, she steps out of my room.

I wish Nic and Glenna could have had more time together. I wish DLD would have never come to my world. I wish I would have made a better decision.

I sigh. There is no point wishing for what would never happen. It does not change the past.

I dress in a black sleeveless shirt and leggings, then head out just as Belthair steps out of his room. He is barechested and barefoot, wearing gray pants and holding a blue shirt in his top right hand.

"Can't sleep?" he asks and pulls his shirt over his defined chest.

"I'm too wound up," I say.

"I was heading out for a sparring session. Care to join me?"

I could use the practice. "Lead the way."

The angled door swooshes open, revealing a spacious and windowless room. Half of the floor is covered in padded mats, while the other half appears to be made of stone. Mirrored walls and weapon racks intersperse throughout the otherwise empty room.

For a second I am in a different sparring room, back on Uhna, with Callum. Where our first kiss happened.

When I don't move, Belthair gestures for me to enter first. "Teague told me that the ship has a lot of these 'sparring rooms,' but this one, due to its proximity to our living quarters, would be empty. The Teryns are not keen on mingling with us." He laughs and closes the door.

I shrug. "They take their cues from Caderyn."

We go through a series of warm-up exercises that we used to do when

Belthair was supervising the rebels' training. When I met him in the rebellion a few months ago, he was angry at me. He thought it was I who betrayed our plan to run away, when in fact it was Beathag. Father ordered his execution on the spot. Sheer luck saved his life—his friends were on guard duty and they let him escape.

"Let's practice a few defensive moves," he says, and heads to the padded mat, stopping in the middle of it.

I nod and take position across from him. "Just like old times."

Belthair nods, smiling. "I do miss the rebellion! Those days, there was always something new to tackle, a problem to solve. I felt useful."

He starts sparring, using all six of his hands, and for a few minutes I am busy deflecting, ducking, and countering punches. "I am glad that you joined my side, even though the first mission is not exciting or glamorous. I am starting at the bottom of the ocean, and it's a long way to the surface."

Belthair shows me a few kicks he wants me to do, then says, "I wasn't complaining, just reminiscing. When Xor recruited me for the rebellion, there were a few of us as ranking officers leading a ragtag band of only fourteen untrained rebels! It took a lot of work and effort to grow the rebellion into what you saw when you ended up joining us. It didn't happen overnight." He takes up a ready stance with arms outstretched and adds, "What you'll have to do is similar, but on an intergalactic scale. The Teryn army is just the tip of the coral reef. You'll have others to convince to support you, the sybil, based on the merit of your title. Prepare yourself for a problematic and time-consuming battle right from the start."

I grimace. "Let's acquire the Teryn armada first before I move onto other matters." I execute the kicks as he directed.

Belthair steps back, signaling to take a break. I wipe sweat from my face, panting. I need to up my endurance.

"You have to be careful with Caderyn," Belthair says, then demonstrates a combination of kicks and punches to practice next.

I repeat the motions a few times, careful not to hurt him, sending jabs and crosses at Belthair's top hands while he redirects the kicks with his lower hands. "What do you mean?" I ask and take a few seconds to catch my breath.

"My instincts tell me that there is more to why he is so adamant against you. He may kill to protect whatever he's hiding."

"That's going a bit far, don't you think?"

Belthair cracks his neck from side to side. "Don't forget how we had to force his hand to allow us to board his spaceship in the first place, and that's after Callum 'argued' with him and won."

I didn't forget that. "It's a bit late to worry now, don't you think?"

Belthair gestures for me to attack, and I rush him.

He grabs my arm, trips my right leg, and I land on the mat on my back. He follows me down and braces his hands by my shoulders, saying, "I worry about you, Lilla. I don't want you to get hurt."

I snort. "I can take care of myself!"

Belthair smiles. "I know you can, because I taught you how!" he says and his expression turns serious as his gaze trails my face. "If Callum ever gets out of the way, I would like to rekindle what we had. We never had a real chance together."

I look at him, surprised. "I had no idea that you feel—"

Belthair jumps to his feet. "Don't worry about my feelings," he says and reaches a hand down to me. "Now let's practice this takedown. This time I'll attack."

CHAPTER 11

It's been two days, six hours, and seven minutes since I've talked to Callum. I looked for him but couldn't find him. I have a feeling he may have been forbidden to visit me.

I glance out the transparent wall into space. It's another morning on the tedious journey toward the Teryn home world.

I have not sparred with Belthair again. In fact, I've been doing my best to avoid him. I had no idea he still harbored romantic feelings toward me. I don't know how to process this new information. There is room for only one person in my heart, and that is Callum.

Dressed in a simple silver dress, I step out of my living quarters and glimpse Isa and Bella's room. I stumble to a halt.

They kneel on the gray carpet in front of their beds. Hundreds of colorful wires, cables, and gadgets lay scattered around them. A rectangular wall panel is missing by the first bed, with the colorful innards of the spaceship showing, full of broken cords and such.

"What are you two doing?!" I ask and enter their room.

Isa studies the rabble on the carpet, swiping a hand through the mess and says, "Just keeping busy." Bella adds, "We are building a remote!"

"For what?" I ask, imagining the worst. If I weren't so upset with them, I would appreciate how fast they learned to navigate technology they never encountered before, and already invented something new out of it.

Isa's emerald green eyes flash with interest as she picks up an oily thing. "Aha!" she says and inserts it into the black square covered in wires that she holds in her left hand. The piece clicks into place. Isa lifts the remote and pushes a tiny button on its side.

The lights in the room turn on and off, repeatedly. Bella jumps up and sticks her head out the door, saying, "It works in the corridor too!"

"Why are you two trying to ruin my mission before it even started?"

Isa turns off the lights. "We were just having a bit of entertainment." Bella adds, "No harm done to anyone. We swear!"

"Can't you two be more serious for once?"

Isa puts down the makeshift remote and gets to her feet. "I think the better question is, why are you so upset over such an infinitesimal issue?"

Bella studies my face and asks, "Lilla, are you okay?"

Something wells up in me and words pour out in a rush, tumbling over each other. "I miss Callum. I am not a Teryn, whatever that means. Belthair still has feelings for me. I'm supposed to acquire the Teryn armada somehow, and I have no idea how to get Guardian Goddess Laoise's blessing!"

I look away, embarrassed by my tirade. Embarrassed at my self-pity. This is not how I imagined my future as the sybil.

"A simple 'no' would have sufficed," Isa jokes. "Though I would like you to expand on how Belthair still has feelings for you."

The twins knew that Belthair and I dated, but not the whole story of what happened.

Bella glares at Isa, then puts her arm around me and leads me to the closer bed, where we sit. "Sweetie, there is nothing for you to be ashamed of! Any one of those things, on their own, can be overwhelming. Combine them, and it's a recipe for emotional catastrophe. You can't keep your feelings bottled up, or an explosion like this one will happen when you least expect it."

"I'm sorry," I say. "You two are my close friends and don't deserve to be snapped at. It's just that—"

"Nothing you do is good enough for the Teryns," Isa says, counting off her fingers one by one. "You couldn't make a good first impression with the emperor, even though you tried so hard. He didn't even want you on his ship."

Bella adds, "Caderyn hates you for claiming his son and wanting his armada. He thinks you are a threat to his empire, which is not true, but he doesn't care about facts. He is too headstrong."

"Hate is a bit harsh," I say, cringing, "but yes, that's a good summary."

Isa and Bella each squeeze one of my hands. "We know how you feel, sweetie," Isa says. "We know what it's like to be judged and held up against a measure that was not your choice."

Bella says, "We know what it feels like to be considered a failure. Never living up to expectations."

I nod. The twins grew up as princesses on a world where science and intellectual achievement were the highest standards. Instead of becoming acclaimed scientists, they choose to be hackers, much to the chagrin of their family and their royal subjects.

"We are here for you," Isa and Bella say in unison, "and we support you!"

I hug them back. "I'm glad you are on my side."

Isa points at the mess on the floor. "Now help us put this stuff back where it belongs before Caderyn figures out we were the ones who messed with his spaceship."

CHAPTER 12

I stomp down the windowless corridor in the middle of the night the follow-ing day, feeling restless.

"If one more person bumps into me 'unintentionally,' I'll . . ." I mutter, biting off the rest of my not-so-cheery thought.

"You'll do what?" Arrov's voice sounds from somewhere behind me.

I retrace my steps until I find him sitting in the back of a mess hall with Glenna.

I make my way to my friends through dozens of empty metal tables with benches attached to them. "I'll bring down the corridor on top of their heads with my mighty Lumenian magic!" I say and raise my arms, shaking them in pretense.

Glenna snorts and lifts a glass mug full of steaming, dark, and orange-col-ored tea to her lips and blows on it before drinking. "More like you'll take down the whole spaceship," she says, "since your control over your magic is anything but predictable."

I laugh. Glenna has a good point.

"Didn't you once tell me," Arrov asks, "that kindness always takes the wind out of mean people's sails?" He pushes a metal tray full of bite-size morsels of food in front of me.

I pick up a tart with blue jam on it and sit next to Glenna. "I did say that."

It was during one of our long sessions of peeling root vegetables together as our assignment, back when we were rebels on Uhna. Arrov and I were allotted to low-level or downright dismissive duties because we were new to the rebellion. How I yearn for those simplistic tasks now!

"You can't sleep either?" Arrov asks and takes a gulp out of a mug that could double as a large vase, full of the same orange-colored tea Glenna has.

I shake my head.

Arrov heaves a deep sigh. "What if I can't change back?"

36

Isa and Bella enter the mess hall, looking fresh and fashionable in their matching red pantsuits. They motion to Arrov, and he scoots down to make room for them on top of the metal table.

"Would it be so bad to stay as a giant?" Glenna asks as she puts her cup down and looks up at Arrov.

"Don't listen to Glennie," Isa says and pats Arrov's forearm—that's as high as she can reach. Bella adds, "You'll change back to your old and handsome self soon."

Arrov sighs again. "Women used to chase me. Now they can't run away fast enough!"

"You are fine-looking just as you are," Isa assures him and pulls a white comb from her pocket. Bella nods in agreement.

"Glenna?" Ragnald's shout sounds from outside the mess hall.

She closes her eyes, struggling to control her temper. "In here."

"You shouldn't be out alone, without, you know," Ragnald says as he strides over to us. I make room for him to sit between Glenna and me, pretending I don't notice her staring pirate swords at me.

"Stop fussing about me," Glenna says. The mage puts his hand on her shoulder and channels magic into her. She closes her eyes for a moment, looking relieved. She adds, "Arrov, what I meant to say is, if there is a cure, I'll find it for you."

"Thank you, Glenna, that means a . . ." Arrov says, and his voice trails off when he notices that the twins are busy combing the long fur on his forearms. "What are you two doing?!"

"Just because you are a big blue giant," Isa says, focused on her undertaking, "doesn't mean you can stop taking care of your appearance."

"This will help get rid of those horrible knots," Bella adds, still administrating the beauty regimen.

Belthair wanders in, rubbing his face with his top right hand. "Are we having a party? Why didn't anyone wake me up?" He heads toward me, then his dark brown eyes widen. He changes direction, nearly stumbling in his feet, striding toward the other side of the table.

Glenna frowns at Belthair. "Why is there this awkward tension between you two?"

"No reason," Belthair and I say in unison, and the twins giggle. "It's not a party," I insist.

"There is food," Belthair says, gesturing to the metal trays piled high with rolls, meats, and tiny desserts, "and there is company. I say that's the definition of a party." He pulls out six small pieces of wood from his pocket as he straddles the bench across from me, then starts whittling away, leaving sawdust scattered around him.

Glenna snorts. "More like the definition of a *boring* party. What about dancing?"

"I don't care for it," Belthair says without looking up. I hide my laughter. He wasn't the romantic type when we dated. Then I remember the first dance I shared with Callum, back on Uhna, and I clear my throat.

"I don't need help with my fur!" Arrov growls at the twins. "I need help changing back!"

"Don't worry," Belthair says to Arrov. Then he blows on the wood pieces he holds. We wait for Belthair to continue, but that's the full extent of his consoling.

"What are we going to do about this army issue?" Ragnald asks.

"What do you mean 'we'? It's my mission."

Ragnald clasps his hands under his chin, showing off his defined biceps under his gray shirt. "You didn't think we wouldn't help, now did you?"

"But aren't you regretting that you followed me?" I ask.

"As I said before, I have no regrets," Belthair says and puts the unfinished wooden sculptures on the table. "There is food and a place to sleep, which is a lot more than I had when I joined the rebellion."

Ragnald nods. "My position on Uhna as Royal Elemental Mage was shaky at best, and once the Ma'ha stepped down, it was over. This allows me to focus on what I want to do more than anything, studying Lumenian magic up close and documenting my findings for history. Not to mention, you are in dire need of magical education. One that I'm happy to provide."

"Great," I say. "I did not realize you'll record my failings so future generations can laugh themselves to death at my expense."

The others chuckle.

"We won't judge you over any magical failings," Isa says and Bella adds, "As long as you don't kill us with your magic!"

"I wasn't planning to," I mumble, "at least not on purpose."

"You know," Ragnald says, "that guardian goddess might know how to help Arrov with his, uh, giant issue."

Arrov's eyes tear up. We women jump to our feet, on cue, and rush to hug him in comfort.

Callum and Teague stride by the entrance of the mess hall and notice us. Callum, with a tight expression, halts and heads toward me.

"We shouldn't be here," Teague says, standing guard by the entrance. "You've just left the brig and—"

"Not now," Callum says, staring at my arm around Arrov. An orange-reddish light flashes across his irises, the only sign to show that he is upset.

"Is that why I couldn't find you?" I ask Callum as I step away from Arrov, "because Caderyn threw you in the brig?"

Callum nods. His jacket looks worn and ragged and his tanned face sports pronounced black stubble.

Teague makes a face. "It was the only way to prevent him from seeing you. Since he was ready to disobey any direct order, which reminds me—"

"Yes, I know. I'm not supposed to be here," Callum snaps. Then he directs his words to Arrov, "Nice tears, giant boy. You would do anything for the women's attention, wouldn't you?"

We women gasp, while Ragnald and Belthair snort.

Arrov growls at Callum in a tone so predatory that the hair on the back of my neck stands up.

Callum raises an eyebrow. "What? Too soon?"

CHAPTER 13

Arrov, with his huge furry hands in fists, heads toward Callum. Belthair and Ragnald hang on him, attempting to hold him back, but Arrov just drags them along until they give up and step back.

"Don't do anything harsh, Arrov," I say. "You'll kill him!"

Callum smirks. "No, he won't."

"Yes, he will," Teague says and checks the corridor, then takes a palm-size dinner roll out of his pocket and bites into the roll while watching the confrontation play out.

Arrov growls again, and bumps into Callum as he storms out of the mess hall.

"Why do you keep provoking poor Arrov?" I ask and slap Callum's arm. It's like hitting a brick wall.

Callum and Arrov have been at odds with each other from the first time they met. It didn't help that Arrov wanted to date me at the time, though later Arrov and I agreed we would not be a good match. After a while the two of them found a more neutral ground—I wouldn't call it friendship—that didn't lead to an outright fight.

"There is nothing 'poor' about that big, giant, attention-seeking—"

"Callum!"

"He was standing too close to you," Callum says. "But enough talk about him."

Callum embraces me, lifting me off my feet. "Gods, I missed you!" He buries his face in the crook of my neck as he holds me tightly.

"Are you disobeying orders now?" I ask and yank a little on Callum's short black hair until he raises his head. I kiss him, conveying how much I missed him. These past days felt unbearable. To know he was on the same spaceship, yet so far away, was torture.

"We can see you, you know," Belthair mocks from behind us.

Callum puts me down and we pull apart, but he doesn't let go of my hands.

"I didn't realize this would be so complicated."

"Getting your guardian goddess's blessing shouldn't be too difficult, right?"

A strange expression crosses Callum's face and he looks torn. He opens his mouth to speak, once, twice, and then says, "I can't—"

"Callum, you have to go now!" Teague urges.

Callum swears under his breath. "Lilla, I wish—"

"Callum, go now!" Teague says with a hiss.

An orange-reddish light flashes across Callum's blue irises again. He kisses me, just a quick peck, and hurries out of the mess hall, cursing.

"Teague, wait a moment, please!" I call out before he can withdraw from the hall.

"I know it's been a strange journey," Teague says when I reach him. "We never had the lights on the whole ship flash like they did yesterday, unless it was part of a shipwide alarm. Don't ask me why it happened because I don't know."

Isa and Bella giggle, but they turn away when Teague glances at them.

"That's not what I'd like to talk about," I say. "Did Caderyn order Callum to stay away from me?"

"Well, the praelor didn't *directly* order him," Teague says and takes out a thin stick of dried meat, "but he strongly recommended that Callum doesn't spend too much time in your presence until further notice. He even set guards to watch him. When Callum was caught trying to visit you, the praelor threw him in the brig until 'Callum can get some sense back into his thick head.'"

Teague pauses to shove the whole dried meat in his mouth, then says as he chews it, "I think the praelor knows that if he commands his son to stay away from you, Callum will break that order without hesitation. Callum is already in trouble from when we were on Uhna. He did not live up to the praelor's expectations about the negotiations. Ironically, Callum was sent to Uhna to take care of diplomatic matters as a punishment for almost disobeying a previous order."

I did not know that.

Teague continues, "I don't understand why this is happening to both of you. I thought the Bride's Choice would work. Why did the Wise Women convey the importance of the Bride's Choice to me five years ago if it means nothing? I despise watching you and Callum suffer like this."

"They told you about the Bride's Choice?"

Teague nods. "Well, not about the Bride's Choice. Every Teryn man knows about it and wish it would happen to them. No, what the Wise Women expressed to me was that there would come a time when someone who is dear to me will need my help and that I should advise his beloved about the Bride's Choice at that exact time. They were adamant that I remember this, and I did."

It's true. Teague did inform me about the Bride's Choice when we were on Uhna, though it's strange that the Wise Women knew *years* ago that Teague would need to do this.

"Their advice clearly didn't work," I say. "What was the point of even suggesting it in the first place?"

Teague pats my shoulder again. "That is the question, love, isn't it?"

CHAPTER 14

"Are you sure this will work?" I ask Ragnald as I roll a pair of large urns into the sparring room a few hours after we met in the mess hall.

Ragnald said we need to practice my magic. He had a surprise to show me that would be a great help in case I lose control. Hence the urns.

"I believe they will withhold splendidly," Ragnald says as he pushes another pair of similar urns in front of him. "I strengthened them with my T'erra magic for a whole week, back on Uhna."

Glenna enters. "That's a bit arrogant of you to declare any guarantee before knowing it full well, don't you think?"

Ragnald ignores Glenna's jab and takes off his black mage robe. His gray shirt reveals a broad chest, visible through his black tank top. She ogles his athletic body with appreciation while the mage is busy placing an urn at each corner of the room.

I look away before I burst out in laughter and study my closer urn, which reaches my waist and sits on a wooden platform with wheels. Its teal color shines brightly under the light coming from the edges of the paneled ceiling. The ones we used on Uhna were navy blue with azure rust on them—they also ended up in pieces. Here is to hope that these will fare better.

"I ask, because if I lose control and they don't hold, it won't end well for the whole ship."

Ragnald waves a hand in a dismissive gesture and points at one of the urns. "These are ten times stronger than the ones you destroyed. I think you'll do better this time, knowing the additional stakes."

"Is that so?" Glenna mocks. "What will you make her do next? Practice in front of a black hole? Or right before a supernova hits?"

Ragnald crosses his arms. "If you cannot bring constructive energy to this magic practice, then I have to ask you to—"

"I'll behave, mage," Glenna interrupts him with her hands up. "Don't get your mage robe in a bunch! Proceed like I'm not here."

Ragnald nods and puts on a pair of yellow glasses that allow him to perceive magical elements. He turns to me and says, "Another approach for studying magic, Lilla, is to go back to its basics. Each element can be represented in its essence: Fla'mma as fire, A'qua as water, A'ris as air, T'erra as soil, A'nima as living things, and Lume as light and energy. Try to form circles that encompass each other, using the purest essence of each element, like so." On his palm, six flat circles appear—like a teeny, flattened rainbow—each circle sparkling in the corresponding color of its element. "Since my affinity is in Fla'mma, T'erra, and A'qua, this is the most I can do with the other elements, but you should not have any problem. As a Lumenian, you have absolute control over these elements."

"In theory," I mutter, but Ragnald does not hear my comment.

With a flick of his wrist, he makes the palm-size circles disappear. "Now it's your turn."

I stride into the middle of the room, where the stone floor meets the padded mat. My reflection in the mirror shows a young, dark-violet-haired woman wearing an amber-colored tunic, black leggings, and a nervous expression. I'm already anticipating the worst.

"You can do it, Lilla!" Glenna cheers from a sideline.

I take a deep breath. Hot-and-cold-and-hot-again feelings envelop my body. My skin glows golden, as it always does when I engage my magic. I close my eyes on the exhale.

At first, darkness waits, then a bright white and pulsing sphere appears in my mind's eye. My magic.

What looked bright white and cohesive is millions of transparent elemental threads, sparkling in their elemental hues.

With an imaginary hand, I pick up a thin, red Fla'mma thread and shape it into a flat circle, then push it away, anchoring it in front of me. For a second I feel an increase in the room's temperature, then the heat banks down.

Next, I choose an azure blue A'qua thread, focusing on shaping it in its basic essence, water, then add it to encircle the Fla'mma one on the floor. I hear a sloshing sound and the air smells moist for a moment.

Then I select a light blue A'ris ribbon, forming it into a soft air current and adding it to the others. A fresh and clean breeze ruffles my loose hair, then dies down.

I look for T'erra ribbons and find a thin one, form it into soil, and let it join to the elemental circles in front of me. The damp scent of forest ground drifts to my nose.

An eager A'nima thread rises to me like a puppy, and I imagine it taking the form of one of Glenna's little dogs. I add it to the others. For a moment there's a sound of running feet and claws scrambling.

I hesitate. One element is left: Lume. The element that caused me the most trouble in the past.

I gulp as sweat breaks out on my palms.

"You are almost done, Lilla," Ragnald says. "Don't stop now."

With utmost care, I reach for a fine ribbon of bright white Lume. It separates from the sphere, willing and pliable. I shape it into its light essence and add it to the other elemental circles. Power saturates the room, raising the hair on my arms, then settles.

I don't dare open my eyes as I wait for that pressure pain to build, one that signals I am about to lose control, but it does not come.

"You can open your eyes, sweetie," Glenna whispers. "It's resplendent!"

I do, and with a surprise I realize I somehow ended up by the entrance of the room, pushed back as the elemental circles grew. In front of me, the whole floor—its edges marked by the four urns—is covered in wide, flat, horizontal circles of elements: fire flows in the center, then water, then wind, evergreen vegetation rustling, then invisible dogs running in place, and a bright white light pulses at the outermost circle. This amalgam of elements hovers at knee height, bursting with power but contained and safe.

Ragnald gapes at the elements. "I think you tackled your control issues! Well done!"

"It does appear so," I say, "for now, at least." I look at the magical rings and have a hard time believing that I made these flawless circles, which represent the essence of each element. Going back to basics was the right place to start.

"Maybe you are getting better at understanding your magic," Glenna says. "How do you feel?"

"I feel relaxed, though surprised," I admit. "I did not have to struggle to reach the elements within the sphere, nor did I have difficulty shaping them, like before."

I still don't understand how my magic works, but maybe I am not so scared of it anymore.

"All it takes is some practice, Lilla. Now let's try something else."

CHAPTER 15

I find Arrov standing in the corridor when I exit my room the next day. "May I join you?" he asks.

After hours of magical practice, I fell into bed, exhausted, and slept through most of the morning. I woke up feeling unsettled. I took a quick sonic shower, letting the gentle sound waves clean sweat off my skin, then dressed in a long blue shirt dress with black boots. I tried to busy myself by reading my mom's journal again, but I couldn't pay attention to the words. I had to leave my room.

"Sure, I'm just going to visit Fearghas. Though I have no idea where he is kept."

Arrov falls in step beside me. "Then let's search for him together."

We take a few turns in the endless gray corridors, heading deeper into the Teryn spacecraft. The rectangular panels with lights around the perimeter give no indication of where we are on the ship. I can't wait for this journey to be over and set foot on solid ground. I sigh.

"Are you okay, Lilla?"

"I would be if I didn't keep thinking about crashing—after all, that's what happened last time I was on a spaceship with you," I joke. We've been traveling for a week now, but it's still hard for me to deal with the fact that we are in space.

Arrov snorts. "It was our first rebel mission for which we volunteered! It sure turned out to be a disaster!"

"We were lucky that Callum was able to save us in time or we would have perished in space!"

I shiver recalling the crash and rub my arms. "I'm glad there are no windows in this corridor."

"I understand what you mean," Arrov says, and gestures to the hide-like walls. "Knowing that the ship is the only barrier against cold and ruthless space is hard for me to comprehend, and I am used to space travel. I cannot imagine what this must do to you. You know, with, uh, your—"

"My claustrophobia," I finish his sentence. "It's okay to talk about it. I know you are not judging me. But yes, it takes constant effort to keep it at bay. It helps that this ship is a thousand times bigger than that cramped spacecraft you and I were piloting."

We stop at another intersection of identical-looking corridors. I peer down to the left, then to the right. I have no idea which way to go.

Arrov points to the left and raises an eyebrow as a question.

I shrug. "We might as well."

"Have you made any progress with your mission?"

I shake my head. "Not much. The inhabitants of this ship are just as unyielding as Caderyn. No matter how many ways I've asked them about their Guardian Goddess Laoise or her whereabouts, the answers were searing looks or complete disregard. I don't understand why they won't talk to me! Unless it was Caderyn who ordered them to keep quiet about it."

"That's possible," Arrov says. "It must be frustrating for you."

A group of four tired-looking crewmen wearing dark blue overalls appears in the corridor. They head toward us. One of the men knocks into me, hard with his shoulder as he passes on my right, making me stumble.

Arrov bellows, his eyes flashing red.

He picks up two crewmen, holding them by the top of their heads, and throws them into the other paralyzed two. "What is wrong with you?!" he roars at them until they run away.

Arrov puts a hand on the wall and leans his head on his thick arm. "My apologies! I have been experiencing, uh, inexplicable anger lately. When I saw those Teryns try to intimidate you, it was too much. You must think I'm a monster."

I touch his arm. "No, I don't think that, but it would be best not to repeat such an outburst."

Arrov lifts his head. "You're right," he says and points behind him. "I think I'll head back to calm down a bit." He retreats from the corridor.

I can't imagine what Arrov must be going through. How scary it must be for him to think he may never turn back to his original self. No wonder he is angry.

I take a few more turns until I am lost with no idea where Fearghas might be or even how to find my way back.

Three warrior men and a woman, dressed in black military uniforms, march into the corridor. "How do I get back to the living quarters?" I ask.

"Via the airlock," a woman with strawberry blond hair says as she passes me without stopping. The men snicker.

"Thank you!" I shout after her.

Buckets of fishguts!

A strange wave of sorrow washes over me. I miss the scents of brine and salt in the air, drifting from the Fyoon Ocean. The sound of waves crashing against the cliffs. I miss the village I used to visit. The beach where Fearghas and I used to gallop, kicking up sand around us. I miss Nic and—

Something whooshes by my left cheek and hits my shoulder, stinging it.

"What on Uhna—" I say but cascading fear and pain sever any logical thoughts. Terror oppresses and crushes my head and my body, cutting off my air.

My head swims. My ears buzz. Black spots rob me of my sight.

My bright orb of magic flares up. I embrace it, grabbing for thick thread of Lume for defense. I let it burst out of me, then my legs give out.

I collapse to the ground just as the ceiling comes crashing down on top of me.

CHAPTER 16

"I'm sorry!" I say to Nic in a bizarre dream that won't release me. With black hair, dark brown eyes, and his six-foot height, he could be the replica of my father. My brother hovers before me in the darkness, his white jacket splattered with red, and a hand covering the slash wound on his throat.

"I wish I could have saved you!" I cry. "I wish I would have made a different choice—"

"I know, and I forgive—" Nic, with forlorn eyes says, then gasps for air. The blood from his wound cascades like the tallest ocean wave, turning everything red.

Lilla, wake up!

When the red retreats, Father smiles at me, his expression tired.

"What are you doing here?" I ask and look around his luxurious apartment, in a prestigious cloudscraper in Uhna's Olde City. "And where is Nic?"

"You know where he is," Father says, and lowers himself next to me on the white leather sofa with a groan. He is still healing from the stab wounds in his chest. "Right by your mom's side. Resting together."

"I regret that I never married your mom," Father says with a deep sigh.

I look away from him. The view from the floor-to-ceiling windows shows Fye Island across the bay, and the ruins of the Crystal Palace. It must be a painful reminder for him. Father will never be a ma'ha again. He will live out his life as a tolerated guest in a gilded cage. The Uhnan citizens showed more mercy toward him than Father ever did toward his subjects when he forced the refugees to work in the underwater crystal mines.

"I know you do," I say. He told me before I left. It was our last conversation on Uhna, one that went better than I thought possible. "Why are we talking about this again?"

Father ignores my question. "There are so many things I would do differently if I had a second chance."

I study his face and notice how pale he is. He's aged decades in the past weeks. His dark brown eyes lost the spark that once defined him.

"I grew up under a lot of pressure," Father continues. "I had royal duties to carry out. There was no room for emotion. It was easy to put my feelings aside. Throughout those marriage contracts, it helped me stay sane. I survived. At least I thought I did. Then Nic was born . . . and my life changed."

He rubs his chest over his heart and winces.

"His birth was the best thing that happened to me. The walls I built around myself imploded. Love made me a different person and I showered Nic with attention."

Father smiles, lost for a moment in the past. "Throughout those years, Nic wasn't happy. I knew he needed a mother. It was the one thing I couldn't and wouldn't give him. Because I had enough."

He nods to himself, his gaze focused on his clasped hands in his lap. "I'd had enough of the royal women of other planets, and the high society women who craved what royalty could give them, who never saw me as a person worthy of love without the title. I couldn't trust anyone."

Father's image and the apartment flicker, turning fuzzy. "Why are you telling me this?" I ask. My question repeats. Over and over like the strangest echo.

Lilla, wake up!

Then the flickering stops.

Father is no longer next to me. I look around and find him by the window, leaning on it. Condensation gathers around his hand on the surface of the glass.

"I truly loved your mother, Lilla. She gave me you and the happiest five years of my life. We were a family—the four of us. I should have . . ."

He clears his voice. "It doesn't matter what I should have done. The fact is, I became the parent I never thought I would be—forceful and out of touch with my children. I ignored both of you. I buried myself in politics. I favored Nic over you, without even realizing it."

"I know! I was there!" I cry out but no sound comes from my mouth.

"I believed I was doing the best for both of you. But in the end, I was taking the easy path by sending Nic to the Coalition Fleet to study and by sending marriage contracts out for you. It took the least effort. I was still grieving over your mother. You reminded me of her too much. A pain that undid me every single day."

I close my eyes against the hurt. Against so many years of pain and disconnect.

When I open them, Father sits by me. He coughs with a rattling sound, his body stooping. He looks into my eyes with bloodshot ones. "Losing Nic—"

The blood drains from my face, turning it cold. "Father, it was my f—"

He grasps my hand. "No, Lilla. If there is anyone to blame, it's me. I was blind and let him walk into a trap."

But I don't believe it was Father's fault. I had a chance to save my family by accepting DLD's offer to relinquish my magic to Him. But I couldn't do that. It was my decision that cost Nic's life.

Father clears his throat. "Losing my son made me realize how precious little time I have left with you. I know this is not something that we can patch up overnight. But maybe it's not too late."

Maybe. I squeeze his hand. In time.

LILLA, WAKE UP!

CHAPTER 17

I groan and blink my eyes open. For a second, I have no idea where I am.

"Finally," Glenna says with relief in her voice.

I lift myself up onto my elbows on the bed. The soft whine of powerful engines breaks the silence. I recognize the minimalistic decoration of my living quarters on the Teryn spacecraft. I try to remember how I got here, but my mind is not cooperating.

"What ha—" I ask, but my words turn into a dry cough.

Glenna hands me a metal cup. "Drink this first."

I take a sip of the hot but sweet, orange-colored tea. Its aromatic scent tickles my nose. "Hmmm. This is not bad. Unlike some of your bitter and horrid concoctions you've made me drink."

"I didn't hear you complain when they helped you feel better."

There is that. "What happened?"

The inward-angled door swooshes open and Ragnald enters. Glenna snaps at him, "Not now!" He turns around without a word and exits.

"You could be nicer to him, you know."

"I could," Glenna grumbles. "What is the last thing you remember?"

"I remember . . . walking down a corridor . . . and . . ." I rub my forehead to concentrate. Sharp pain jabs where my finger touches skin. A trickle of heat emits from the Sybil talisman on the back of my neck, healing.

"Your Lume magic took a nice chunk out of three levels of corridors, most of it landing right on top of you. It's a miracle that you didn't take out the whole ship. Frankly, it's a miracle you survived. Thanks to how some of the big pieces landed, creating a makeshift tent above you and protecting you from the brunt of the crash. You barely had any scratches on you."

"How did I end up back here? Shouldn't I be in a medical center?"

"I insisted on treating you in your room, surrounded by your friends. As to how you got here—it was Callum."

I sit up so fast the room starts spinning. "Where is he?"

"He couldn't stay," Glenna says and steadies me with a hand. "He tore apart the wreckage and carried you here in his arms. He would not let anyone near you except me, and guarded you for two days before he was forced to leave. Callum wanted to stay, but . . ." she trails off when she realizes the effort it takes to keep my expression schooled and not burst into tears. "You were poisoned," she blurts.

"What?!"

"When Ragnald confirmed that there were traces of Lume magic over the, um, holes you tore through the levels, we both thought that something must have triggered you to use your magic. Unless you were practicing and it backfired. You know, like it did with the library, back on Uhna." Glenna raises an eyebrow in question.

"No, I wasn't practicing my magic." I wave the half-empty metal cup around for emphasis, splashing some tea on my blanket. "Besides, I only burned down the library twice!" How long do I have to be reminded of that?

"That's what I told Ragnald, but it's good to know in any case." Glenna takes my cup before I can turn the white blanket orange. "I found a pinpoint-size wound by your neck, which makes me think that whoever attacked you must have used some sort of dart. Either made of magic or for injecting you with the poison. Since no one could find the dart, it is highly possible that it was the former."

"Did Ragnald confirm the magic poison?"

"No, he didn't."

"Then how do you know I was poisoned with magic?"

"Maybe the word 'poison' isn't quite accurate. For two days your body fought whatever you were injected with. I don't want to scare you, but I was getting worried when I couldn't wake you."

"Last time you were knocked out for days . . ." Glenna's voice trails off. She turns her head away and wipes at her eyes, pretending to fuss with her dark crimson hair.

Was after the battle with DLD, when Nic died.

I hug her shoulders for a long moment and squeeze my eyes shut to keep my tears at bay.

"What we know," Glenna continues, "is that there were no other magical traces at the scene besides Lume. It was a targeted attack on you. Something triggered you to use your magic, which in my opinion proves at least the magical aspect of the dart."

"I recall feeling repulsed, which is my reaction to the dark Acerbus element."

"It could have been Acerbus," Glenna says, "but I can't confirm that. We didn't find any trace of it. I don't think this attack was meant to kill you. You would be dead if that was the intention and not chatting here with me."

She is probably right.

The door to my living quarters swishes open and Callum steps in.

Glenna jumps to her feet. "I'll, uh, I'll be back in a few minutes!"

Callum nods at Glenna as she hurries out of my room. Then he sits by me and pulls me into an embrace. "Gods, I thought I lost you!"

I close my eyes for a second, inhaling his scent of sun, sand, and the intriguing scent that is his own. "I'm fine, and I even remember who I am," I joke, referring to the first time we met, when I couldn't remember who I was or how I'd gotten to his spaceship.

"That's a relief." Callum pulls back. He cups my face in his hands and kisses me.

Before our kiss can deepen and turn too passionate, Callum leans back. "Gods, if anything would have happened to you . . ."

Belthair's warning about Caderyn flashes in my mind. "I didn't think that journeying on your father's ship could be so dangerous," I say, and realization sinks in—whoever shot me with that magical dart is still out there, somewhere on this spacecraft!

Callum frowns. "Are you implying that I can't protect you?" He gets to his feet and paces in front of my bed.

"It's not that! Ever since I've boarded this ship, the crew acts unhappy with my presence and then this incident happened—"

"Do you think that it was the praelor who orchestrated it?"

I stare at him. "He could have done that," I say, thinking out loud. "He has thousands of warriors at his disposal. This attempt was just strong enough to knock me out for a few days but not kill me. I could even imagine why Caderyn would do this—I am not a Teryn, as he likes to point out; I tried to acquire his army and have an unwanted Bride's Choice claim on his son; not to mention I was asking too many questions about the Teryn guardian goddess. Hypothetically, it does make sense."

An orange-reddish light flashes across Callum's eyes. "How could you think that it was my father?"

I throw my hands up. "I wasn't thinking that! You put the idea into my head and now it's there! Are you happy?"

"Not particularly!" Callum says and storms out.

I gape after him. Did we just have our first spat?

CHAPTER 18

ANKHAR

I observe the Teryn general storm out of the Sybil's room and feel satisfaction. I enjoy watching the Sybil hurt; always did, even before I became the Ankhar—general and right hand to the Archgod of Chaos and Destruction.

The attack I arranged did not work as planned. The Acerbus should have incapacitated the Sybil long enough for me to kidnap her, but I underestimated her wild magic. I was lucky to get out of there in one piece!

I touch my aching shoulder where the Lume grazed it and clench my hands, staring at the door leading to the Sybil's room. It's so tempting to burst in there and take her out! Though I cannot do that. The Archgod of Chaos and Destruction gave specific orders, and I am not strong enough to go against Him. Yet.

It is a miracle that I am standing here, hidden behind a cloud of Dusky A'ris, when I should have died plummeting to my death.

I am learning how to use the dark elements of Murky A'qua, Black T'erra, Shadowy Fla'mma, Dusky A'ris, and Acerbus. Their power surges in me, filling me to the brim, making me feel invincible for the first time in my life! I want to slaughter and drain the whole ship, including the Sybil, a desire that pumps through my veins irresistibly, but I am on a short leash. For now.

I am still new. I shiver recollecting how I came to be the new Ankhar.

I woke up in a white room, lying on a white floor, and gazing at the white, seamless walls, trying to remember what happened.

He stood across from me in His original form, bursting with divine and lethal power, His long, black hair floating around Him, wearing a loose black tunic and matching pants, barefoot. He was painting a beautiful and ethereal meadow with three women, two blond and one dark-violet-haired, when He looked at me and said, "Welcome, my Ankhar. I have an errand for you. I want you to bring me the Sybil. I need to syphon her magical powers."

"Why?" I asked, confused. My body was on fire one second, then chilled the next. My skin tingled, then stretched too tightly over my bones.

"Because I need to absorb the last Lumenian's power! Now do as I said and do not fail me!"

Shaking the memory off, I exhale. Though I do not need air anymore. It's a habit I cling to, denying the truth of what I have become. Something that is not quite alive. Something *different* altogether.

A Teryn crewman strides by me, oblivious of the danger I pose, trailing the tantalizing scent of fresh blood, triggering my fangs to descend. Hunger, never satisfied hunger urges me to follow, and I give in to the temptation. As long as I feed, I do not need rest to recuperate. I heal in an instant. My elemental magic replenishes in seconds. A secret the Lumenians never discovered, though if they did, I bet they abhorred it! Foolish, arrogant creatures!

I laugh under my breath, making the crewman look around nervously in the empty corridor, unable to perceive me.

The Sybil has no idea that there is a new Ankhar in place. Her ignorance will be the demise of the Lumenians!

CHAPTER 19

LILLA

"We're here," Callum says and stops at our metal table in the mess hall the next morning. There is a line around his mouth when he looks at me.

"This trip cannot end soon enough," Teague mutters and takes out a handful of nuts from his pocket. "Flashing lights, dozens of exsanguinated crewmen! We might as well be cursed!"

I raise my hands. "Don't look at me! I had nothing to do with any of it," I say. Isa and Bella giggle and I just hope they did not reassemble that remote they used on the spaceship's lights the other day.

At the word "exsanguinated" I remember how I found those bodies, back on Uhna, lying in a pile on the beach, among them Deidre. "Do you know what happened to those crewmen? Did you find any corruption?"

The hair on my neck stands up. I look around to find who watches me, but there is no one else in the room outside of us. A repulsive feeling makes my skin itch, and I rub it.

Teague shakes his head as he pops the nuts into his mouth by the handful. "No corruption," he says, and I exhale in relief. DLD is not here to turn us into His dark servants. He adds, "It seems that they suffered a freak accident. They, uh, stumbled over the railings in the hangar and, uh, ended up hanging—"

Ragnald interrupts him. "That is enough of the gruesome details. There are ladies present."

Glenna snorts. "I am not queasy like you, mage."

I glance at Callum, and he turns his head away. I have no doubt that this time he avoided me on purpose. But that's fine with me. I'm still upset with the way he stormed out in the middle of our conversation.

Teague chews for a second and winks at me, smiling, but clears his expression when Callum glowers at him, then heads toward the closest counter with metal trays full of rolls.

"Are we already on Teryn?" Glenna asks from my left, twirling the white strand around her finger.

Ragnald, sitting on her right, reaches for Glenna's shoulder, but she bats his hand away. "Stop driving me crazy!"

Ragnald takes a deep breath and says, "It's been a few hours. I think you need your—"

"I'll let you know, mage, when I need your help, thank you!"

Only Glenna can make the word "mage" sound like an insult.

"Glennie, you are not being nice!" Isa says. "Just take your medicine and stop complaining." Bella adds, "Wasn't that what you used to say to us?"

Glenna shrugs. "I did say 'thank you.'"

"That doesn't make it better," Isa says, laughing. "Oh, Glennie," Bella adds, "your temper always gets away with you!"

Glenna glares at the twins. "Stay out of my boat!"

I look up and find Callum studying me with intent blue eyes. Glenna notices too. "I can move if you want me to," she offers, but I shake my head. She raises an eyebrow in response but stays put.

"We've arrived so fast?" Belthair comments, sitting by the twins. "I thought it would take months, not weeks, to cross from Galaxy Five to Galaxy Six."

"Or forever," Arrov mutters, sitting hunched at the other end, on top of the metal table.

Isa's eyes light up. "How is that possible? What type of space travel are you using?" Bella adds, "It can't be FTL."

"What's that?" Glenna asks.

"We are not using FTL, or Faster Than Light," Teague says and settles by Arrov with a tray of meats and offers some to the giant, who declines it. "We are traveling at the light-bending speed of one hundred CWP, or Cosmic-Web Propulsion."

"Say what?" Belthair asks, then makes a gagging sound. He picks a long, light blue strand of fur out of his mouth. "Ugh, Arrov! You're shedding!"

"I can't help it!" Arrov whines and scoots a bit farther away from Belthair. He could crush Belthair with one of his hands, which are the size of the metal trays. The fact that he is not doing that is a wonder.

Isa and Bella, with hopeful expressions, each raise a comb, but Arrov growls at the twins. "I'm still picking out beads from my fur. Beads!"

"There is nothing wrong with looking pretty," Isa says, and Bella wiggles her eyebrows at Arrov.

"The simplest explanation," Teague says, waving a piece of dried meat, "is that we are using the cosmic-web like a space highway to lay out our course. We collect space particles with the help of the long-beaked salamanders. They filter those particles down to hydrogen atoms for us and we use those atoms to slingshot to our destination along the charted path on the cosmic web, practically appearing at any galaxy in a few weeks or so. One side effect, though: we tend to push space rubble ahead of us."

"There was nothing simple about that explanation," Belthair says, crossing his top two arms.

"That is why we ran into the asteroids when you arrived near Uhna," Arrov grumbles. I add, pointing at Callum, "I always knew it was not an accident!"

Callum raises an eyebrow. "Still complaining after I saved you? I deserve more gratitude."

"You held the space crash against me, and even called me a spy!" I sputter.

"So cute!" Isa says, and Bella adds, "Lilla is blushing!"

"Anyway, I think you should call it 'asteroid-pushing speed,'" I say, ignoring my burning face. "It would be far more accurate."

"Or APS for short," Isa says, clapping her hands. Bella adds, "I like that better, too! More scientific."

Callum frowns at the twins across from him. "We will *not* call it that. Ever!"

"But—" the twins insist, only to get interrupted when the ship shudders and creaks.

"No time to argue," Callum says as he flows to his feet. "Get ready to depart."

CHAPTER 20

ANKHAR

I stare at the Sybil. My not-beating heart fills with hate knowing she is so happy and fitting in with her friends. I never had friends. Not trustworthy ones, anyway.

Oh, how I want to kill her! Make the Sybil suffer! Like she made me suffer! She ruined my life. She destroyed my dreams and killed me. It's what she deserves. Then I can be free of her and find a way to be free from the archgod.

My hands shake and I force my fangs to retract.

With this new body comes urges that are not natural for how I used to think or behave. I was always good at holding my temper. I used to think clearly, past my emotions that did not dictate my actions but rather fueled me, helping to work toward my goals. I did not operate on such pure, basic urges and near-animalistic drives, as I do now.

The Sybil looks around, her gaze passing over my hiding spot. She must feel something is amiss, sensing danger.

I snigger in silence. Good! She should fear me!

I study the Sybil's allies, my enemies. I curse their existence and loyalty. They surround her, providing protection, making it difficult for me to isolate the Sybil again. I cannot fail my task!

I need an ally, too. I know who could help.

What I am about to do is unheard of! No Ankhar has ever attempted such a thing in the history of six era wars! It's plain insanity!

I float away from the Sybil, out into space, a useful skill. I set my eye on a half-desolated planet, my new destination. I know without a doubt that my plan will work. I will have the advantage of surprise on my side.

I throw my head back and laugh in the vacuum of space, though no sound can be heard.

CHAPTER 21

LILLA

"This is not how I imagined Teryn," I say as I step out of the shuttlecraft after Callum and Teague.

Lush forest surrounds us. Among the evergreen trees hills roll covered in bright green plants. On top of the hills, ancient-looking fortresses nestle, built with light gray bricks. The fortresses cluster together in a circle, grouped in six, with the largest one, in the center, towering above the others. I glimpse dozens of such clusters in the distance, like strange cities, but no sign of advanced technology.

Callum strides up to me. In his calloused palm he holds a yellow, button-size thing, with tiny copper parts glinting on top of it. "Take this."

"What is it?" I ask and lift the round thing up. Thin legs descend, running in place, and I almost drop it. "It's a bug!"

Isa and Bella step close, pointing at their ears. "We have one too!"

I try to hand it back to Callum. "I'll be fine without whatever this is."

"The last thing I want is you getting lost and not have the means to communicate with anyone," Callum says and points to his ear to show he has one too.

Belthair taps his earlobe, and his voice comes out magnified from the bug in my hand. "Without me, she'd still be haunting the Uhnan smuggling tunnels, thinking she is heading in the right direction!"

My friends laugh.

"Ha-ha!" I say and allow Isa to help me "install" the bug device behind my ear. "I'm sure I would have found my way out of the tunnels . . . eventually." I shudder when I feel the thin legs clutch onto the edge of my ear. "I can't believe I'm bugged!"

"It's called the k'bug. Push at its back by pressing at your earlobe when you want to talk," Callum explains. The thin, long hairs on its legs resonate, creating sound waves that can reach far distances to another bug, even out in space. It feeds off died skin particles and can survive a long time, even in horrible conditions."

Fascinating. A living technology. "I didn't see you use one of these on Uhna."

Callum snorts. "No. I used a previous, archaic version for communications, one I knew would get the attention of a certain rebel."

"Speaking of that 'archaic' device," I say, ducking my head, "have you ever found out who sent the report from Uhna that led to your father to rush to my home world?"

"No I didn't, but I have my suspicions. There aren't that many who had access to it. I just need more proof."

Callum sighs and places a hand on my forearm when I turn away from him. "Listen, I shouldn't have left like that."

I put a hand over his. "I realize now that it couldn't have been Caderyn who attempted to magically poison me." I had a lot of time to think about it these past few days. "Knowing how Teryns prefer technology with biological components, I concluded that Caderyn would not have tried to magically poison me." I rise on my tiptoes and kiss him. "We're good?"

Callum hugs me to him. "We're good."

"I'm waiting!" Caderyn's voice booms into my ear from the bug device.

CHAPTER 22

We turn toward the most dominant and elegant gray fortress, towering in majestic glory in front of us.

At least twenty stories in height, it reaches for the blue sky with peaked roofs of various heights on narrow towers. A gray brick wall with siege towers pops up from among the viridescent trees along the outer edge of the courtyard. At the base of its hill, in the pine woods, runs a curving stream before disappearing from my view.

Round wooden doors open, and three monks step through.

A dark-haired monk, dressed in a red robe with two sashes on its front—A'nima yellow and A'ris blue—smiles as he approaches. "Welcome to Pada," he says. The other two monks, wearing beige robes and white head covers, with black fabric in the middle, stand behind the dark-haired monk, with their hands clasped in front of them.

"Pada?" I ask. Never heard of it.

"The Pada are famous for being the greatest hosts in the whole Seven Galaxies," Teague says. "Their pies and cakes are the most delicious. Padan dinners have been coveted for hundreds of years—wars have even been fought over their reception times."

"Is that so?" I ask, embarrassed about my meager knowledge of the Seven Galaxies. Growing up, my education was mainly limited to royal rules and etiquette. Most of what I know beyond that I've gained from reading ancient tomes at the Royal Library whenever I had the chance.

"They love hosting us and our guests at their monasteries," Teague continues, "and making our weapons for this Era War. We didn't have a chance to fight in the previous Era War, we were too new, but we are ready now."

"I thought blacksmiths are the ones skilled in crafting weapons," I say.

"We taught them how, so they can participate in the Era War with honor," Teague explains. He eyes the four monks who just stepped outside, carrying wooden trays with plates on them. "It's true that they enjoy hosting gatherings more, which is a good thing."

"Why is that?" I ask.

"Because no outsiders are allowed to step foot on Teryn," Teague says. "If they do, on the rare occasions when we allow them, they will never return to their home world."

I blink at Teague. Callum never told me any of this!

"I am Devotee Zimon," the lead monk says without a head cover. "Please accept our humble welcoming gifts from my disciples." He gestures at the monks with hands full of trays. "Do not engage them in discussion. They are not allowed to speak. Feel free to direct your questions to me or to any other devotees."

I take my plate and marvel at the pieces of food, arranged in the shape of a dark-violet-haired fighter, with a black horse, and bright white magical blasts around her. "That looks like Fearghas and me! Did they know we were coming?"

"No, they did not," Teague says. "The praelor made an impromptu decision to stop here. Not only do the monks know when we'll be here, but who will be with us, and they never make a mistake."

"This looks a lot like me," Glenna says and shows me her plate. On it is a red-haired herb gatherer, with a thin white streak in her crimson hair, in a green forest, surrounded by animals. She peeks at mine. "Surreal!"

"I don't like mine," Arrov grumbles. His plate has a light-blue giant with an ice-covered mountain on it.

Ragnald presents his, beaming. "That's one tiny handsome mage with triple elemental affinity!" Glenna checks it out and picks up a red berry that represents Fla'mma magic and pops it into her mouth. "Now it has dual elemental affinities," she says.

Isa and Bella giggle. "Even our miniature versions are fashionable and smart!" Their two food figurines wear minidresses and carry laser guns with numbers floating around their heads.

Belthair points at his dish, where a six-armed fighter stands, each hand holding something different—a serrated pirate sword, a dagger, a flower, a rifle, a laser pistol, and a money bag. "Yep. That's pretty much who I am."

Callum picks up the head of the tiny black-clad warrior on his own plate and tosses it behind him. "I don't eat flowers."

Teague shrugs. "I have no such problem. Most Teryns consider eating flowers dangerous, as it can be toxic to us, but I doubt the Pada would try to kill me." He shoves the snacks into his mouth, eating faster than usual.

"What's the hurry?" I ask Teague, while still undecided whether to eat mine. It's almost too beautiful to consider it as food and not art.

Teague chews with his mouth full and lifts a hand, counting from three fingers backward. When he reaches one, Caderyn shouts, "Get that thing away from me!" A black plate flies by us, scattering pieces of food.

Callum sighs. "Every single time."

CHAPTER 23

After finishing with our welcome plates, Devotee Zimon leads our group through the round double doors. We enter into a corridor with high arches that opens to a rectangular courtyard full of fruit trees. Disciples harvest ripe red and purple fruits into baskets by their feet. We take a left turn and pass by another courtyard, this one full of planters with leafy vegetables that are on the ground, on shelves, or hanging from poles. Another courtyard contains disciples hard at work crafting porcelain clays into plates and curing them in outdoor brick ovens. Yet another turn and we stride past a courtyard where red and beige sheep are being sheared in an orderly fashion.

"These monks are quite self-sufficient," Glenna comments from next to me and I nod in agreement.

Our last turn shows a courtyard in disarray with wooden and stone stations set up in a haphazard fashion for blacksmithing. Disciples run around in a chaos, carrying long swords, and piling them high wherever they can find room.

We pass through another wooden door into a foyer with stone tiles and a steep stairway leading up to the second floor. The walls are covered in numerous paintings, metal, clay, and glassworks, all the way to the ceiling. Ancient arms and other weapons are interspersed among them. Judging by their pristine state, they are more for decoration than use.

Ragnald glances my way. "In addition to their culinary talent, the Pada are well known for collecting and preserving art from the Seven Galaxies. They are formidable experts in magic as well."

Glenna studies Ragnald. "You know a lot about the Pada."

"I had the good fortune to study with a Pada monk," the mage explains.

"I didn't realize there was a Pada monk in the Pax Septum Coalition," I say.

Ragnald shakes his head. "There aren't any in the coalition, but there was one advising the H'rarh Dynasty."

"The nemesis of the coalition!" Glenna says. "How could you?"

"I was not assisting the dynasty," Ragnald explains. "I was simply granted a rare apprenticeship with their Pada. I'd be a fool to pass it up. I didn't ask permission from the Academia nor the coalition. Neither of them had any business telling me what I can or can't do with my time."

"Mage, this is not like you to do something against the Academia's wishes," Glenna mocks.

"In my two hundred years, I have done many things. Besides, I was young and couldn't resist the opportunity to learn from a fabled Pada monk who was rumored to be able to fight like a shadow."

"And did he?" I ask.

Ragnald gives me an enigmatic smile in response.

Belthair elbows his way between Glenna and the mage. "I heard they can also fight with wild animals by their side!"

Arrov pushes Belthair to the back. "I heard they can outsmart coups and usurpers without fail!"

"Come to think of it," Glenna says, "I read somewhere that they can bring life to any dying world's nature."

"That's awe-inspiring," I say. "Who knew these Pada monks were so legendary?" Evidently not me.

Caderyn overhears my last words and stops to face me. "None of that is true! They are nothing but fables spread by the weak in hopes of the illusion of protection. Look at them. We conquered the Pada world without any resistance. Does that sound so 'awe-inspiring' to you?" Caderyn mocks. "I thought you would know better, since Lumenians are supposed to be legendary, and yet here you are as anything but."

CHAPTER 24

"P̲raelor—" Callum says, and I interrupt him before he says something he'll regret.

"I am humbled to meet you, an expert of the Lumenians! I hope to learn so much from you," I say.

Teague and the others snicker.

"You do have a lot to learn from me, little girl. You have a rare chance to witness what it takes to run an empire—ruthless iron fists! Anything else, and you'll have rebellions on your hands. A lesson your father learned the hard way, didn't he?"

I grind my teeth to hold back my opinion.

I can't antagonize the praelor, or he will never allow me to recruit his army. There is too much at stake. Every minute I spend waiting, DLD makes progress, spreading His corruption, enlarging His army with half-corrupted dark servants and dark fiends. Once those nightmarish things reach fully corrupted levels, nothing but Lume magic can stop them.

We enter the cavernous banquet hall. The wooden coffered ceiling and walls, covered in brown and gray stones, dominate the large room. Alcoves and balconies jut from among the intricate adornments and landscape paintings. A'ris magic sparkles on their surfaces, keeping them clean and dust-free. Half a dozen wooden, circular chandeliers with Fla'mma-infused candles that never burn out provide ample light. T'erra magic clings to the bricks, remnants of when the fortress-monastery was built. Judging from the thick magical residue, they must have used a lot of T'erra elemental magic. The inviting room, full of circular tables with white, silk tablecloths and matching high-back chairs, buzzes from more than a hundred guests' conversations.

There are plenty of signs of magic or magic-infused technology here. It's a surprise to find such a blatant showcase of magical proficiency outside the Pax Septum Coalition. Based on how the mages asserted control over all things magical in the coalition, everyone believed that they were the ones controlling magic in the whole Seven Galaxies as well. A belief they fueled as they took on themselves to combat the Turned—mages or healers who have overused their magic, becoming corrupt aberrations that desired destruction and killing in the name of DLD. Glenna's family paid a high price for the mages' overzealous hunt.

"Teague!" a slender man with dark brown eyes shouts and jumps into the colonel's arms. "I thought I'd . . . when they took me . . ." His voice buckles. Then he kisses Teague, embracing him in a passionate hug.

"Love," Teague says and pulls back, "would I ever let anything happen to you?"

A blush appears on the other man's tanned face. "I shouldn't have doubted it," he says and smooths the wrinkles of his elegant silk tunic. "I was just so worried since they said that if you don't comply—"

"Love, it's not important anymore," Teague insists nervously, then turns to us and says, "Allow me to present you my love and life, Consuasor Steaphan a'vaan, who also happens to be a Brainiac."

Steaphan laughs and slaps Teague's shoulder. "Don't use that horrible nickname where the other consuasors, senators, can overhear you! Especially Chief Consuasor Graeme," he says and points to the left at a black-haired man in his thirties. The chief consuasor has a goatee on his tanned face and is dressed in a red silk tunic. "You know how the consuasors despise it when you and the other warriors call us *that*. We all know you warriors are strong and broad-shouldered"—he clears his throat and continues—"unlike us."

"When the Brainiacs quit bragging about how intelligent they are, and stop interfering with the Ground Rules," Teague says, "then we will cease calling them that." Teague touches Steaphan's face. "I never thought you weak for a moment, love. You are the smartest and kindest person I know."

Steaphan's blush deepens, then he smiles at us.

"Greetings to you, Steaphan!" Callum says and clasps the consuasor's forearm in greeting, slapping the other man's back a few times. "Don't let Teague tease you. Give me the word and I'll put him in his place."

Steaphan laughs. "There is no need for that! I refuse to be the cause of your 'argument.'"

"You don't have to worry, love," Teague says. "I can listen. You are so much wiser than any of us."

Steaphan smiles. "Do stop that or these nice people will think you are a hopeless romantic, ruining your tough warrior image." He turns to me and bows. "It is an honor to be in your presence, Sybil. You have the consuasors' support."

Caderyn appears by our group. "Is that so, Consuasor Steaphan? I don't remember declaring my support for the Sybil."

Steaphan straightens his back and faces the praelor with surprising strength. "I believe Chief Consuasor Graeme has informed you of this. *Multiple* times. It is our job to stand by the side of the Archgoddess of the Eternal Light and Order. We just need to discuss a few details and—"

"That Brainiac chatters too much," Caderyn says, crossing his arms. "Graeme shouldn't be agreeing to things without coming to me first. Not that I'd pay much attention to the gibberish he spouts!"

Caderyn bursts into laughter but no one else joins in.

CHAPTER 25

Teague and Steaphan excuse themselves, and the others disperse. Callum and I wander deeper into the banquet hall, mingling with dapper guests. I'm relieved that the crowd parts for Callum and I don't have to battle with my claustrophobia.

"Who is this Chief Consuasor Graeme?" I ask.

"He is the ambitious leader of the Teryn Senatus. Though the way he acts, I am sure he imagines he is the one ruling the Teryn Praelium and not the praelor."

I glance at him. "You don't like this Consuasor Graeme much either."

"He is just another Brainiac who failed at the, uh . . ." His voice trails off.

"Failed at what?" I press but Callum stops by a group of chattering women. Their fashions vary from pantsuits and dramatic evening gowns to minidresses, or barely anything. The only common denominator is their age—they are in their early twenties.

Callum inclines his head to a black-haired, tanned woman who looks a lot like him. She has blue eyes, just like Callum, but they are almond-shaped, unlike his. "That's my younger sister, Rhona," he says to me. "She wants to be a general, and the way she's heading, she will be the first nonme"—he stumbles over a word, then continues—"I mean the first female general in her, uh, age group." His fondness for his sister is clear in his voice.

"I didn't know you had a sister," I say.

"There was no time to talk about my family," Callum says. "We had other important matters to deal with. Not to mention, it never occurred to me that you'd ever meet them."

I frown. "These are the things we are supposed to share with each other."

Callum raises an eyebrow. "If these things are important to you, then I shall do my best to share them with you in the future." He looks around, and his gaze snags on his father badgering a horrified-looking Devotee Zimon over silk-covered chairs Caderyn keeps shaking.

Callum curses under his breath. "You stay here, I have to go before the praelor does something rude. Again!"

Callum strides away and I look back to the group of young women.

A blonde turns to Rhona and says, "You know, with a bit less muscle, and without that ugly black uniform, you could pass as something *almost* feminine."

The other women giggle behind their hands.

"Did they run out of material when they made your dress?" I ask, cutting into their laughter. The blonde's garment in question has the quality of rags. Expensive rags. Peppered with large "holes" that are held together with thin threads around her back and waist, the minidress showcases her black lacy underwear.

The blonde's green gaze travels up and down my body with a mocking and scrutinizing expression. "Who are you supposed to be with that outfit? The waiter or the maid?"

I glance down at my simple off-white evening gown with silver threads woven into its top layer that sparkle in the Fla'mma-infused candlelight. If she considers this servant's attire, what do the rich people on her planet wear?

"After you," I say.

She raises her chin. "I am Crown Princess Intonia Varia Yanna, heir to the Marauders' Syndicate, or as my friends call me, Princess Ivy."

I doubt that she has many friends. "Like the clinging plant?"

"Exactly like that," Princess Ivy says, and swipes her long blond locks over her shoulder. "Though Callum never complained about my 'clinging.'"

CHAPTER 26

I push against the well-dressed guests, fighting to hold back my tears as I rush through the crowded room. Running away from Ivy. Away from Callum.

How could he not have told me about her? What did he like in that arrogant Ivy? He just promised me he'd tell me more about his life, but he forgot to mention his lover?! I don't understand!

The crowd closes around me, and my claustrophobia flares up. I break out in a cold sweat. Clamoring starts up in my ears, and I struggle to breathe. The urge to *flee!* becomes overpowering.

"Lilla," Callum shouts, catching up to me, "where are you going?!"

"Where do you think?"

He reaches for my arm, but I pull away. "How could you not tell me about your lover?"

"Who?" Callum asks with an uncomprehending expression.

"Do you have so many that you need a reminder?" I turn away but he grabs my forearm.

"Would you please stay put for one second?"

"Why? So you can lie more about Ivy? You promised me to always tell the truth!"

"Guardian Goddess Laoise, give me patience!" Callum mutters under his breath, then says, "I have been telling you the truth! I should have known she'd try something like this with you."

I glare at him. "Is that all you have to say? Blame it on Ivy?"

A loud gong sounds. We turn to see a man in his forties with rune-like tattoos on his right cheek; he is standing on a half-moon-shaped wooden platform at the opposite end of the room.

"Welcome back to Pada," the man says. "I am Devotee Zorion. It is my pleasure to host you. Please, take a seat. Dinner will be served right away. Enjoy!" His dark blue ceremonial robe, with a silver ruffled cape, covers his neck and ends at the edge of his wide shoulders. He wears two sashes, which run down in front of his chest—one is A'ris blue, the other is Fl'amma red.

I head to the right, but Callum touches my shoulder. With a nod to the left, he indicates where our table is. I shake his hand off and take a seat next to Glenna.

"Where is Ragnald?" I ask her, ignoring Callum, who sits at my right with Teague, across from Caderyn and Rhona.

"I have no idea where that mage is, and I don't miss him!" Glenna snaps.

"I never told you about Ivy," Callum says in a low voice, "because there is nothing to tell. I never dated her. I didn't encourage her. No matter how hard she tried to change my mind."

"Is that so?" I ask and he nods with an earnest and solemn expression.

My anger dissipates, leaving behind relief and embarrassment over my little outburst. I've never thought myself the jealous type before.

I glance at Ivy, sitting a few tables away from us. I must admit that she is pretty and confident. She looks perfect on the surface, someone who has it together.

Curiosity gets the better of me and I ask, "Why didn't you date her?"

"I was waiting for you," Callum says, looking into my eyes. "You are my whole world, Lilla. My everything."

Speechless, I stare at him, unable to look away from his intent blue gaze. The whole room disappears, leaving Callum and me. My one wish in life is to be with him, together.

Then Ragnald arrives at our table, breaking the moment. He whispers something into Teague's ear. Teague nods and moves down a seat, and Ragnald sits next to Glenna, taking the last available chair.

After the noise of seats scraping on the stone tiles subsides, disciples carrying packed trays flood the reception hall. Tantalizing scents drift through the air.

I look down at the white ceramic plate with octopus legs arranged as if rising from waves of blue vegetables and my stomach drops. "Bucket of fishguts!"

I'm sure the Pada think they are doing me a favor by bringing signature dishes from my home world, but this is a culinary nightmare to me. I can't stand seafood. Not the smell of it, and not the taste of it. Maybe their foresight is not so unlimited after all.

Recognition and humor shine in Callum's eyes as he switches his plate with mine without a word. His has thin slices of red meat piled on it, without any artistic arrangement. I smile in thanks and dig in.

My next course consists of slices of fish wrapped in seaweed. I turn to Callum, but he also got a sea creature, one that's still wiggling. Callum checks Teague's plate, nods, and takes it from him before Teague digs in.

"Hey! What's that supposed to—" Teague's voice trails off as he follows his plate's journey to me, while my plate makes it to him. "I see. No pun intended."

A telltale scent betrays the innocent-looking white square, drizzled with beige sauce, on my next plate. Fish!

Callum checks his and Teague's plate, but they both have seafood offerings.

A gentle tap comes from my left and Glenna hands her plate to me. "I've got it covered, sweetie."

"We want to play too!" Isa and Bella say in unison and even Arrov snaps out of his gloom, sitting on the floor by the twins with his elbows on the tabletop.

I cringe. "Technically, it's not a game we're playing—"

Belthair pipes up, "It doesn't matter, I'm in too!"

"You don't even know what the 'game' is," I say with exasperation, and turn to Glenna, hoping she'll help me out. Instead, she shrugs her shoulders and says, "What the ship, let's play!"

A disciple places another seafood offering in front of me.

Belthair shoves his under my nose, knocking Arrov's plate out of the way and shouts, "I win!"

Murmurs rise from the tables around us, picking up on the fun and mimicking our game, with some of their own rules.

A clamor of laughter and shouts spreads through the reception hall.

Feeling like someone is staring at me, I accept a plate from Arrov and look up, right into Caderyn's eyes.

I freeze. He must think I was raised on a coral reef and not in a palace!

After a long moment, Caderyn nods and smiles. . . . Wait, Caderyn is smiling?

The praelor waves a disciple over, whose serving tray just got ravaged by the closest table's guests. He grabs one of the disciple's sashes and pulls them closer. "I want meat. None of this artsy stuff. Make it happen."

The scared disciple scrambles away in a hurry.

The warriors, scattered around the reception hall, jump to their feet and bang their fists on their tables, shouting, "Sing, Praelor! Sing! Sing!"

Caderyn gestures for them to settle down and bursts into a ballad, to the joy of the Teryn warriors and to the shame of the consuasors, who cover their eyes. The song tells the story of a gory battle the Teryns fought against half-corrupted dark servants and won, full of extraneous details and with a chorus of "And the strong will win while the weak will die!" that repeats too many times.

Belthair and Arrov enjoy the song and belt out the chorus along with the warriors.

Callum glowers. Teague, too preoccupied with eating, doesn't participate in the singing, though he does lift his right hand up and shake it to the rhythm.

Devotee Zimon, looking dismayed, stops by our table. "It was going so well until that plate game."

CHAPTER 27

"I hope you enjoyed your dinner," Devotee Zorion says from the podium, "and the new dinner game brought to you by the Teryn table, along with the musical entertainment."

I duck my head as laughter and applause erupt.

Devotee Zorion waits until it quiets down and says, "Allow me to welcome you to Pada."

This time mild and polite applause comes from the guests.

Teague picks up a piece of cheese from one of the after-dinner trays left on our table. His gaze searches the room until he finds Steaphan sitting in the back, and winks at him.

Many Brainiacs mingle among the other guests wearing colorful silk tunics like Steaphan's. The occupants of the tables are as varied as the colors of the senators' outfits, with skin tones ranging from stone gray to light coral red.

"Love," Teague says to me, "pass me those tantalizing rolls."

I hand him the whole tray full of pastries, rolls, and slices of dark breads. Teague takes it from me with an excited look. How he can eat so much after eight courses, I can't fathom.

Devotee Zorion gestures to a table far on the left. *"Welcome representatives of the Miners' Coalition."*

A round of applause. A short man, sans the coal smudges one would expect of a miner, springs to his feet and bows his head.

"I found the elementalist mage assigned to the Pada world," Ragnald says, leaning toward me so others won't overhear us.

"The Academia of Mages has a far reach," I comment.

Ragnald nods. "Yes, they do, throughout the Seven Galaxies and with strict guidelines when it comes to magical knowledge and its usage. We monitor the worlds, and they must petition us for permission to practice magic. Hence the assigned elementalist mage."

"Welcome representatives of the Marauders' Syndicate."

Another round of applause and Princess Ivy jumps to her feet. She makes an awkward curtsy and waves a hand around while chewing something with an open mouth. Classy.

Ragnald continues, "It took me a while to get some information out of the elder mage. He wasn't coherent. What he told me is interesting. Or disturbing. I can't decide."

"Welcome representatives of the Industrial Conglomerate."

An older man with white hair slicked back and wearing elegant black suit, stands up and bows from the waist.

"According to the old mage, his appointment is a formal gesture," Ragnald says, "and it's the Pada monks who are in complete control over elemental magic here in Galaxy Six. They ignore guidance from the Academia and even restrict the elderly mage's ability to report back."

"That does not align with their peaceful nature. Why would they do this?"

"Welcome representatives of the Merchants' Vendere."

A wiry young man stands up, four of his ears twitching on top of his head, covered in shaggy, greasy-looking hair. I clap along.

"I am not sure, to be honest," Ragnald says, "but there is more."

"Welcome representatives of the Free Traders' Consortium."

I don't even bother to clap this time when a stout man tumbles out of his seat in his effort to get to his feet. His white shirt is covered in food stains, and his pants are stretched to their limit on his sickly pale body. He swipes a long, black wisp of hair off his shiny forehead, pushing the hair back to the top to hide the substantial bald spot in the middle.

"What do you mean?" I ask.

"Last, welcome representatives of the Farmers' Partnership."

Lukewarm and scattered applause greets an older woman dressed in a simple homemade green dress.

"This is not a reception, no matter how many times Devotee Zorion 'welcomes' the assembled," Ragnald says. "This is a mandatory meeting between the conquered worlds and the Teryns. They even rank the worlds in tiers, based on their size and usefulness. For example, Pada and these worlds are part of Tier One. Uhna and the Pax Septum Coalition would have been Tier

Five. Anyway, each world must report their progress on the industrial or agricultural production that the Teryns forced on them, without payment made in exchange, like what you saw with the Pada blacksmithing. Each world has a 'job' to fulfill to preserve their 'honor' in the Era War by supporting the Teryn Praelium in any way the praelor deems necessary."

"That's horrible!"

"They report to the Teryn consuasors," Ragnald continues, "who run the whole Praelium despite what the praelor believes. The praelor 'visits' to remind these worlds that if they fail to attend these 'meetings' they will be punished, and by that they mean blown to bits."

For the first time I look around with the new context in mind and notice the strained looks on the attendants' faces.

Caderyn watches the whole ceremony with voracious glints in his eyes, then glances at me with a pointed look.

Now I understand why we stopped here. This was not just a lesson in what Caderyn meant by ruling with a ruthless iron fist, but also a show of the power he has over the conquered worlds. A fate he wants for Uhna and the Pax Septum Coalition, despite the existing agreement Callum was able to garner during the diplomatic negotiations.

This is also the reason why Caderyn will never respect me. I came from a world that cannot compete with the Teryn Praelium and only managed to buy itself some time before the inevitable takeover happens.

Sea of
Sorrow

Rending Ridge

Blood Mountains

The Bleeding Steps

Witless Maw

Plains of Mourning

River of Death

Mountain of Pain

SAVAGE
RANGE
MOUNTAIN

Pillars of
The Broken Crown

Beware Hills

CITY OF
HONOR

CITY OF
GLORY

OUTPOST

DEFENSE
SILO

BUNKER

EMERGENCE

WISE WOMEN
CAVE

CHAPTER 28

Callum helps me out of the shuttlecraft. I step onto a landing platform surrounded by red sand. Oppressive heat shocks me, burning my skin.

We left Pada right after the dinner reception and arrived on Teryn at dawn.

The sun rises, illuminating the red sand into a rippling red sea. Two moons, one huge and one significantly smaller, touch the horizon behind the curving mountains.

"It's, um, nice here," I say. Sweat breaks out on my back, plastering my white blouse to my skin, saturating the waistline of my black leggings. If I'd known it would be this hot on Teryn, I would have opted out of wearing boots. Too late now.

Callum smiles with pride. "It is, isn't it?" He helps Glenna and the twins out, turning his back right when Arrov appears at the exit.

Arrov jumps out of the craft. "It's hotter here than DLD's as—"

"It's not that bad," I interrupt Arrov, "is it?" If I keep saying it enough times, maybe I'll believe it too.

Belthair crosses his six arms in answer, while Ragnald stares at me, lost for words.

"It will get worse down here, as this is the beginning of the hot season," Teague informs us. "We live on the Mountain of Pain, in the City of Honor, where it's much cooler. We'll be heading there." He gestures to the top of the mountain, where twisting stone-tiled streets run among square and midsize cloudscrapers, blending into the red-hued environment. At the base of the mountain, fields of solar panels glint in the bright sunlight.

Mountain of Pain? I hope that's an endearing name and not a literal one.

Glenna puts a hand over her eyes. "It's a bit of a trek."

"You'll take the elevators," Callum says just as Caderyn's shuttle lands to the right of us, blasting us with hot wind and stinging sand. The warriors pile out, beginning their disembark routine of light sparring. At least Callum and Teague forgo that tradition, probably too excited to get home.

"Lead the way," I say.

"You'll love it here," Callum says as we head toward the base of the mountain. "We just started the Foundation Month observance. Celebrating how we Teryns came to be after the previous Era War ended."

"That's, um, great!" I say, wiping sweat from my face. My bones feel like they are boiling in my body.

"We missed the First Week," Callum says, "and the First Day of the Second Week, but tomorrow will be full of the First Victory, Days of Reflection, and Foundation Month celebrations."

"That's a lot of festivities," I say as we stop by a strange group of animals. The animals in question are supported by six powerful lion-like legs that look double jointed. Their two thin arms, with leather pouches underneath, end in paws with seven long toes. Wooden chair-like contraptions are attached to their backs with complicated harnesses.

Callum stops by the closest one and investigates it. "It's not a lot when we are celebrating life itself," he explains without looking up. "This is a k'mountain lion." He gestures for me to come closer. "Our elevator."

The k'mountain lion turns its flat head with huge black eyes and brays, foam spattering from its mouth.

I lift both of my hands and back away. "I changed my mind. I think I'd rather walk."

Teague snorts. "Love, we'll be running up the mountain while you enjoy a leisurely excursion as the elevator takes you up five hundred levels or so."

Five hundred levels? "I still think—"

"Trust me, Lilla," Callum says, "you don't want to run with us. The praelor keeps a fierce pace."

I glance at Glenna and the twins. They shake their heads, uninterested in climbing the Mountain of Pain. Maybe that's where the mountain received its name—it's a pain to scale it.

"Callum could carry you on his back," Isa says, and Bella adds, "It would be so dreamy! He is certainly strong enough to do it." Then they sigh and bat their eyelashes at the unimpressed-looking Callum.

"Callum could," Teague agrees, "but at the speed we'll be going, Lilla would end up throwing up on him. Again." Referring to the first time when I met Callum on his ship.

"I had a concussion!" I say. "Fine! We'll use the, uh, elevators."

CHAPTER 29

Caderyn, Callum, and Teague help us women out of our seats once we reach the top of the mountain. Rhona ignores us, sighing in impatience. The dozen guards that followed Caderyn have disappeared. The stone-tiled street leads to a dead end, with a large, fifteen-story building dominating it.

More streets with small to midsize cloudscrapers zigzag over the mountain, some built into the mountain wall, others on top of it. The style of the buildings is modern, reminding me of barracks. The flat rooftops create the illusion of tiered terraces that blend into the dark red color of the mountainside. They form an elongated city, with others like this visible in the distance, on the long and curving mountain ridge.

Callum clasps my hand and points to the east, toward a desolate and rocky area. "The Teryns first emerged at the bottom of the Bleeding Steps, earning their name from the painful crossing the Teryns had to endure over the sharp, volcanic rocks cutting up their feet. They crossed the now inactive volcano, Rending Ridge, named after the predators who tore many pilgrims apart. They had to swim across the Sea of Sorrow, which is more like a lake than a sea, earning its name from all those who drowned in the process," he says proudly as he tracks the historical journey with his hand, encompassing a flattened volcano and a reddish lake. Then he turns toward the northwest, pointing at a long and curving mountain range. "Then those early Teryns scaled Blood Mountain, where they were honed into warriors. They ventured into Witless Maw, aptly named after the foolish expedition that cost even more lives. But they had a goal—they wanted to settle at the most defendable location. They did not stop until they arrived here, at the Mountain of Pain, the hardest mountain to climb, at the far side of the Savage Mountain Range, which dominates this continent. They established the City of Honor, where praelors and praelias lived for centuries. My home."

"That's quite an expedition your ancestors took," I say. "Where did the Teryns come from?"

"No one really knows," Callum says. "Some of those early tribes decided to stay behind at the emergence location and founded the City of Glory, near the Plains of Suffering, called that because of its lack of viable resources. Others chose to form wandering tribes, roaming the Beware Hills, full of dangerous wild animals, in search of honor. But no one ever steps foot in the Pillars of Broken Crown." He points to the south of us where a ruin is visible. "Look at those ribbonlike pillars that form a crown. We think it's haunted by those who died before our emergence. They left behind advanced technology that allowed us to become spacefaring hundreds of years before we could have invented it. We did have to modify and enhance it with biological components. Unfortunately, much of that society's knowledge and culture has been lost. There are many other ruins of cities scattered all over Teryn, but none is as intact as the Pillars of Broken Crown."

How sad! I wonder what happened to that extinct civilization.

Arrov climbs up next to us and wipes his massive hands together. He ascended the steep cliff wall on his own, going as fast as the k'mountain lions.

"The view was amazing," Glenna says, looking over the ledge.

Belthair steps out of an Umbrae portal next to her and taps the worn leather gauntlet to close the swirling shadow gateway. "I've seen better." Though where he could have, I don't know.

"I, for one, have never seen such things in my two hundred years as those huge lizards with wings, five eyes, and a deadly scorpion stinger hunting to the right of you, Lilla," Ragnald marvels. He steps off the makeshift stair he built out of chunks of rocks using his T'erra magic. "Fascinating wildlife!"

I look around, wide-eyed. "You saw a *what* hunting by me?"

Glenna's wearied expression lightens up. "I saw them too! They were beautiful!"

"They are called k'scorpions," Callum says. "When tamed, they are great for the children to ride. Teague had one as a kid."

"I loved that old temperamental k'scorpion till the day it died," Teague says and waves at Consuasor Steaphan who appears followed by Fearghas. "Love, I'm glad you were able to join us."

A black-haired warrior sprints to us. "Praelor, I . . . couldn't . . . stop the

. . . horse!" he says, panting. Most of the uniform's right slide is tattered, appearing to be gnawed on.

Caderyn snorts. "I would have been surprised if you did."

Fearghas stops by me, nickering. I pet his thick, black neck. "You are so stubborn!" I cannot admonish him when he looks so mischievous. I turn to Caderyn and ask, "Where can he rest?" Hopefully in a safe place, somewhere he can't get out to hurt others.

A bearded warrior exits the fifteen-story building and jogs toward us. Caderyn nods at him. "He will take care of Fearghas." He looks at my horse and adds, "Fearghas, go with that young man and no biting! He will settle you down and give you something to eat."

Fearghas neighs but obeys the bearded warrior without any incident.

Steaphan bows to Caderyn, then smiles at Teague. "I can stay for little before I have to go back. The senatus is adjourned but they will start a new assembly soon." He points to the left, to an elegant round building down the street. It is nothing like the other cloudscrapers. Its intricate decoration and jutting balconies showcase an elegance that the rest of the buildings in the City of Honor do not have.

Caderyn slaps Steaphan's shoulder, making him stumble. "They can wait. Son, you'll stay for breakfast."

"But Chief Consuasor Graeme won't be happy if I'm not—"

Caderyn grunts, heading toward a wooden stairway that runs the vertical length of the building. "The chief consuasor knows where to find me if he has a problem. Now let us go before Sorcha complains that we're late."

We pass by the ground-floor entrance of the building, from which young, military-clad warriors go in and out. At my questioning look, Teague says, "The first ten floors are for unclaimed warriors who are either in training or don't want to live on their own yet. The rest is the praelor's armory and living quarters for his family."

Caderyn takes the wooden stairs at a brisk speed, with Rhona and Teague following him. I sigh, and climb up the steps, holding onto the railing the higher we get. Somehow it doesn't look safe enough as protection.

We enter through a square stone door on the fifteenth floor, into a spacious room decorated to the brim with weapons.

Our party spends a few minutes removing their various swords, daggers, crossbows, and laser guns, piling them up on a metal table by the door.

A bell gongs in the distance.

"It's the First Hour of Significance bell," Steaphan says when he catches me looking around for the source. "Time for the third and largest morning feast."

"That's a lot of feasts in one morning," I mutter. This explains why Teague always munches on something!

A tall, black-haired woman wearing a loose white shirt and matching pants enters the room from the right. "You're late!"

This must be Sorcha.

Caderyn laughs and hugs his wife, lifting her off her bare feet. "See? I told you she'd complain." Then he kisses her in greeting.

Sorcha steps back from Caderyn, smiling, and opens her arms wide. "Teague, my son!" she says and hugs him and then Steaphan. "I'm glad you're joining us, Steaphan dear."

I glance at Steaphan, puzzled. Is Teague his brother?

"Teague was adopted by the praelor's family at a young age after his warrior parents died in battle," Steaphan whispers.

"I had no idea," I say. Callum forgot to mention that tidbit.

Steaphan nods. "I'm not surprised. Warriors are trained to hide familial ties to outsiders. Someone can use that information against them, weakening them. They consider any sign of weakness a stain on their honor!" he says and laughs. "It took years before Teague even introduced me because they consider the consuasors outsiders too. The fact that you are here, meeting them now, even though the praelor didn't honor your Bride's Choice, is a true testament of how much Callum loves you."

This does put Callum's secretiveness into perspective.

"Rhona, my daughter," Sorcha says, "I'm glad you are home!"

Rhona hugs her back, saying an embarrassed, "Mother."

Sorcha glances at Callum as he strides up to her to give a hug as well. "Callum, my son, back from your long journey and you've brought a few souvenirs, too."

Callum laughs and introduces my friends to his mother. Then he takes my hand and pulls me forward. "This is Sybil Lilla, my love and life."

"Not until I say so," Caderyn grumbles, but Callum ignores him.

"Lilla, this is Praelia Sorcha a'ruun, my mother."

I reach out to shake her hand, but she clasps my forearms instead, in a strong grip. "I heard you claimed my son."

I hold Sorcha's dark brown gaze. "I did."

"You are the Sybil, and a Lumenian," she says, and lets go of my arm. "It is an honor to meet you in my humble household."

"You mean *our* household," Caderyn corrects her. "Besides, she doesn't look like one."

I roll my eyes. Not with that again!

Sorcha cuts a sharp look toward her husband before focusing back on me. "I have a feeling she'll surprise you."

Caderyn shakes his head. "I doubt that."

"Underestimating again? I thought you'd learned your lesson by now," Sorcha says and turns on her heel. "I hunted a k'boar yesterday. We better sit and enjoy it before it gets cold."

CHAPTER 30

"I bet you were expecting a palace or something luxurious like that," Caderyn says to me as we stand on his home's rooftop, getting ready to watch Callum—and his two older brothers I've yet to meet—play in a so-called Valleyball game. We came up here after we finished eating the third morning feast, which was awkward and plentiful at the same time.

"I don't need *luxury*," I say, turning to him. Luxury came with strings attached in the Uhnan court. I learned not to depend on it or expect it if I wanted to be free. "What I need is to get on with earning your Guardian Goddess Laoise's blessing." If I didn't know better, I'd think Caderyn is stalling me. "Where did you say I can find her?"

"I am not in a hurry," the praelor says, confirming my suspicion, "and you know *well* that I didn't tell you where you can find my goddess. It wouldn't be much of a challenge if I did, would it?"

Cheers sound from the Teryns around us. I turn my attention to the open valley in front of me. How is Caderyn not worried knowing that with each second he delays my mission, DLD gains more power?

Callum, wearing a red and white striped tunic over black pants and plated boots, lines up in midair among twelve warriors dressed alike. He adjusts the modest silver shield on his forearm, then grins at me.

Across from Callum, thirteen warriors wearing blue and white stripes face him. Both teams ride manta ray-like birds with flat and round bodies covered in fur. Their feathered wings beat fast in place. Multiple horns protrude from their narrow heads. Eight spider legs are tucked under the birds' bellies. They let out high-pitched twitters, adding to the growing noise of excited chatter and shouts from the crowd.

Sorcha points ahead. "Those are domesticated k'birds. They are fast and agile, able to catch a warrior with their sticky claws before they hit the ground."

"What's the point of this game?" Arrov asks from my right.

A loud horn sounds and the two teams scatter, taking up positions in the air.

"Valleyball is a game of strategy," Caderyn explains. "The goal is to knock the most players off their k'bird. Each player is equipped with three dozen rocks that they throw at one another. Players can deflect the stones with that shield attached to their forearms. This game is played over a valley, hence its name." He watches the game with a pride and adds, "I have many fond memories from when I played this game. I'm glad my sons participate in it too."

"Knocking players off their ride sounds brutal," I say, and Glenna nods in agreement. Ragnald rubs his chin as he studies the players but does not add to the discussion.

"It might appear to be brutal," Caderyn says, "but this game is crucial for young warriors to learn to follow orders and for older warriors to practice how to be a leader in continuously changing and unpredictable situations. Maybe for the next game you should join them. There is a lot for you to learn if you want to be the general of *all* armies. Including mine."

"I'm sure there are better ways for me to learn," I mutter. Ones that don't include throwing rocks.

Callum hovers in midair with Teague and two other men. One of the men tries to shove him off his k'bird and bursts into laughter. Teague kicks the harness of the laughing man's flyer, and the k'bird spirals in place a few times.

Belthair asks, "Who are those men with Callum? They look like him."

"That's Sachary and Sawney," Rhona answers, "our dear older brothers. They didn't join us because they were busy getting ready for the big game they love so much." Her voice does not hide her dislike toward them. "Half brothers to be precise, from Dad's previous Bride's Choice," she adds. "But their mother sadly passed away when they were young."

My grief wells up. Nic and I had a much different sibling relationship. He was always there for me. I loved him very much and I miss him dearly.

Teague, Callum, and his two brothers pick out a few rocks from the leather pouches attached to their k'birds. They fly in a zigzag pattern over the battlefield until Callum signals. Then they pelt five players with rocks in a methodical way, knocking them off their k'birds.

The crowd clamors when the k'birds pluck the warriors out of the air and carry each one off the playing field and out of the valley.

"I can't say I find much tactic applied, other than brute force," I say.

"That's true," Sorcha says, "but there is a lot more to it once you understand the game. Each player can have the role of a *fielder*, who tries to intercept the attack to protect their teammates; or they can be the *frontiers*, who throw the rocks. The difficulty comes from the limited number of rocks the teams have, and the ability to switch between the two roles as they think best."

I nod in understanding. "That does make this game more complex."

"Tell me more about that pirate sword you brought for me," Caderyn says, turning to me.

With help from Callum, I collected a few items before leaving Uhna. I didn't realize they would be gifts for his family. I only knew that they were in line with Teryn visiting traditions. I gave Sorcha a jar of cherished boomberry jam made by Deidre; a serrated dagger for Rhona; and a pirate sword for Caderyn. Callum failed to take his two half brothers into consideration. I can't wait for the uncomfortable scene when they learn I've brought them nothing.

"My ancestors were pirates," I explain, "hunting deep-water sharks and other sea monsters. Those serrated teeth on the blade are from those sharks and can cut through most metals. The rifle attached on top of the sword was originally designed to shoot poison darts but later was converted into laser enhanced with Fla'mma magic as our technology progressed." In a way, the sword is like Uhna's history materialized.

"It's quite a weapon," Caderyn says, "and I am happy to have it in my collection."

I nod. I saw the arms collection on the walls of the royal residence and I'm glad Caderyn considers it a fitting addition.

Four more blue players get knocked off their k'birds by Callum and Teague's coordinated attacks, earning shouts from the spectators gathered on the rooftops below us.

I hold my breath until the last warrior is saved by her own flyer, not too far from the ground.

"Just to be clear," Caderyn says, watching Callum and Teague knock the last four blue players off their k'birds, "it takes more than a gift to earn my respect. The Teryns are nothing like your pirate ancestors. We rely on honor and not bribes."

"I wasn't trying to bribe you," I say.

Callum soars above us, grinning, as he flies a victory lap before heading back to his team.

"Good," Caderyn says and bares his teeth, "because bribery would not make me see you in a better light."

CHAPTER 31

Terraquakes jar me awake. I sit up under the wooden canopy of the bed. For a second I have no idea where I am. Then it comes back to me. The trip to Pada, and then arriving on Teryn. The Valleyball game in the heat.

As I predicted, Callum's older half brothers, Sachary and Sawney, were not happy about receiving no gifts. They didn't look happy to meet me in the first place. It felt like I was the cause of a strange tension between Callum and his half brothers, and that made it difficult to stay in their company.

Feeling exhausted, I decided to take a nap. Too tired to even undress, I woke up to pitch darkness outside, visible through the window of my bedroom, tucked away at the end of the fifteenth floor.

The weapons hanging on the wall rattle. I jump to my feet, unsure of what to do. There were a few terraquakes on Uhna, caused by DLD when he disrupted the natural balance on my world.

A sword clatters to the ground and I run out of the room, down the dark hallway. I stop in the main room as the building shakes under my feet, swaying, with more weapons ending up on the floor.

I look around, searching for the way out. I did not pay attention to how I got to my room, and now I can't recall which one of the multiple hallways leads to the exit.

Then as suddenly as the terraquakes started, they stop.

Rhona enters the room, barefoot and wearing a green sleep shirt that reaches past her knees. She rubs her eyes. "The terraquakes are normal. No need to run around panicking."

"I wasn't panicking." I will not admit it to her that I did, giving her a reason to judge me weak.

Rhona grunts in response—so much like Caderyn—and shuffles to the closest weapon on the floor. She picks a big mace up and places it back on its spot on the wall. "This was my great-great-great-grandmother Praelia Ayleen's favored weapon. She was a much-feared general on the battlegrounds."

I hand a longsword to her.

"This belonged to my great-great grandfather, Praelor Caden. He was the most cunning tactician among the Teryn generals."

Rhona gathers the last weapon, a shield in an immaculate condition.

"Let me guess," I say, "this was the shield belonging to one of your relatives, who was also an amazing general and ruler."

Rhona frowns. "Now, why would you say that? This is part of the altar for our beloved Guardian Goddess Laoise," she says and rises on her toes to place it back on the wall. "A true Teryn only uses shields in a game or as part of an altar."

Good to know.

A round, purple insect, the size of a pillow, with ridge-like bumps covering its back, skitters into the room. I shudder, getting ready to shriek if it nears me.

"It's just the cleaner, a k'zoombug," Rhona says as the purple thing with hundreds of legs whizzes around us, making sucking noises before it exits. "Why are you so scared of bugs? That's not a great quality in a general."

I grind my teeth and ignore her verbal barb. Instead I say, "You don't like using magic, do you?"

Rhona shrugs her broad shoulders. "Magic can backfire. Not to mention we would need mages or Pada monks. Both tend to reach beyond what is theirs, always hungry for control and power. You should know, since Uhna did fight off the mages in a battle, no?"

I'm surprised she knows anything about the history of my world.

"A lot has changed since then," I say. Though I find her explanation about magic and mages a bit simplistic. Maybe it has to do with the magical immunity, like Callum has, one I witnessed firsthand when both he and Teague withstood my magical explosion back on Uhna.

I yawn and move around a sofa, heading for one of the six wooden chairs to sit down. "Don't get too comfortable," Rhona snaps.

So territorial!

I straighten back out. "I didn't realize it was your chair."

"It's not about the chair. I meant don't get too comfortable *here*. As in, on Teryn. You have complicated my poor brother's life enough. If you love Callum, you will depart now. You've caused enough trouble as it is."

I stare at Rhona. "What do you mean 'if you love Callum'? Of course I love him!" Even if my Bride's Choice claim never gets honored.

"And I love you," Callum's voice sounds from behind me. "What are you doing, Rhona?"

I turn with a hand on my throat.

Rhona just glares at her brother. "Trying to help you. She shouldn't be here!"

I frown. "You do realize I am on a mission—"

"I know what's at stake," Callum says, crossing his arms, "but I decided that Lilla is worth it. It is my duty to help her succeed as a Sybil."

"You decided?!" Rhona asks, laughing. "We must follow the rules but not you?"

"What rules?" I ask.

Callum points at his sister. "Stop meddling!"

"I am not meddling, I am being reasonable!" Rhona says and slaps Callum's hand away. "She is not a true Teryn! That's a fact!"

"It's enough that's what I have to hear from Father and my brothers," Callum says, and an orange-reddish light crosses his eyes, "but I was expecting otherwise from you. Go away if you can't say anything nice!"

"I am on your side, you fool, but there is no room for the Sybil! Don't say I didn't warn you!" Rhona storms out, bumping into Glenna, who is heading toward us.

"What's with the shouting?" Glenna asks, yawning.

"Callum, what was this whole thing about? Why does Rhona want me to desert you?"

Callum drags a hand through his short black hair. "I wish I could explain, but I am not allowed."

Glenna wanders around the room to give us some privacy, invested in studying the weapons on the walls.

"Why aren't you allowed?" I ask.

Callum exhales, looking frustrated. "Because you are not a Teryn."

It hurts more coming from him. To know that I am not good enough because I wasn't born on his home planet is almost too much to bear. I was never good enough to fit in at the court on Uhna, and now I'll never be good enough for the Teryns.

Callum swears under his breath. "It's true what Rhona said that things are complicated. I am fighting to change the rules. I thought we could force the praelor's hand by having the Brainiacs support you as their Sybil. It was a long shot to begin with."

"A long shot is what the Seven Galaxies have against DLD," I say. My magic against His innumerable and corrupted armies makes this Era War look bleak compared to the others. Especially without the Teryn armada.

"What on Uhna is that?" Glenna asks and points at something outside.

Callum and I peek out the window. In the semidarkness, illuminated by the two large moons, a shabby-looking tree towers in a corner of the walled-in courtyard. It looks like a disturbing cross between a tropical plant and a giant spider. A black critter approaches the tree. A branch snaps out, ensnaring it. The tree drags its wiggling victim close until the poor critter disappears inside the ragged-looking branches covered with wide fronds.

"Isn't it adorable?" Glenna asks.

"Not even a little," Callum and I say together.

"It's a k'tree, our scrap food eliminator," Callum explains. "Want to visit it?"

Glenna claps her hands. "Absolutely!"

We trail after Callum, exiting at a side door, down fourteen flights of wooden stairs, and enter through a metal gate into the courtyard.

Callum and I stop at a safe distance, but Glenna keeps heading toward the k'tree.

"I wouldn't do that if I were you," Callum warns but she just waves it off. "I'll be fine."

"Glenna? Are you sure you want to do this at night? In the dark?"

She waves again, dismissing my concerns and focuses her attention on the k'tree.

It stops its movements. A pair of large, black, and segmented orbs of eyes peek from among long leaves.

Glenna begins cooing in a soft voice and reaches out with her hand in a fist. She takes a few more steps before stopping in front of the thirty-foot-tall k'tree.

The k'tree doesn't move for a few seconds. A branch that looks a lot like a spider leg stretches toward Glenna's hand. When it nears her fingers, she opens them up to reveal a piece of a carrot on her palm.

"Where did she get that carrot?" Callum asks.

I eye Glenna's ankle-length yellow nightgown. I can't detect any pockets in it. "Who knows?"

The branch hesitates over the carrot, but after a few seconds it snatches up the snack without touching Glenna's hand.

"Look at this marvelous creature!" Glenna murmurs in a kind voice. "Just because it looks scary and different on the outside doesn't mean it is evil on the inside."

I have a feeling she's not referring to the tree.

Callum lets out a deep breath. "That's good it didn't touch Glenna's skin. It has poisonous glands at the end of its branches."

"You're telling me this now?" I hiss in a low voice; I don't want to startle the k'tree.

He shrugs. "She's doing great. Look."

When I turn back to Glenna, she is sitting on the ground, talking to the k'tree, and feeding it with more carrots.

He laughs. "Can't wait to see the praelor's face when he realizes that Glenna has tamed and thus ruined his savage and prized scrap food eliminator."

CHAPTER 32

The next morning, I stifle a yawn as I hurry down a wide and stone-tiled street, dodging meandering Teryn warriors and consuasors.

Right at dawn, Caderyn insisted we go spectate another game in which Callum and Teague had to participate, called Swordplay. We gathered around an open, stone-tiled area in the middle of the mountain with midsize cloud-scrapers crowding around it. There were a pair of wooden posts at each end of the field, with just enough distance between them for a person to fit. Rushing through the open frame was the goal, but often the game broke down into sword fights, as it did with Callum stuck in the middle. The team with more players left standing would win. But I didn't stay long enough to find out the result. Glenna and the twins created a distraction, and thanks to their help, Caderyn didn't even notice when I slipped away to start my search for the mysterious Teryn guardian goddess.

I slow down my steps once I am far away from the game.

All around, red dominates. It has a pinkish hue that does not appeal to me. Not many other colors break up the monotony. Red dust covers *everything*, even stuck in my teeth.

As the street declines, it becomes busier too. My claustrophobia flares up, and I break out in a cold sweat. My breath hitches and I almost bolt down the street.

I step to the side and lean on a wall to catch my breath. Loud conversations surround me. Unbearable summer heat beats down my back, sweat soaking through my gray shirt.

I'm glad Caderyn or Rhona is not here to witness my weakness. This is not the way a legendary Lumenian, or Sybil, should act.

I have a goal and I can't stop now! I don't know when I'll have another chance to wander off, since Caderyn has been going out of his way to keep me busy, preventing me from completing his requirement. I need to make the most out of *now*.

I force calm on my frayed nerves and continue down the street. I do my best to ignore the pressing bodies of the crowd until I run into a dead end with a large gathering around a half-empty fight circle marked by three horizontal ropes. A huge, bald man wearing tight black military pants paces around with open arms, waiting.

I step up to a brown-haired and tanned warrior woman. "Did he invoke the, uh, seventh Ground Rule to argue with a family member?" I ask, trying to recall what Teague told me.

The warrior woman, without taking her eyes off the circle, says, "No, that would be the sixth. This is the fifth, permitting celebratory fights. Addendum number twenty-seven specifies to avoid dismembering if possible."

"If possible?" I repeat, eyeing the half-naked bald man with an arrogant expression on his face. His thick and tanned body, reaching almost seven feet in height, is covered in bulging muscles and crisscrossing scars. I don't envy the warrior who will end up fighting this behemoth.

"Accidents do happen," the warrior woman says, distracted in thought, "but we have the best battle surgeons in the whole Seven Galaxies, posted on the space station that orbits the first moon. I mean it; we picked a few up from each galaxy."

That must be nice.

Seeing how this warrior woman is more prone to disperse information, I press on, "Where can I find Guardian Goddess Laoise?"

The warrior woman scoffs. "In the Wise Women's cave, of course." She glances at me, and her dark brown eyes narrow. "You are not a Teryn!"

Before I can respond, sharp fingernails with serrated edges dig into my back. Someone pushes me and I stumble forward, over the ropes, and into the fight circle.

The huge bald man gives me a wicked grin, showing sharpened teeth like fangs as he hits his open palm with a fist.

CHAPTER 33

The whole crowd goes silent.

I try to step out of the circle, but the brown-haired warrior woman shoves me back by my shoulders.

"I didn't mean to enter the circle in the first place," I say. "It was an accident."

She shakes her head. "It doesn't matter."

The man grabs my gray shirt at my upper chest, bunching it in his meaty hand. He picks me up, dangling me a few feet from above the ground. "How dare you try to abort before the fight even started? I will teach you the Ground Rules by the time this is over!"

He throws me back into the middle of the circle.

I land on my left side, catching myself with my hand and hitting my head on the stone tile. Bones in my wrist crunch. Stars dance in my vision. White-hot pain bursts from my left wrist, tearing up my eyes. I exhale from the pain.

"Ground Rule number one: no fighter or fightee abandons a fight circle without concluding their fight."

"Get up! Get up!" the crowd shouts.

I force myself to my feet, cradling my left hand. I have to get out of here! Then I remember the bug behind my ear, the Teryn communication device, and I reach up with my right hand.

The huge man slaps my hand away before I can touch my ear. "Ground Rule number two: no one can interrupt a fight in a fight circle for any reason."

I back away from the menacing man, until my heels touch one of the ropes. The crowd propels me back into the fight circle.

My left wrist throbs and trickling warmth spreads down my spine, from my Sybil talisman to my hand. It's just good enough to take the edge of the pain but not to heal the broken bones.

"Ground Rule number three: no friend or family member of the fighter or fightee can seek a grudge fight after a fight circle is concluded," the bald man says and lunges at me, faster than I thought he'd move.

I sprint away from him. He swipes at me, tearing into the back of my shirt with his long nails, shredding it. Blood spreads over my back.

I cry out from the pain and reach for my magic in panic. But the pulsing white sphere is not there! The damage from magical poisoning must still be in effect!

"Ground Rule number four: no rank difference of the fighter or fightee matters in the fight circle," the bald man says, cracking his knuckles.

Another trickle of heat spreads from my talisman, down my back, acting slowly against the pain.

"Ground Rule number five: celebratory—"

"I know rules five and six," I mutter. He bares his jagged teeth at me, looking enraged that I dared to speak.

"Ground Rule number seven: allows killing as the fighter or fightee sees fit." The bald man kicks out, but I fail to avoid it. It lands in my stomach. I stumble back, sucking in air, but nothing comes for a few seconds.

I am powerless against this man!

The bald man prowls toward me. Gasping, I jump straight up and kick out, aiming in the middle of his chest. He grabs my extended leg before my kick can connect. "Ground Rule number eight: fights cannot be held inside a building," he says and twists my leg to the side without letting it go.

Something pops in my knee, and I scream.

"Ground Rule number nine: fights cannot start on a spacecraft." The bald man lifts my injured leg, with the swollen knee up, and pushes me to the side.

I hit the ground, landing on my back, and jolting my broken wrist. Blackness floods my vision for a few moments. When I come to, the man bends down over me.

"Ground Rule number ten: non-Teryns cannot benefit or receive protection from the Ground Rules."

The words sink in, and I scramble to get up, gasping for air. "What about the addenda and clarifications?" I ask to buy some time.

The bald man raises his right fist.

I know without a doubt he will kill me.

Unable to move my legs, I use my arms to gather energy toward me, as I learned it from the Saage Women, letting my instincts guide me. With a desperate shout, I shove the gathered energy at the man.

He stumbles back, tripping over the ropes.

I collapse from the force of releasing the energy and welcome the darkness enveloping me.

CHAPTER 34

My head throbs and the pain wakes me up.

I open my eyes. Above me, an intricately carved wooden canopy frames the bed I am lying in. Weapons cover the wall. I'm still on Teryn.

I push the white blanket off, struggling to sit up, and the room spins.

Callum's head snaps up from his elbows; he is kneeling by the foot of the bed. "Thank Guardian Goddess Laoise, you are up!"

He springs to his feet and sits by my side. "I shouldn't have let you wander on your own!" he says and pulls me into a hug.

Sharp pain jabs into my shoulder. "Not so tight, please!"

He relaxes his hold on me and props me up against the bed frame. "How are you feeling?"

Blood drains from my face and cold sweat breaks out on my forehead. I fight down the horrific images. My body feels healed, though phantom pains remain from the broken bones and sprained knee. I could have died in that fight circle, and it would have been within bounds according to the Teryn Ground Rules. No one, not even Callum, could have changed it.

"I'm glad to be alive."

A mixed expression of guilt, sorrow, and anger crosses his face. "It's my fault! Rhona was right. I should have never let you claim me!"

"Hold your ships for a second."

"This whole mission is too dangerous."

I frown at Callum. "Are you saying I can't handle danger?"

Callum exhales, frustrated. "That's not what I'm saying at all! I believe in you, but that doesn't mean I don't want to keep you safe."

"There is no safe, only the illusion of safety."

Callum laughs. "Even so, I will never stop worrying about you." He takes a thin leather necklace, with different sizes of fangs at its end, off his neck. He hands it to me as he says, "Here, I want you to have this."

I take the still-warm necklace from him, the fangs clicking from the movement. "What's this?"

Callum makes a face. "I know it's nothing elegant. I earned it with my bare hands when I was fifteen."

I touch the sharp and curving fangs, still shining white. "Are you telling me that you slayed an animal? With your bare hands? When you were just fifteen?"

"Yes, a k'alligator. I had been preparing for my trial since I was five."

I try to imagine Callum as a young boy, dreaming of being a warrior. While I was at the despised Uhnan court at the same age, grieving over the loss of my mom. How different our lives have been!

I examine the fangs with fascination. "What is this 'trial'?"

"All Teryn children, male or female, must go through their trial at age fifteen. With nothing but the clothes on our back, we embark on our individual journey. To prove our worth as a warrior. Or fail and end up as a weak Brainiac or a civilian supporting the praelium to earn their honor back. Many kill a k'boar or k'mountain lion, but I wanted to do something no one had done before. I ventured into the River of Death to hunt a k'alligator and I won. Though my memories of it are a bit hazy."

River of Death? Another charming name.

I have a feeling there was a reason many Teryns chose not to face that k'alligator. "I shouldn't have this."

I try to give it back, but Callum stops me. "I want you to have it. It has brought me luck. Unless you don't like it—"

"No! I love it," I say and slip the necklace over my head. "Thank you."

A terraquake rattles the walls of my bedroom and the weapons on them.

"Another one?" I ask.

"Nothing to worry about. As long as I can remember, there have been terraquakes on Teryn."

After a minute, the shaking dies down.

"What happened after I blacked out?" I ask.

"I found you and carried you back. I transported you to our space station, where the best med specialists worked on you, along with Glenna, who used her A'ris magic. You were out for days."

Hopeful that my magic healed too, I check for my pulsing bright white sphere, but it's still not accessible. The magical poisoning must still be blocking it.

"Oh, good," Glenna says, entering the room with Ragnald on her heels. "You are awake."

Glenna touches my forehead, checks my eyes, and lifts my left arm. Slight pain flares up from my shoulder. I don't even remember dislocating it. "Good, it's much better," she says.

She grabs my right leg and moves it around. "What Callum forgot to mention is that Teague and Rhona had to physically drag him away from that vile man, because the general was ready to throw reason to the ocean."

"Did he now?" I ask and glance at him. His face is unreadable until an orange-reddish light flashes across his blue irises.

Glenna's gaze fills with uncharacteristic anger. "Ground Rules aside, I'd love to give that man some of my *medicine*! He would suffer for days, in the worst pain imaginable, begging for my mercy!"

I gape at Glenna. The white strands seem to encroach more of her dark red hair.

Ragnald places his hand on Glenna's right shoulder, channeling red ribbons of Fla'mma into her until the rage drains from her face. The mage steps back, clasping his hands in front of him, looking like nothing out of the ordinary happened. The white streak retreats in Glenna's hair but does not disappear.

Glenna rubs her forehead, confused. "Why are you staring at me like I've grown lobster claws?"

Ragnald shakes his head, indicating to keep this episode a secret.

"Nothing," I say.

Glenna glances at Ragnald. "Did the mage do something? Again?"

Ragnald spreads his arms and says, "You know me, I couldn't help my arrogant charlatan self."

"You got that right," Glenna says, unsure.

I study the pair of them. Just how many times has Glenna lost it that Ragnald had to make an excuse to hide it?

"So it took three days to heal me?" I ask. "Isn't that a bit long?"

I don't feel too bad, considering the damage. My knee and shoulder ache a bit but nothing like that pain I felt in the fight circle. My wrist is not in a cast, though it troubles me more than the other injuries.

"No, sweetie. It took ten days to bring you back from critical state due to a severe concussion and internal bleeding, and another three days for you to regain consciousness."

CHAPTER 35

The door to my living quarter opens and Arrov peeks in. "May I come in?"

"No!" Callum says, just as I say, "Yes."

Ragnald steps to the side to allow Arrov to shuffle closer to my bed, across from Callum. The giant, with a sad expression, kneels by my side.

Arrov picks at a loose thread on my white blanket. "I am so sorry, Lilla!"

A knock sounds on the door, and before I can say anything, Isa and Bella sashay into the room and sit by Arrov.

Arrov wrinkles the blanket. "With this new body, I get so exhausted that when I fall asleep, I can't easily wake up. Just like today."

"We tried to shake him awake," Isa says, and Bella adds, "But he nearly clawed my face off!"

Isa nods. "It's a good thing Bella has freakishly good reflexes."

"She does have that," I agree.

Arrov's mouth trembles and the twins hug his shoulders, or at least attempt to hug them but can't quite reach all the way across his back. "I have let you down, Lilla. Can you forgive me?"

Callum glares at Arrov. "I wouldn't."

I glare at Callum, then look at Arrov, and say, "There is nothing to forgive."

Belthair strides in and drops down at the foot of my bed. "I'm glad you're up," he says. "I was getting worried that the Teryns succeeded where DLD didn't. Not to mention, I'd hate to be stuck on this despicable world for too long."

Callum glowers at Belthair. "What did you call my home world?"

Teague opens the door, holding a large roasted k'boar's leg. Seeing the room so crowded, he leans on the wall by the doorway and tears into the roasted meat. "Lilla, I should have found a way to get out of that game," he says around a large bite.

Glenna covers her mouth and says from behind her fingers, "I helped to create a distraction!" She looks at Ragnald for comfort. The mage blinks at

Glenna in shock, then pats her shoulder in consolation. "You were trying to help your friend," he says to her.

Belthair raises an eyebrow at Callum. "You heard me. I say it how I see it! This planet is the worst I have ever stepped foot on. The only reason I'm here is because Lilla is the Sybil, and she needs your army. Without her, I would be away from this place faster than you can say my name."

Callum jumps up and leans close to Belthair. "Take it back or I will make you!"

Arrov gets to his feet. "Why?" he asks. "Did we hurt your feelings?"

Isa and Bella stand up, giggling. "We didn't know Callum can be so sensitive!"

My room shrinks to the size of a handkerchief as they crowd around my bed, shouting. My anxiety spikes, fueled by claustrophobia, and sweat breaks out on my body.

Glenna reaches a hand down. "Why don't we go for a nice stroll?" she asks.

I nod in relief.

CHAPTER 36

With Glenna's help I escape but we don't go far. Once at ground level of the building, we hear soft whining coming from a wooden fenced kennel that's hidden underneath the stairs. We stop to investigate.

"No! Don't open that gate!" a gangly warrior yells, running toward us.

Glenna swings the gate wide open before he can stop her.

A dozen black-and-white colt-size dogs rush at us, jumping up and down on their six legs, sneezing from happiness.

Glenna and I land on our bottoms on the stone-tiled ground, laughing as we try to deflect long, wet tongues.

"I'm dead," the gangly warrior says with a groan as he watches us with a hopeless expression. "The praelor will kill me. I'm so dead!"

"Don't worry about the tide gone, I will take responsibility," she says and shoos the gangly man away.

The puppies, judging by how playful they are, settle around us, fast asleep from happiness. From where we're sitting, I can see most of the City of Honor spreading out in front of me. Unassuming. Faint hollers sound from a distance. The Foundation Month celebrations are still going strong.

But now I know what lies underneath that unassuming surface. Constant fights, for one reason or another, that can end up killing you, regulated by rules that do not care for non-Teryns.

The ground shakes, like something heavy hitting stone. Fearghas trots toward us from around the corner. He bares his sharp fangs at the puppies. The puppies crack an eyelid open to acknowledge my horse, but they don't move. Then Fearghas sniffs my hair, neighing.

Glenna hands me fruit slices wrapped in wax paper, and I feed them to him. "I guess I don't have to search for you," I say, patting his warm, black neck. It seems that Fearghas had no trouble getting accustomed to the hot Teryn climate. His spirits are up, and he looks robust, his black hide shining in the sun. I wish I could be more like him, adapting to any new situation with ease.

Glenna glances at me. "I'm worried about you, Lilla. This mission is killing you."

"It was my own arrogance that got me in trouble. I assumed that it was safe for me to just venture out."

"That is an oversimplification of what happened, and you know it," Glenna says as she runs her hand over the back of one of the sleeping puppies. "You are becoming reckless. I don't want to watch you die too."

I study her downturned face. "I didn't choose this mission, Glen; it was The Lady who insisted that She needs the Teryn army and that no other will do. I can't throw in the pirate hat and declare it a loss just because I encountered a bit of hardship along the way. This is my life now, as Sybil. I have a duty to carry out."

"You also have to think of the others," Glenna says. "We have upended our lives to follow you."

"Don't you think I know that? I'm steering the boat as best I can! I thought you'd support me."

"I do support you! I just want you to be careful."

"You've ruined my prized scrap food eliminator!" Caderyn booms as he steps around the building, sneaking up on us on silent feet. "Now you're ruining my treasured k'hounds?" He stops by Fearghas and pats my horse's neck and sneaks him a slice of fruit.

The puppies get to their feet in a flash and surround Caderyn, though they don't jump on him. They sneeze and whine in their doggie language, greeting their owner.

"We didn't ruin anything," I say and straighten. "They deserve a bit of love and care, don't you think?"

"Your love and care will make them soft and weak," Caderyn says. "They need to be tough and strong to survive on Teryn. A lesson you should learn as well."

I point at Fearghas. "Does he look soft and weak to you?"

My horse bares his sharp fangs, bobbing his head, looking insulted.

Caderyn grunts in answer.

"I'm glad you're conscious, little girl," he says. "It will be much easier to send you back to your watery world, along with your annoying rabble. I'd hate if you'd die here because you are not a Teryn."

I'd hate that too. Though what being a "Teryn" has to do with anything is beyond me.

"You won't get rid of me," I say and step closer to Caderyn with a finger pointing at his chest. "I am here to recruit your armada. The sooner I can accomplish my mission, the sooner you'll be rid of me!"

Caderyn laughs. "I admire your spirit! There is honor in not giving up, but you are in over your head, little girl."

"Stop calling me that!" I say, then take a deep breath to calm down. "I am committed to earn your guardian goddess's blessing."

Caderyn grunts. "You don't even know where to find Guardian Goddess Laoise. Forsake this foolish mission and go home. It would be much easier for us, including my son. You do care about my son, don't you?"

I grind my teeth. "More like it would be easy for you! Just admit it. Why don't you want me here?"

Caderyn crosses his thick arms. "You bring nothing but headaches. You have no idea what's at stake here."

"That's because no one will enlighten me about said stakes!"

Caderyn leans down. "You want enlightenment? Here it is: you are not cut out to be a Teryn."

"What does that even mean?" I ask. "Besides, I know where to find your goddess. She is in the Wise Women's cave." He doesn't need to know that's as far as I got.

"Someone talked, I see," Caderyn says, then looks away. He narrows his eyes with a frustrated expression, watching three skeletal men, with a square red cloth covering their groins, shuffle toward us.

Caderyn curses, and his expression turns calculating. "I see I have no choice in the matter now that Guardian Goddess Laoise interferes. However, I can put a limit on how long I will tolerate you. You have seven days to earn the goddess's blessing."

"I take it!" Shouldn't take too long, now, should it?

The skeletal men stop in front of us, staring at us without blinking.

"I see you, attendants of the Wise Women," Caderyn says and bows to the skeletal men. Wisps of gray beard hang on their face and chin. Light corral-red skin stretches on their sharp cheekbones, bald heads, and emaciated bodies, their feet bound in rags. Their dark, sunken, and beady eyes show no emotion, reminding me of the dark servants but without the rotting or corruption.

They wait, motionless.

"Fail," Caderyn says to me, "and you and your friends will never leave Teryn."

"Now hold your ships! I cannot agree to this without my friends'—"

Caderyn scoffs. "You said you won't quit. Or was that for show and no real strength?"

I shake my head. "I meant it."

The thinnest skeletal man opens his mouth, and a female voice comes forth, saying, "The Wise Women will see the non-Teryn now."

CHAPTER 37

"It's a lot bigger inside than I would have thought possible," I say once we enter the Wise Women's cave, careening my neck as I look around.

The inside of the circular cave consists of one main room with dark red walls, multiple dark tunnels branching off, hidden on the other side of the Mountain of Pain. Ginormous rocks blocked the path here, forcing us to go around them, creating the illusion of hitting a wall as their red color blended. I never would have found it on my own.

"We were expecting you," say the three black-haired women in unison, wearing sleeveless bright red dresses and lining up on the left side of the cave. "But you were late."

"I did not realize I had a standing appointment," I say, keeping my distance from the strange column of air that whirls with rocks inside it. It begins in the center of the cave floor and exits through a large opening in the cave's ceiling.

Two of the skeletal men disappear in one of the tunnels, while the third sits by the feet of the women, who look young yet ageless at the same time with their tanned and flawless skin and perfect bodies—neither too thin nor too athletic. There are no individual markers to differentiate one from the other.

Another terrashake rumbles through the ground, much stronger than before, originating from the swirling column of rocks.

"Is this normal?" I whisper to Ragnald and gesture toward the Wise Women and their mysterious attendant.

"There are many things that do not fit the definition of normal here," Ragnald says. "I don't even know where to begin."

The ground shakes again, but this time it's because Arrov drops down from his nine-foot height into a seated position near the column of rocks, mesmerized by the swirling currents. The twins snicker and Glenna rolls her eyes. Belthair, with his arms crossed, leans against the wall by the entrance, studying the scene with mild interest.

"This is a waste of time," Rhona says. "We all know she is not compatible and won't be able to complete the meld—"

"Just because you couldn't do it," Callum interrupts Rhona, "doesn't mean Lilla won't be able to! I believe in her!"

"Complete what?" I ask, looking from him to Rhona, but neither bothers to answer.

"Enough!" Caderyn snaps and Rhona glares at me. Great, now she blames for this, too.

Ivy waltzes inside, wearing a flowing white dress. She elbows her way through the others and stops between Callum and me. She wiggles her elegant fingers, ending in sharp and serrated nails. "I hope I am not too late," she says. "I am here to have my Bride's Choice honored."

"What is she doing here?" I ask. "Since when does she have a Bride's Choice claim on Callum?"

"Crown Princess Intonia made her Bride's Choice claim *before* you did," Caderyn says and smiles at the smug-looking Ivy. "I invited her to Teryn to discuss it, since I'll never honor your claim. The crown princess enjoys my protection and does not plan to stay long enough on Teryn to cause any issues."

I look away from Caderyn. I don't understand why he won't allow Callum and me to be together but has no problem with Ivy. Then I narrow my gaze on Ivy's sharp and serrated nails. I remember how they felt on my back. "Even knowing it was she who pushed me into the fight circle? What do your Ground Rules say about that?"

An orange-reddish light flickers through Callum's eyes. "Did she now?"

Ivy gasps in an exaggerated way and swipes her long blond hair over her shoulder. "You can't prove that."

Callum drags Ivy, despite the princess's protest, to Rhona. "Hold her," he says and then points at Caderyn. "You can invite whoever you want, but it won't matter to me! I want Lilla!"

"You got that right, son, that I can invite whoever *I* want," Caderyn snaps, "and you'd best keep that in mind. We are not here to converse about Lilla's Bride's Choice. We are here to figure out *if* she can earn the blessing of Guardian Goddess Laoise. I anticipate that this will be over fast."

Caderyn steps forward, preventing any more disputes. In a respectful tone, the praelor says to the three Wise Women, "We present Sybil Lilla to Guardian Goddess Laoise. Will our cherished goddess accept our plea and bestow Her blessing, or will She find the Sybil unworthy?"

Ivy struggles against Rhona's hold and yells, "She'll fail!"

The Wise Women raise their arms to the ceiling, chanting indiscernible words. An energy fills the cave, making the hair stand up on the back of my neck. Then they point at me and say, "Guardian Goddess Laoise will consider the Sybil's plea once the Sybil obtains the Heart Amulet."

"That is not the honorable way of our tradition!" Caderyn snaps. "I do not agree to this!"

The Wise Women turn their heads as one and look at the praelor. "Your agreement and your honor do not interest the most venerated Guardian Goddess Laoise."

Caderyn's tanned face turns dark red and a blue-reddish light flashes across his irises.

A strong wind picks up, swirling around my friends and me like a powerful current.

Ragnald touches my arm. "Lilla, I think you should reconsider this. I have a bad—"

The wind sucks my friends; Rhona, who holds Ivy; and me into the column of air and rocks.

Leaning Ridge

Bluid Mountains

Bluming Steppes

Whitle Maw

Sor'ow
Sea

Cave Ve'Lena

Green Forest

Mount Pa'Aina

Lake of Tears

Inlet of Deatha

SUN'SET
MOUNTAIN
RANGE

Morning Glade

Bell'air Archipelago

CITY OF
CR'WN

TOWN OF
HA'RMONY

TRADE
PORT

SENTRY

FARM
CO-OP

FISH CO-OP

CAVE
VE'LENA

CHAPTER 38

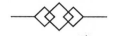

DAY 1

"—bad feeling about this," Ragnald finishes as he stumbles to a stop by me. We land in a bright green meadow speckled with yellow flowers. For a second, I think it's the place The Lady always transports me, but She's never brought any of my friends there, and I dismiss the idea.

I look around for clues.

Rolling hills, like bumps under a plush green blanket, spread all the way to the horizon. Its thick green grass gives the illusion of soft-looking moss. Far on the left, evergreen trees stretch toward the blue sky, running down the side of the hill like a fence. On our right, hillocks rise, with groups of trees peppering them, like green stubble. Behind us, even more small hills spread out, until they reach snowcapped mountains.

"What did the Wise Women mean by 'obtains the Heart Amulet'?" Belthair asks.

"We are on an adventure!" Isa says and Bella adds, "On a quest within a mission!"

"I rather be lapidified than be here with you!" Rhona barks, pointing at me. "Your misfortune is contagious!"

"Do you think any of us wants to be here?" I ask her.

"What's 'lapidified'?" Glenna whispers to Ragnald. "She means turned to stone or petrified," he explains.

"Then why didn't she say that?" Glenna asks.

"Where is the exit?" Arrov grumbles, pulling at the long, light-blue fur on his face. "It's too hot here and—"

I put a hand on Arrov's arm to comfort him. "It will be fine." He takes a deep breath and smiles. It takes a lot of effort to remain composed, facing yet another obstacle in my way, to execute my duty as a Sybil.

Ivy yells skyward, "Let me out of here! I have nothing to do with this

117

pathetic group! This is a misunderstanding!'"

I snort. I don't think the Wise Women care one way or another.

"Where are we?" Glenna shouts over the princess's shrieking.

Isa says, giggling, "This is going to be so much fun!" and Bella adds, "Finally, something interesting is happening," earning looks from Belthair and Ragnald. Glenna rolls her eyes, muttering, "Spoiled brats."

"Somehow I doubt that this is going to be anything like 'fun,'" I say. "I have to find this Heart Trinket—"

"Amulet," Ragnald corrects me.

"—and a way out of here."

"You mean *we* have to find the Heart Amulet and *we* have to find a way out of here," Rhona says with an eyebrow raised. "I am downright juberous about this 'quest' and can't wait to get away from you."

I glare at Rhona. "You are not alone."

"What is 'juberous'?" Isa asks Ragnald, not even pretending to be quiet about it.

"Uncertain or dubious," Ragnald explains.

Isa frowns. "Then why didn't she say that?"

"One thing is for sure," Belthair says, "we are not on Teryn anymore." He taps on his leather gauntlet, then says in a frustrated voice, "I can't even activate the Umbrae gateway!"

"Great job figuring out the obvious," Arrov says with a growl. "I could have told you that."

Ivy points at me. "This is your fault! You *are* the bringer of bad luck!"

"Don't be dramatic," I say. "Besides, you were the one who showed up, uninvited, at my, uh, blessing ceremony. You got what you deserved."

"I was not uninvited. The praelor—"

"Yes, yes, we know that Caderyn summoned you," I say. "Now try to make yourself useful."

The princess pouts. "Don't tell me what to do!"

I turn my back on her. There is only so much patience I can force on myself before it turns unhealthy.

Belthair points toward the forest. "We will head—"

Arrov scoffs. "You're wrong, ex-rebel! We should go toward the sun."

The others start arguing, forgetting about Rhona and me.

I turn to Rhona. "Listen, I'm sorry you ended up here."

"Don't ever think I am on your side, *Sybil*. I will be watching you! If I find you lacking, then our little group has one less person to worry about. Understood?"

"What did I ever do to you?"

"I told you to go away, didn't I?" Rhona says. "Now, because of your self-centeredness, *I* have to pay the price!"

"You can't blame me for being stuck here too!"

Rhona ignores me, and says in a loud voice to the others, "We will head that way"—she points forward—"toward that mountain. I think I recognize it—"

Ragnald perks up and interrupts Rhona, "—with its shadows on cliffs that look like gaping mouths! It's the Mountain of Pain!"

I study it with my head turned to the side. Ragnald is correct! "How is that possible? This is nothing like the Teryn we came from. Did we time-travel?"

"I don't like being interrupted," Rhona says. "I cannot disentangle what's possible or what's not possible, though I doubt we time-traveled here. The Teryn world has never been so *green*. It doesn't matter anyway. We have one goal: get the Heart Amulet and go back to Teryn."

Who died and made her captain of this pirate ship?

Isa chimes in, "Those are two goals," and Bella adds, "though they are dependent on each other and can count as one."

Belthair crosses his six arms. "There is no reason for us to follow *Walking Dictionary*. I was a captain with the rebellion, and I have experience in leading large groups successfully—"

"What did you call me?" Rhona interrupts him and shoves at his shoulder.

Belthair shoves her back. "You heard me, *Walking Dictionary*."

Rhona gets into Belthair's face and he leans into her, not backing down.

Glenna, along with Ragnald, hurries over to them. "There is no need for violence!" she says and attempts to pull Rhona and Belthair apart. "We need more help!" Arrov and the twins join in as well.

I step back from them and turn away, whispering, "Archgoddess of the Eternal Light and Order, please show yourself."

Nothing.

Then, out of nowhere, near-complete darkness descends, turning the day into night. Two moons, one giant-size and one much smaller than the first, appear in the sky, providing some light.

We stop and stare. They are so much like the ones we saw on Teryn.

"We will make camp," Rhona states.

Why is The Lady not answering? I try a few more times but to no avail.

"When you are done with your mumbling," Rhona says to me, "maybe you would care to help."

I sigh and head back toward the others. It never took this long to get The Lady to answer my appeal. Could She be ignoring me?

I reach back and rub my neck, expecting the usual zap, but it never comes. Then my hand freezes as realization hits.

The Sybil talisman is missing!

CHAPTER 39

DAY 2

"Lilla, can you hear me?" Callum's voice breaks into my nightmare, where that bald man kept beating me, over and over again. Pain emanates from my wrist, shoulder, and knee, a stark reminder of how close to death I got.

We made camp in the middle of the green meadow, sitting back-to-back to fight off the cold of the night.

I blink against the morning sunlight and open my tired eyes. A hologram-like image hovers in front of me, showing a partially visible Callum, who holds the beard of one of the Wise Women's skeletal attendants. The image is no bigger than three feet square, cut off at his chest, and blurry around the edges.

"Callum," I ask, "how is it that you can talk to me?"

"See?" Teague says from somewhere next to Callum. "I told you she is alive."

He ignores Teague and says, "The Wise Women's attendants can create holographic projections. As long as I hold onto their beards, that is. How are you holding up?"

"Why did you think that I was dead?" I ask.

"You all dropped to the ground like dead k'flies. I tried to wake you, but I couldn't."

I rub my eyes. "Hold your ships for a second! Are you telling me that my body is still in the Wise Women's cave?"

He nods.

"Then where am I?"

"I wish I knew. Teague had this idea of how to communicate with you since your k'bug stopped working."

I touch my ear and the k'bug is gone too. I search for the necklace Callum gave me. To my relief, my fingers brush against a leather string with sharp fangs at its end. How is it possible that the necklace made it but the other items didn't?

"Whatever you do," Callum continues, "try not to die there. Or you won't ever come back."

"I wasn't planning on dying," I mumble. "Do you know anything about the Heart Rock?"

"You mean amulet," Callum corrects me. "No, I don't know much about it. Ask Rhona. She was the one who paid attention to fables, not me."

I can't wait to ask her. She's always so helpful. Not.

He exhales in frustration. "It kills me that I am not the one who has to do this!"

"But you can't be the one. I must earn your guardian goddess's blessing. To show your father that I am capable as a Sybil; then he'll cooperate with me."

Callum's expression turns upset, and he tugs on the skeletal man's beard, almost toppling over the poor attendant. "I still don't like it. I worry about you!"

"Who are you talking to?" Arrov grumbles and tucks me closer to his side with his left arm while still seated. "Don't crush me!" Glenna's yelp comes from the other side of the giant. She and I both had the fortune to sleep tucked in next to Arrov, protected from most of the cold.

Callum narrows his eyes. "Did you sleep with that blue giant?!"

I duck my head. "Only for warmth. I have to go now!"

Callum lets go of the skeletal man's beard, reaching through the hologram-mirror to throttle Arrov, and the connection breaks.

Arrov stretches and I get to my feet. The others wake up as well.

"Whoever said that camping outside is relaxing," Ivy complains as she scratches red bug bites on her neck, "has never done it."

"Camping *is* done outside," I point out. Belthair adds, "This doesn't count, though. We had no choice."

Ivy stamps her foot. "As long as I see a tree, it counts!" Cursing under her breath, she picks grass blades off her not-so-white dress, stained with green and dirt smudges.

"We should get going," I say, fighting my urge to order around my friends to pick up the pace. "We don't know how much daylight we'll have." We already lost one day.

Arrov points to the knolls on the right while Belthair throws a thumb over his back, toward the forest, both declaring, "We should hunt there first." The twins and Ivy gather around the two men, voicing their opinions on the matter.

Ragnald pulls his long silver hair into a ponytail and ties it with a leather strip he found in his black mage robe's pocket. "Lilla, can you feel your magic?" he asks.

I cover the absence of the Sybil talisman on my neck with my hair. "Of course I can!" I say. "What kind of question is that?"

Shame scorches my face, but I can't confess to Ragnald that I don't have my magic. Or that the Sybil talisman is missing. Not when Rhona is watching for any sign of weakness. I want to look like someone who knows what she's doing.

Ragnald scratches the stubble on his jaw. "Oh, I'm just checking because Glenna and I can't feel our elemental magic. It must be because Lume is not an element tied to nature but exists in its own right—as a direct element of the Archgoddess of the Eternal Light and Order. Just as Acerbus is a direct element of the Archgod of Chaos and Destruction."

I make a noncommittal noise, feeling the heat burn my face even more.

"Lilla, are you okay?" Ragnald asks. "You look a bit flushed."

I wave the mage's concern away. "Since I have seven, no, six days left to find the Heart Bauble—"

"Amulet!" Glenna says.

"I think that finding it should be our priority over hunting," I say, just as my belly grumbles.

Isa and Bella say, "We haven't had anything to eat since yesterday's breakfast."

"We can find something on our way," I say.

Arrov shakes his head. "I'm hungry *now.*" The others join in, debating where to go in search of food.

I don't engage. Each second we waste increases the chance of failure. I'm supposed to be the Sybil, who *leads* her people. I can't even lead my friends!

The argument over food turns heated. "We should calm down!" I say, but no one pays attention.

"Quiet!" Rhona barks and the others focus on us.

"I hope you observed," Rhona says, "how a good general gains the attention of her people."

I grind my teeth. "That was not necessary. I don't need your or anyone else's help."

"That's mistake number one," Rhona says, smirking, "overestimating your own capabilities while ignoring the tools at your disposal—your friends, in this case." She sounds so much like Caderyn. She irritates me like broken seashells caught in sandals.

Rhona turns to address the group, "My phronesis is—"

Belthair raises a hand. "What in the name of a turtle are you talking about?"

Rhona sighs. "It means that *in my wisdom* I believe that finding food is our priority, and *the means of attaining it* might be easier than you think."

"Well, why didn't you say that?!" Belthair asks.

Rhona points to a hillside behind us. "Do you see those bushes full of berries?"

I turn and squint.

There are a few sea-green plants, waist high, with dark blue berries peeking out from wide and dark green leaflets. I would not have noticed them if I didn't know where to look.

"Those berries will be enough to prevent us butchering one another to feast on the corpse," Rhona says.

"Somehow," Ragnald says, "my appetite has lessened."

I turn to Glenna. "Are those poisonous?"

Glenna shakes her head. "Berries that have blue, black, or purple colors are usually safe. If they were white or yellow, I would say not to eat them. Those can have a higher probability of being deadly."

We each pick a shrub and tear the berries off with vehemence, gulping them down for a few minutes in silence.

I straighten, feeling full. Then my belly rolls, bubbling and cramping. I drop the handful of berries I was planning to save for later.

I don't feel too well!

The others make worrying noises.

Then there is no time to think. I burst into a sprint, heading for the closest tree line, in a desperate race with my friends.

CHAPTER 40

"This was your plan," I say to Rhona. What a cruel torture! To enjoy food for a precious few minutes, then have it taken away when your digestive system revolts.

Ivy nods in agreement. "I hold you liable for this disaster, too!"

Rhona pushes Ivy back. "I was right there with you, uh, *struggling*, you overindulged little—"

"I had no idea," Arrov says as he rubs his stomach, "that I still had so much left in me when I can't even remember my last meal."

"Great job dawdling away our time," I say, pointing at Rhona. "Do you not want to get out of here? Because the only way out of wherever we are is to find the Heart Brooch." At least I assume that once we finish the Wise Women's task, we will be allowed to go home.

Gods, I hope so!

"It's amulet," Rhona says, "and of course I want to go home!"

Ivy collapses to the ground by the twins, drumming her heels in the grass like a toddler. "I just want to wake from this nightmare and get out of here!" she wails.

I remember what Callum told me and I turn to Rhona. "Why don't you help by telling us what you know instead of trying to poison us?"

Rhona grinds her teeth. "We'll have to start with 'The Fable of the Weak, the Wimp, and the Wuss.'"

Sounds delightful," I say.

Rhona smiles. "It does, doesn't it?" she says, missing my sarcasm by a carlin. "It's one of my favorites!"

"Fascinating tidbit about Teryn literature," I say, "but how will this fable help us?"

Rhona crosses her legs at the ankle and drops down in one smooth move. She gestures for us to sit. "The elder warriors often spoke of this story, one from *The Hundred Fables of the Frail*."

"Are you kidding?" I mutter but settle down on the grass as well.

Glenna puts a hand on my arm. "Let's hear her out. It's not like we have a better idea."

Glenna is right.

Rhona clears her throat and waits until we quiet.

"This is a true story of redemption," Rhona intones, "of trying to earn honor for oneself!"

"How can it be a true story if it's a fable?" I ask, fighting the urge to get up and just start heading in a random direction instead of sitting here like I have nothing better to do.

My friends lean closer in interest, and I begrudgingly follow their example.

"It's the story of how the lost souls, dreaming to be honorable warriors, embarked on their quest for vindication." Rhona raises her eyebrows and smiles in anticipation.

The group watches Rhona, fascinated but in silence.

Oh, for the love of seagulls! "What quest?"

"I'm glad you asked," Rhona says. "It's 'The Quest for the Heart Amulet.'"

All we need is some drums in the background to enhance the intrigue.

"Tell us more," Belthair says and plucks a long strand of grass and puts it in his mouth.

Rhona's eyes twinkle in excitement. "'The Quest for the Heart Amulet' is not for the fainthearted," she continues. "It will test your commitment. Your endurance. Your—"

"Thank you, Warrioress of Negativity," I say, rolling my eyes. "We get it. It's an arduous quest."

Rhona glares at me. "To get to the point, the Heart Amulet can be found: 'Beyond the river. Over the last hill. Where the two halves of the sun join.'"

"Logically speaking, that's nonsense," Isa says. "The instruction is too generic to be useful." Bella adds, "What I wouldn't give for my trusty intergalactic compass! Too bad I left it on Barabal when we ran for our lives."

"So how did these, uh, heroes of yore find the Heart Amulet?" Arrov asks.

"They didn't," Rhona says cheerfully. "They died trying."

CHAPTER 41

MOIRA

"It is hard to believe that today my son turns eighteen summers old," I say and put down the wooden picture frame that shows a smiling image of him. Keelan has my black hair and dark brown eyes, and his dad's aquiline nose and high cheekbones.

"You mean *our* son?" Edan asks and hugs me from behind.

Taller by a head at his six and a half feet height, my husband's strong body fits flush against mine. Holding me with hands on my hips, he leans down and kisses my ear. "I almost lost both of you that day," he murmurs and crosses his arm over my flat belly.

I'll never forget those difficult days after my son's birth. Looking now at his striking physique and attractive face, no one would know how hard my baby boy had to fight to stay alive after being born too early.

Edan kisses my neck, his hands questing up from my hips.

"Stop that"—I slap at his hands, laughing—"before anyone catches us!" After being together for more than twenty years, he still acts like a young courting man, making me forget about my royal duties.

Through the oval window, my gaze lands on the light-gray marble buildings that look like elegant, twisting ribbons with fuzzy green sides, from the bright plants covering their facades. My people have come far from the simple village lifestyle to this modern one in a relatively short time. It was the dream of my great-great-great-grandmother, who was queen then—to live in such luxury. But not mine.

"I can believe that Keelan is eighteen," Edan says. "He demanded yet another fiddle, ahead of his celebration day, because he 'inadvertently' broke the previous one. He has too many 'accidents' if you ask me. Brattish and stubborn *child.*"

"I wonder where he gets that from," I say, smiling as I pull away from him. "You know full well that Keelan has the spirit of an artist. He is a great musician, a talented painter, poet, and dancer, too."

Instead of letting me go, Edan grabs my hand at the last second, turning my step into a complicated dance move as he pulls me back to his chest. "He couldn't have inherited it from me," he says, looking serious, but his eyes shine full of humor as he kisses my nose, then my lips. "I don't have a single artistic bone."

"Says the long-reigning dance champion!" Sometimes I am surprised that he picked me from among those beautiful girls, knowing our life together would be anything but easy. Full of obligation to the court and my people.

He winks at me. "Let's go to the bedroom—"

"I hope I am not interrupting." A beautiful and ethereal voice sounds from behind us.

"Gigi!" With burning face, I disentangle from Edan and look at the woman in her thirties. "You are always welcome in my humble suite." Edan scoffs at my words but covers it up with a cough when I scowl at him. I turn to look out the oval window.

Gigi glides next to me and gazes out too, observing the green parks and picturesque lakes between the elegant buildings. "I am amazed at how skillful your people are. So much elegance and beauty in your society. Nature and technology exist in balance. Your society flourishes in peace. You have achieved harmony." She gestures to encompass the whole city with a thin hand. The sunlight on her pale, gray-toned face lends her beauty, but she would refuse that compliment. She always said that the best anyone can call her is handsome. She could be more attractive if she would not insist on wearing a brown, straight dress that hangs on her almost six-foot frame.

"I have more bad news," Gigi says and tucks a long black strand of hair behind her ear. Her expression is concerned. A first since I've known her.

"Has the Era War advanced that much to cause you worry?" I ask. Edan hugs my shoulders, giving me strength. We knew this day might come. I just hoped it wouldn't be during my generation or my son's.

"It's not just that." Gigi's intelligent and dark brown eyes fill with dread. "The Archgod of Chaos and Destruction has dispatched a half-corrupted squad, backed by an armada of dark fiends, to attack us."

CHAPTER 42

LILLA

"What is the point of this quest if we end up dying?" Ivy whines as she fidgets with her stained dress. "I am too young! I have not lived long enough to fulfill my dreams. Now I will perish here, never to be free."

"No one is going to die or perish," I say. Not if I can help it. "It was just a fable. Rhona exaggerated it."

"I didn't!" Rhona says. She crosses her arms in a move I've seen Callum do dozens of times. Missing him, I touch the fangs at the end of the leather necklace.

"The point is," I say, shaking off my sadness, "we have to get going. Staying here is not an option. We can sort out the rest on our way."

"We still haven't decided who will lead us on this quest," Belthair says. "As a captain in the rebellion, I have executed many successful raids against the Pax Septum Coalition armory to retrieve weapons without getting caught."

Isa glides up to Belthair and puts a hand on his bicep. "You are so brave!" Isa says, and Bella adds, "Please tell us more." They flutter their eyelashes at him.

Belthair puffs his chest out. "I'd be happy to expand on how I—"

"There will be no expanding!" I snap.

Belthair frowns at me. "In any case, you have the worst sense of direction. You aren't the best candidate to lead us."

Isa and Bella nod, saying in unison, "That's true, sweetie."

Belthair continues, "I think we can agree that I am the most qualified—"

"It's your quest, Lilla," Arrov says, pushing Belthair out of the way. "What would you have us do?"

"We will go . . ." I look around, hesitating. A light breeze sways the long grass, bringing with it a hint of wood smoke from the direction of the down-ward-sloping mounds, lined by a dark green forest on its right edge. I search for the source, and my gaze lands on a thin, curling column of smoke. I continue, "toward the smoke."

"What smoke?" Belthair mocks. "There was nothing . . ." his voice trails off when he notices the smoke spiraling in the cloudless blue sky.

CHAPTER 43

Out of nowhere, a thick evergreen woodland cuts into our path. Rhona and I halt. I could have sworn it was on our left side as we trekked parallel with it. Impossibly, the trees must have shifted until they were blocking our way.

I shake my head. I must be hallucinating—maybe a side effect from those wild berries we ate earlier. Nothing else can explain this.

I glance at Rhona, but noting her closed expression, I decide not to talk to her. No matter how fast I was going, she kept pace with me, pretending to lead this quest *together*.

"We have to go through the forest," Rhona states.

"I know that," I say. Nothing good ever comes from entering dark woods, though she is right. We don't have much choice. It's the shortest path toward the curling smoke, as opposed to trying to go around it. Maybe we can find something to eat there.

"We will cut through the forest," Rhona and I say at the same time. The others catch up to us, then glare at each other.

Glenna holds out a handful of wiggling white worms and offers them to us. I shake my head. Hungry as I am, I am not ready to eat bugs. Yet.

Rhona takes a few. "I see the ex-princess is too good to eat like the rest of us," she says, chewing the worms like they're the tastiest morsels she has ever had.

I grind my teeth. I won't let her provoke me.

Arrov accepts a handful, shoving them into his mouth. A few worms end up stuck in his facial fur. "They are a bit salty, bitter, and chewy, but not bad."

I shudder. Not my favorite combination of flavors.

"I hate nature!" Ivy shouts, the last one to arrive. "I hate being hungry!" She leans on her knees, breathing hard, but slaps away Glenna's handful of worms. "Eating bugs is *not* the Marauder way!"

Rhona watches Ivy with a smirk. "Who knew you have so much in common with Lilla? This must be a *princess* thing, to be so spoiled and *weak*," she says and raises an eyebrow at me.

If she thinks I'm weak, I'll just have to prove her wrong.

Belthair makes sympathetic noises for Ivy, gathering a bunch of wildflowers with his right three hands and handing them to her.

My jaw drops. He never once bought me flowers when we were dating. Even Isa and Bella surround Ivy in comfort and support, while she complains of aches and dirt and bug bites. I scratch a few red and itchy ones on my arm. I can relate to the bug bites.

"Are you done?" Rhona asks when Ivy takes a deep breath.

"I hate you too," Ivy gripes, glaring back at Rhona.

"Don't worry," Rhona says, smiling, "the feeling is mutual."

Rhona raises her arm. "We are going in!" she shouts and wades into the green darkness of the forest without a backward glance. "Stay close, don't get lost, and we will be fine."

Said the pirate captain before his ship sank.

CHAPTER 44

Cutting through clinging vegetation, we enter the evergreen forest. Wading deeper, we can barely see the sunlight through gaps in the thick canopies. The air smells moist, with scents of rotting foliage.

Silence stalks us, and chills run down my spine from my clamoring instinct. "We are being followed," I whisper to Rhona.

She glances at me. "I know."

I rub my arms for warmth and look around. The others trail after us, with nervous expressions.

"OW!" Ivy exclaims and stumbles on a twisted root, making us jump.

Rhona looks back at her. "Be quiet!"

Belthair steadies Ivy with one of his lower right arms around her waist. "I've got you."

Glenna leans closer to Ragnald. "I should gather some mushrooms or worms," she says.

Ragnald and I exchange a look. It's clear that neither of us thinks it's a good idea for Glenna to wander off. "Maybe it's best not to—"

Loud clicking-purring sounds interrupt him. Goose bumps break out on my skin.

Isa and Bella whirl around with wide eyes. "What was that?!"

Rhona lifts a hand, and we stop.

More clicking-purring echoes, multiplied by the dozen.

Rhona gulps and barks, "RUN!"

CHAPTER 45

"OH, MY GODS!" Arrov bellows. He races past us as we charge out of the forest, straight into high grass that reaches two feet above our heads and to Arrov's neck. We follow him, grateful that he cleared a path for us.

Hundreds of huge, threatening red eyes, grouped in fours, glare out of the dark. But the dark, monstrous shapes those eyes belong to don't follow.

"What were those things?" Glenna asks. "I've never knew so many fangs can protrude from a maw!"

"I'm just glad none of their poisonous spit landed on me," Isa says. "Those plants shriveled up whenever their spit missed their marks." Bella adds, "Or those black spikes that they shot out of their tails? I saw them cut chunks out of a tree trunk!"

"Are we all out?" I ask, looking around.

Belthair helps Ivy get rid of green thorns that got stuck in her blond hair.

Isa and Bella throw rocks back into the forest, taunting the predators still lurking in the shadows. I put my hands out and they give me their rocks, muttering, "You are spoiling our amusement!"

"It's better to be alive than to die of too much excitement," I say and drop the rocks by my feet.

Glenna shakes her fists at the forest. "I despise being stalked! You are lucky I can't use my magic, or I would blast you to bits!"

Ragnald shakes his head and puts a hand on her shoulder. "Glenna, it's best to keep your calm. Do not feed the corruption."

Glenna pales. "I didn't even notice . . . that I was doing that . . ." She exhales and adds, "It's getting worse, isn't it?"

Ragnald and I exchange a knowing look. "Let's not worry about that now," he says. "We'll deal with it once we get out of here."

I'm glad the mage didn't say "if" we get out of here.

"At least we are all safe," I say.

Glenna shakes her head. "Check again."

I realize she is right. "Where is Rhona?"

Branches snap and twigs crack under running footsteps. Rhona bursts out of the forest, shouting and waving her arms. The right sleeve of her black military jacket is missing. Blood wells in fresh claw marks on her tanned and defined arm.

"I think those were bear-wolves," Rhona says with a dazed look on her face. "They're supposed to be extinct for hundreds of years!"

"I don't care what they were," Belthair says. He flicks the top of his left hand, which has shallow scratch marks. "What I want to know is, why aren't they following us?"

"It doesn't matter," I say. "We must make up for lost time and . . ." I trail off when I notice that the others are not paying any attention to me. They stare at the twins behind me.

"Okay, what's going on?" I ask and turn around. "What did you two do this time?"

Isa and Bella swallow. "We know why those bear-wolves didn't follow us," they say in unison and point above the white, fluffy tops of the grass stalks.

CHAPTER 46

My gaze trails the height of the grass, landing on a brown insect with a reddish hue to its chitin. Bigger than a personal space shuttle, it reminds me of a dry stick. Two long antennae grow out of a flat, round head that is too tiny in proportion to its long and thin body. Three pairs of thin legs support it, each ending in four sharp claws.

"Nobody move," I say out of the corner of my mouth.

My friends obey.

The twig insect stares at us with kaleidoscopic eyes, its antennae twitching. Two pairs of mandibles click a couple of times. It is either trying to talk to us, or it finds us appetizing.

"Let me try something," Rhona says and inches toward it.

"Don't you dare kill that poor thing!" Glenna says with a hiss and Ragnald restrains her with a muscular arm in front of her chest.

"I won't."

Rhona opens her mouth and sings in her own language. Her voice sounds clear and beautiful. Her song evokes feelings of calm and comfort. When she reaches the chorus, she takes a few steps forward and pauses. She repeats this until she is right in front of the insect.

I hold my breath as Rhona reaches her hand up, still singing.

The twig insect bends its head, allowing her to place her palm on it. Then it lowers its body to the ground, peacefully.

I exhale in relief. I am glad Rhona didn't end up as a snack. It would have been difficult to explain it to Callum and his family.

Glenna steps up to Rhona. "That was impressive!" she says and digs into one of the deep pockets of her dark blue overalls, rummaging until she finds a few seeds to offer the twig insect.

It clicks its mandibles, showing interest. Glenna steps closer, until it can pick a few seeds off her palm, then she rubs its flat head too.

Rhona grins. "Who wants a ride?"

CHAPTER 47

"Well, that didn't last long," Belthair says with his top right hand above his eyes as he watches the twig insect being carried off by an immense bird that looks a lot like a lobster with leathery wings and a long beak.

"We were lucky to survive the encounter," Ivy huffs with a pointed look at Rhona. "How about next time we don't repeat this mistake? Hmm?"

"Ungrateful little . . ." Rhona mutters. "I couldn't have known that a k'hawk would spot us!"

"Don't mind her," Glenna says to Rhona, "this is nature at work. We experienced something special for however a short time it lasted." Thanks to the twig insect, we covered several days' worth of ground in a few hours as it crossed over the grassy plains at breakneck speed.

Despite her comforting words, Glenna looks sad, and I hug her. It's hard to witness nature's cruelty and not do anything about it. Especially for Glenna, who had dozens of rescued animals and insects in her room back on Uhna. She nursed them back to health with much love and care. Sadly, none of the animals in her care survived the devastation DLD wreaked on Fye Island.

"Fine," Rhona says, then heads to the hill on our right, toward the spiraling smoke. I hurry after her, while the others lag, discussing their favorite meals that they will eat the second we are out of here.

If we ever make it out of here.

I touch the fangs at the end of my leather necklace. I cannot give into despair and lose hope! I will get back to Callum even if it's the last thing I do!

Rhona and I ascend to the top of the hill. Arrov drops down into a cross-legged position next to us while a heaving sigh, facing the slope where we came from. That is why he doesn't spot it first.

I stumble as my mind works hard to make sense of what I'm seeing. Projectiles heading toward us like a lethal black swarm.

"Retreat!" I shout just as Rhona orders, "Charge!"

CHAPTER 48

"Retreat!" I shout again and look back at Rhona and Arrov.

She stays and pulls a black, hand-size box out of her jacket. She slaps her other hand on top of it. The box unfolds into a short sword. Arrov doesn't move; he stares at his clasped hand, oblivious and lethargic at the same time.

Rhona takes up a ready stance as arrows rain around them.

Muttering curses, I sprint down the hill "Run!" I yell at the rest of my puzzled-looking party, then stumble but manage to regain my footing. Isa, Bella, Glenna, and Ivy turn on their heels and hurry down the hill. Belthair and Ragnald hesitate before deciding to follow.

Something flashes by. A large, dark-green blur, dashing between Glenna and the twins, then around the men and me. Too fast to discern who or what it is.

"You can stop!" Rhona shouts, lowering her sword with a grimace. She heads toward us, looking frustrated. "It's over."

We stop, panting for air.

"I'm exhausted from all this running!" Ivy says. "It's cowardly and nothing like the Marauders' way! I have never shied away from confrontation, though I do prefer to operate out of sight, from the shadows. By the time you perceive me, it's already too late."

Belthair nods along Ivy's words. "That's an admirable tactic!"

She glances at Belthair, blushing, and tucks a blond strand of hair behind her ear. "It is? I mean, exactly!"

Isa and Bella lie down on their backs, staring up at the sky. "Why did we have to withdraw?" Isa asks and Bella adds, "You could have used your magic, Lilla—"

"Never mind that now," I say, interrupting Bella and she studies me. I don't know how long I can keep my lack of magic secret from them.

I turn to the approaching Rhona. "How come you have a sword?"

"Why wouldn't I have a sword?" she asks, sneering. "A good general is never without one." The *unlike you* is implied loud and clear.

"Sometimes a conversation can do wonders," I say in my defense. It's better than lying outright.

"That's what the weak use as their excuse," Rhona mocks and taps the bottom of the short sword's hilt. The blade snaps back into it, leaving behind the small, black box. "This is my compact travel sword. I always have it with me." She points at various pockets and adds, "I also carry a few daggers; and a knife; and—"

I raise a hand to stop her. "I don't need to know the full extent of your arsenal."

Rhona pockets the black box. "Just like you don't know any other military command than 'Retreat'?"

Funny! "There was no reason for us to stay and fight when we didn't even know who was attacking," I explain. It sounds logical, even to me. Almost better than the truth.

"At least we won," Glenna says with an encouraging expression as she puts a hand on my arm.

Arrov ambles down the hill. "You left me behind!"

"Arrov," I say, "don't tell me you missed the commotion!"

A dark blue blush appears on Arrov's fur-covered face. "I was, um, trying to change back and must have gotten lost in thought. I didn't hear a thing."

"At least you don't feel them," Glenna says. She twirls her finger, indicating for him to turn around.

"Is there something on me?" Arrov asks as he complies, looking over his bulging shoulder.

Arrows. A dozen of them stuck in his strong back, sticking out amid his long, light blue fur. He looks like an overgrown, melancholic porcupine.

He doesn't even wince when Glenna pulls out a few of the arrows.

"Amazing!" she says while she removes the rest. "You are not even bleeding! This must be one of your superpowers."

Arrov's expression cheers up. "It must be!" He flexes his arms, and Isa and Bella giggle in appreciation.

Rhona shakes her head. "I don't want to poison your well, but this was no win, Glenna. This was a test of our strength. Not a true attack, just a lick."

I turn to Rhona. "What do you mean?" I gesture toward Arrov's now clean back, and the arrows scattered around him. "He almost got killed!"

Rhona waves toward Arrov. "That is why I know this was a test! No one else got hurt except Arrov, because he wouldn't move when he was supposed to."

I frown. "I don't think—"

"I believe they found out what they needed from this skirmish," Rhona insists in a cold voice. "We won't be so lucky next time."

CHAPTER 49

"You can never trust a food that's green," Ivy declares after Glenna hands her a few flowers and leafy greens she'd been collecting for our dinner along the way.

Glenna kept a cautious distance from the darker parts of the woods, but we haven't seen those bear-wolves for a while now. Maybe they prefer a deeper forest, like the one we encountered earlier today.

"I gather you are not a fan of vegetables," Ragnald says, and studies his "meal" without much enthusiasm.

"Who is?" Ivy asks, then gives her portion to Belthair, who perks up at the unexpected attention.

"Don't worry," Glenna says to us, once finished handing out what she had in her pockets. "These are edible and should tide us over a bit longer."

"I don't like the word 'edible,'" I mutter. When Glenna raises an eyebrow in question, I add, "Because what it means is that whatever you put 'edible' before is not meant to be eaten. Like edible flowers. Edible bugs. Or edible wild berries. Technically you *can* eat them, but should you?"

The others agree, except Rhona, who says, "A good general always provides for her troops."

"You didn't hunt for us," I point out. "Not once."

"We need meat," Arrov says with a growl, staring off through the trees. "Roasted, cooked, or raw, I don't care at this point."

Isa and Bella sigh. "Preferably roasted."

"Quiet!" Rhona says, raising her right arm with the missing jacket sleeve. "I hear a k'rabbit rummaging—"

We laugh.

Rhona frowns. "What's so funny?"

"We don't believe in your 'help' anymore," Belthair says, "not after the, uh, berry incident."

Just thinking about it makes me sick to my stomach.

"Fine," Rhona says, and with a flourish she flicks her wrist. "Then you figure it out."

Something large and beige-colored, at least four feet tall and two feet wide, dashes on our right, snorting and huffing, then disappears among the trees.

Arrov raises his head, sniffing and staring after it. Nothing of the once handsome and mischievous prince is left in his dark blue eyes that now glint with a red predatory light.

"That's a k'boar, and it's too dangerous without any spears or . . ." Rhona's voice trails off as Arrov charges after the beast on fast but silent feet.

"K'rabbit and k'boar; how imaginative," Ivy mocks as she turns to Rhona. "Though you did say bear-wolves and not k'bear-wolves."

"The 'k' is silent," Rhona says.

A few trees topple to the ground, and a loud screech pierces the air.

Arrov ambles out of the woods, carrying a dead k'boar on his shoulder while dragging two saplings after him.

He throws the carcass at Rhona's feet. "Dinner is served."

CHAPTER 50

After feasting on roasted k'boar, night came again, forcing us to make camp on the spot.

I sit wide awake, with my back against the others, next to Arrov. Sounds of snoring intersperse with screeches and other animal noises. Bugs add harsh twittering and cheeping sounds to the cacophony of the night, playing with my nerves.

Not that I need much at this point to achieve that. The wildlife in this place is more aggressive and dangerous than I would have imagined, though the incident that Rhona believes was a test of our strength worries me more. I cannot fathom who would attack us or why.

Nothing makes much sense in this fog-cursed place!

Isa mutters in her sleep, "Just divide it by two hundred and fifty!" Then she puts her head on her sleeping sister's shoulder.

I look up to the dark and cloudless sky, filled with trillions of bright stars. The two moons provide soft illumination. A feeling of humbleness envelops me as I take in the vastness of space above, but I cannot find peace in it as I used to.

Those millions of worlds out there, full of inhabitants who have no idea that the Era War has started, what will they do? Will DLD vanquish them next, to add to His corrupted army? Who will protect them? Not their Sybil, who cannot even recruit an army to start with.

Their Sybil is stuck and there is no way to help them.

Fighting the urge to do something, *anything*, I look back down and stare ahead at the dark shapes of our surroundings. My imagination fills it with predators and mysterious raiders, waiting to pounce. I hug my knees to my chest and rest my forehead on my hands.

I don't feel strong enough to keep going; to keep pretending that my magic hasn't disappeared; that being trapped here does not make me scared to death.

143

I touch the fangs at the end of the leather necklace and conjure Callum's attractive face, with his intent blue eyes. My heart fills with so much love, it surprises me anew. I miss his directness. I miss how he supported me without trying to take over. I miss *him* so much!

I squeeze the fangs until they cut into my palm.

I won't let this place intimidate me! I will keep going!

My eyes close on their own and I yawn.

Tomorrow will be different.

CHAPTER 51

DAY 3

"It's gone!" Rhona shouts, waking us up at dawn.

"What's gone?" I ask, yawning. I look at my palm that still shows the imprint of a fang that I'd been clutching in my sleep.

Rhona points at the flat top of a boulder, where we laid out pieces of salted and roasted k'boar meat after we finished eating. There was enough left to last us for at least another day, but they are gone now. "What kind of general are you if you can't even protect our food for one night?!"

Buckets of fishguts! "I was sleeping, like you!"

Ivy glides next to Rhona. "It must have been that giant," she says, gesturing toward Arrov, "his stomach kept growling the whole night."

We turn to Arrov, who is busy grooming his facial fur with his fingers. He glances up and asks, "Why are you gawking at me?" Then he notices the empty stone. "I was looking forward to breakfast!"

"Glenna or I would have woken up if Arrov tried to get up," I say. "He was sleeping between us."

Isa stretches. "It's clear it wasn't Arrov who took the food." Bella nods in agreement.

Belthair studies the crime scene. "Maybe it was the same people who attacked us on the hilltop."

"How would you know?" Glenna snaps, her dark crimson eyes flashing. "Unless this is your way to deflect from your own guilt! Don't try to lie, you bottom-feeder shrimp!"

Belthair looks taken aback. "Is that what you think of me?"

"Of course she doesn't," I say to Belthair, then turn to Glenna. "He was sitting by you, remember? You would have felt him move."

Glenna takes a deep breath, but Ragnald places a hand on her shoulder, and she looks up at the mage, surprised. Then her expression turns shocked,

145

ashamed, and sad in seconds. "I, uh, didn't mean it, Belthair . . ." she trails off and rubs her face with both of her hands.

The others gather around Rhona and the large stone, discussing the possibility of sabotage.

Ivy glides up to me. "Mark my word, this *is* your fault," she says with a hiss. She keeps her smile in place, and her gaze focused on the others. "It's because of you that I ended up in this godsforsaken place. It's because of you we are tired and hungry and lost. It will be your fault when I die here!"

"How is this my responsibility? You pushed me into that fight circle, almost killing me, then followed me to the Wise Women's cave. Maybe it's time to take accountability for your actions, don't you think?"

Ivy shrugs. "No one would believe you without any proof."

I look at her sharp and serrated nails. "That might be so for now, but that doesn't mean I trust you. How do I know it wasn't you who destroyed our food?"

Ivy narrows her eyes. "I should have taken care of you the Marauder way!"

"What *is* the Marauder way?"

"Kill you in your sleep!" Ivy says and swipes her blond hair off her shoulder as she stomps away.

"Wait your turn," I mutter after her.

CHAPTER 52

MOIRA

Nothing is left of the luxurious new city with its light gray marble and twirling, ribbonlike buildings covered in green plants. Or any of the other cities, for that matter.

It took one year for the Archgod of Chaos and Destruction to crush our planetary defense artillery and then our cities. Our lakes and seas dried up from the heat of the bombardments. Our mountaintops leveled. Our land burned and dead along with most of its animals. Half our planet is blackened from the spread of corruption the monstrous dark fiends brought with them.

The second year of the invasion had many of us dying at the hands of the Turned, corrupted elementalist mages, who lead the armies of the archgod. We retreated to the ruins of the mountains.

Many were caught. The archgod tried to corrupt the prisoners so they would become His dark servants, but to no avail. Our secret, the natural resistance to most magic, made us valuable but not indispensable. Our fortune was that the archgod hasn't given up finding why His corruption didn't work on us; otherwise He would have annihilated our planet. If He can't turn us into dark servants, then the Archgoddess of the Eternal Light and Order shouldn't have us in Her army either. For Him, it's a win-win either way. For us, caught in the middle, not so much.

This is the third year of our resistance, the beginning of spring. I fear we won't last long. Half of the population is already gone, millions of souls lost. Those still alive are exhausted, starving, and weary. Though we are not ready to give up just yet.

Gigi predicted this would happen, but I refused to believe it. Because of her warning, we were able to survive. She offered an alternative solution, but I am not ready to take her up on it. It is too drastic. I am not sure if I have the right to make that decision on behalf of my people. If I *should* make that decision. It's wrong. It would be like giving up, but worse. So much worse!

We must keep fighting! For as long as we can.

While we have the magical resistance, our home world doesn't. Trying to fight when the Turned conjured erupting volcanoes or threw gale winds at us was nearly impossible. That is why I came up with this plan to even the odds from impossible to nightmare-but-there-is-a-chance-it-might-work level.

We set traps at the foot of the mountain, in the hopes that a few thousand dark fiends would plummet into the wide trenches hidden there, halting their progress. Then instead of charging down the mountain straight at them, as they would expect us to do, we would attack from the side and from around the mountain instead. There still would be hundreds of thousands of dark fiends, outnumbering us ten to one; but that never stopped us before.

"Almost," I say in a low voice and crawl back from the rocky outcrop of the cliff while the scout remains behind.

Crouching, I head to the group of militias, holding swords and makeshift weapons. "When they are closer, we will attack," I say. "Don't forget: our main target is the Turned leading the squadron of dark fiends."

Once we take out the Turned, the confusion and lack of leadership will make slaying the hundred thousand half-corrupted dark fiends *easier*, for lack of a better word.

Ten thousand dirty, tired men and women, in rags, gather wherever they can fit on the twisting mountain "street" the bombardments left behind. My order spreads through their ranks, then their signal of acknowledgment returns to me.

Thousands of groups like us will attack from multiple locations at the same time, following the same plan. We hope to crush most of their forces and drive the archgod's army out of our home world in a last-ditch effort.

Edan and Keelan are among the fighters, grasping their longswords. I wish they wouldn't have to come with us, but I cannot show favoritism. Not that they would *let* me spare them anyway. Their blood burns with vengeance, too, from the losses we've suffered.

At a whistle from the scout, I jump to my feet, shouting, "Attack!"

CHAPTER 53

LILLA

"I don't think it's a good idea to cross this river," Arrov says, backing away from the wide stream that flows in front of us. It is carved into the green hills with steep dirt banks, surrounded by lush viridescent grass and amber-colored flowers.

I point at the muddy water. "We don't have a choice. We've lost precious time going around the last forest. Besides, this might be the river from our 'directions' to the Heart Amulet. How does the fable go again?"

Rhona sighs, exasperated. "Beyond the river, over the last hill, where the two halves of the sun join. How could you forget it already? Having trouble with your memory?"

I ignore Rhona and turn to Arrov. "The river doesn't look too difficult to cross," I say and gesture ahead. "Not to mention that smoke is visible over the woods on the opposite bank. I think we are getting closer."

Gods, I hope! We are three days into our quest with nothing to show for it. If I didn't know better, I'd say that smoke keeps moving *away* from us.

"I wouldn't wade into this river," Rhona says. "It reminds me a lot of the River of Death that's full of k'—"

Yet another charming name! "There is nothing threatening about this river," I say, interrupting her as I observe the slow-moving water. "You are being Warrioress of Negativity again."

Rhona glares. "Have it your way then."

"Enough talking!" Belthair says and tucks his gray shirt into his pants, then leaps off the steep riverbank. He lands in waist-high water and wades in deeper. The twins, Glenna, and Ragnald follow him, soon switching to swimming.

Arrov shakes his furry head. "I don't know if I can swim in this giant form! I will just have to—"

Rhona shoves Arrov. He stumbles, landing in the river and disappears under its surface.

"Arrov!" I shout and move to go after him, but Rhona grabs my forearm. "Just wait."

After a moment, Arrov's light blue head breaks the surface of the water. He swims better and faster than the others, leaving them behind with a few long arm strokes. "Look at me!" he shouts. "Who knew I am so aquatically inclined?"

Glenna and Ragnald laugh. "Another superpower!" she says.

"See?" Rhona asks and jumps into the water.

I hurry after her and meet the group halfway in.

Before I reach Rhona, Isa and Bella shriek.

"What happened?" I ask, paddling in place.

Something slimy with sharp scales brushes against my foot. "What was that?!" I yelp, looking around, but I cannot see anything in the murky water.

"Swim for your life!" Rhona shouts and picks up speed.

CHAPTER 54

"Why didn't you tell us?" I ask, breathless, as I crawl out of the water and drop on my back on the rocky riverbank. I shove long, wet strands of hair out of my face and shiver when the cool breeze hits my soaked tunic.

I've never seen anything like what chased us! It reached twenty feet in length, with dozens of legs ending in sharp claws. Its elongated head, with three sets of black orbs for eyes, sported a long maw full of fangs.

Rhona strides out, not even breathing hard. "I tried to tell you. Remember? But none of you listened! Plus, I was betting the k'alligator was alone and wouldn't come after such a big group as ours."

K'alligator? Like the one Callum had to slay with his bare hands when he was just fifteen? I reach for the leather necklace with fangs. I am astonished he survived the encounter with that dreadful creature at such a young age.

"You were betting?!" Belthair asks, lying on his back with his six arms spread out.

Isa and Bella sit next to each other with their knees pulled up. "We've never swam so hard in our whole lives!" they say in unison.

"I do not care to repeat the experience," Arrov says and stretches his long legs out in front of him while he leans back on his hands, "but I am glad your bet paid off. Otherwise I never would have learned that I am a great swimmer in this form." Most of his fur looks halfway dry, like it's water-repellent.

Rhona grins down, standing over me. "A good general would have known when to listen and avoid danger!"

Not with that again!

Ivy snickers as she looks me over. "If Callum could see you now, he would run straight to me!" Somehow she looks pretty and collected even soaked, with her long blond hair combed back and her dress looking immaculate.

I didn't have such luck. There is a huge tear in my black leggings, and my tunic is covered in mud, looking more like a rag.

"Is delusion a Marauder characteristic?" I ask her. "It goes well with spoiled."

Ivy raises her chin. "You can pretend you still have time to finish your little quest, but we know you'll fail. Then Callum will be mine. Now who's delusional?"

I open my mouth to retort when a hand touches my arm.

"Don't mind her," Glenna says, "she is just jealous that Callum loves you and not her."

"I'm not jealous of her," Ivy says, then shivers and glances at the woods behind us. "I feel eyes on me!"

"No one cares about your phobias!" Glenna snaps. Ragnald puts a hand on Glenna's forearm, and she closes her eyes in a forced calm.

"It's time to get going before nightfall," Rhona says.

No one moves. Even I am too exhausted to stand.

Isa whines, "Can't you just let us rest a minute?" Bella agrees.

Rhona narrows her eyes on the forest and murmurs, "That can't be possible."

"What are you muttering about?" I ask.

"Get on your feet, right now!" Rhona barks. "We are about to get attacked!"

CHAPTER 55

The thick timberland behind us separates into two sections, leaving a wide path for a group of rushing dark green blurs heading straight for us.

"No forest would naturally part like that," Ragnald says, scrambling to his feet. His worried expression betrays his calm tone. He lowers a hand for Glenna and helps her to her feet.

"I agree," Arrov says and shakes his whole body, spraying us with remnants of water from his fur.

I jump to my feet. "This is the second time a forest shows such strange shifting ability. It cannot be a coincidence."

"What should we do?" Ivy asks, hiding behind Belthair's back. He postures, enjoying the attention from her.

The twins shiver and hold hands. "We'd rather not go back into that river," Isa says, and Bella adds, "Ever!"

"We must stand our ground," Rhona says, pulling her compact sword's box from her pocket, "and fight here!"

"Or Lilla could use her legendary Lumenian magic and save us!" Ragnald says, smiling at me with pride. "You should have seen her obliterate a throng of fully corrupted dark servants until nothing was left. It was a sight to behold!"

Buckets and buckets of fishguts!

They turn to me, waiting for my magic to save us.

My gaze darts around, looking for a solution, but the attackers are getting close.

"LILLA!" they shout.

Without thinking, I raise my knee with arms out in front of me. I step forward and spread my arms at the same time, pushing energy out.

The force of the energy repels the attackers. They slide back to where they came from—to the other side of the forest.

It's not magic, but the Saage Women's energy manipulation trick has saved me more than once.

Ragnald crosses his arms. "This wasn't what I had in mind."

"Now what?" Glenna asks.

"Now we run!" I shout and burst into a sprint, up the rocky riverside.

CHAPTER 56

"Why did we stop?" I ask, huffing and shivering in my cold, wet clothing. In front of me towers a hillside with dozens of flat boulders protruding from it.

We ran as far as we could on the riverbank, jumping over dead tree trunks and washed-up moss-covered debris, before venturing into the forest. We risked it because Rhona believed she could see the other side, and it turned out that she was right. When she glimpsed these knolls with their white and almost gleaming stones, she changed direction heading toward them.

Arrov ambles next to me and touches one of the large, jutting rocks and tries to jiggle them, then nods, satisfied. "This would make a good site to rest."

"A better question is," Rhona says to me, her black military-style jacket still dripping water, "why did you not use your 'legendary' magic? A good general would know—"

Something unpleasant rears its head inside me and words I kept pressed down, burst out. "I've never asked for your help!" I say, whirling on Rhona, and pointing into her face. "I've had enough of your lectures! I've had enough of you criticizing me! I have had enough of your haughty attitude with this 'good general' whalecrap! How would you know what that means when you are not even a general!"

I glance away from Rhona. I immediately regret shouting at her, wishing I would have taken the high tide.

The group quiets, and my friends eye me.

Rhona, with a blank expression, turns her back on me and begins stomping on a spot on the ground. She is either making a place for fire or working out her anger.

"I'm impressed," Ivy says, smirking. "You asserted yourself like a true Marauder. You must have been holding that back for quite a while."

I grimace.

Isa shakes her head. "The probability of Lilla losing it grew each time Rhona needled her." Bella adds, "This was unavoidable."

"In my humble opinion, garnered through two hundred years of hard work at the Academia, honesty is a cornerstone of any relationship, whether it is on professional level or not. Maybe work on your delivery a bit more?"

I nod to Ragnald, but I'm too embarrassed to look at the mage. I despise each second that I hide the truth about my magic or lack thereof. Whether Rhona had it coming or not, does not make me feel better about the way I handled her "needling."

Glenna frowns at Ragnald. "I thought you said you are two hundred years old. Or were you born in the Academia and started working right away?"

Ragnald ducks his head. "I am two hundred and forty years old, but two hundred sounds better."

Glenna rolls her eyes at him. "I didn't realize mages can be so sensitive about their age."

Arrov touches my shoulder with a hand. "Are you okay, Lilla? I've never seen you so upset."

No, I'm not okay. "I'm fine, Arrov." I can't admit that this quest is getting to me.

He smiles in response and wanders away, gathering sticks for the fire.

I look at Rhona dragging dry branches into the stone circle she built. "I am so sorry—"

"We will make camp before night," Rhona says, interrupting my apology, "that is why we stopped here, to answer your question." She squats by the campfire site when Belthair steps up to her.

"Allow me," he says, and checks to see if Ivy is watching him. Then he shoos Rhona away from the branches. "This is a job for an experienced leader."

He picks up two twigs and gauges a spot on one with his fingernail. Then he places the other stick on the spot and spins the vertical stick between his palms, back and forth.

"We should keep going," I say, "and make the most of what's left of daylight. We cannot let them throw us off track."

Rhona watches Belthair with mild interest. "We need rest, and time for our clothing to dry," she says. "We can use those flat rocks over there for drying our clothing."

Ivy rubs her arms as she glances around, looking troubled. "Isn't anyone worried that whoever attacked us will find us and kill us, since we are trapped here?"

Belthair stops to wipe sweat from his forehead with his middle right arm, looking exhausted, but there is still no sign of fire.

"We will set a watch," Rhona says, "and take turns." She pulls her sword box out of her pocket. She unscrews the bottom and takes a tiny lighter out of it. She kindles it, then places the flame near the sticks. Within seconds flames bursts so high, they almost singe Belthair's eyebrow off, forcing him to scramble away.

"I will take first watch," Rhona says. "Besides, I am not worried." When we keep staring at Rhona, she adds, "We've confused them with Lilla's 'legendary' magic. Now they will regroup and try to come up with a new tactic. We have a bit of time before they attack again."

"How do you know that?" I ask.

"Because a good . . ." Rhona pauses and clears her throat. "Because that's what I would do. Now go to sleep. You'll be up next."

CHAPTER 57

DAY 4

Rhona's shouting cuts into a gibberish nightmare about yesterday's attack and I open my eyes. The sun's pinkish-orange light paints the bottom of the still-dark sky.

I glower at Rhona, wishing she would refrain from shouting so early in the day.

"What happened?" I ask Glenna, rubbing my face. Ragnald offers a hand to help me up. I accept it, but avoid ogling his athletic body, wearing only a pair of black briefs.

I cross one of my arms in front of the white tank top while doing my best to cover my matching panties with the other. This earns a raised eyebrow from Ragnald. "Do you not think that I have seen my fair share of female bodies?" he asks.

"That doesn't mean I want to add *my* body to that long list of yours," I grumble.

"I don't know what happened," Glenna answers my question in yellow bra and matching panties. "I just woke up, too."

"It was you who stole our clothing!" Rhona shouts, pointing into Ivy's face. She is dressed in black hipster panties and a bandana bra.

"What did Ivy do this time?" I ask Rhona.

Ivy, with trembling lips, backs away from the furious Rhona. "Why would you even think that I would do such a horrible thing?" Ivy asks, her slim body clad in strips of pink lace that would be a stretch to call underwear with how little coverage they offer.

"Because . . ." Rhona trails off and frowns at Arrov, who lifts a few large boulders, searching underneath them. "Do you think that somehow the garments we laid out on *top* of the boulders managed to drop *under* them?"

Arrov, holding a large rock in his hands and looking downcast, says, "I was just trying to help."

Belthair laughs. "Maybe the longer Arrov stays as an A'ice giant, the dumber he'll get. He was never this senseless in the rebellion!"

Arrov just stares at him, looking stung.

"That was not a nice thing to say to poor Arrov," Glenna says, and turns to him, muttering soft words of comfort.

Ivy slips behind Belthair. He preens from Ivy's attention and says, "I have two questions—"

"Yes, you are stupid," Rhona says with a snarl. "No, you weren't born like this!"

"Okay, Warrioress of Negativity," I say and step in front of Rhona. "That's enough insulting of my friends because you need an outlet to vent!" I pause and cringe. I did the exact same thing to Rhona yesterday, didn't I? It takes a pirate to know one . . .

I clear my throat and ask, "Why do you think this was Ivy's fault anyway?"

"Because she was the last one on watch duty," Rhona says, "and I found her asleep."

Ivy peeks out from behind Belthair. "I made a mistake! I was too tired and . . ." Rhona glares at Ivy until the princess bursts into tears.

"Because of your irresponsible action," Rhona says to the sobbing Ivy, "the attackers had a chance to steal our apparel and destroy whatever little we have left of our morale! Are you happy now?"

"You can't prove it!" Ivy shouts back, still crying.

"I think you are doing a great job destroying our morale on your own," Arrov says to Rhona.

I sigh. It is a setback, not to mention the humiliation to continue our journey in our underwear. This would be comical any other day, but right now it's the last drop on the sand castle.

Belthair scratches a red bug bite on his chin with his top left hand. "That answers my first question, but not the second. Why would they sabotage us when they could have killed us in our sleep? What does that achieve?"

Rhona shrugs her wide shoulders. "To intimidate us, play with us, or both."

Belthair raises his left three arms to the sky and shakes his fists. "We won't be intimidated by you, stealthy attackers! You hear? We—"

Arrov clamps a large hand over Belthair's face. "Stop shouting or they will come back with an *answer* to your challenge."

Rhona turns to me, her eyes furious. "What is the big plan now, *general*?"

CHAPTER 58

MOIRA

Something went wrong. The trenches didn't work as we expected.

The Turned tricked us. They drew us out of our hiding place. Once we reached them, they surrounded us on our flanks in a pincer move, with unexpected reinforcements from not one but two more Turned-led battalions!

The Turned had never worked together like this before! They are known to be too selfish and crazed for such cooperation. Often they end up killing each other if they come in close proximity. Somehow these Turned elementalist mages found a way to unite against us.

I should have expected them to learn our tactics! I was arrogant. I underestimated them. Now we are paying the price for my carelessness.

I raise my short sword and cut across a dark fiend, a cross between a tremendous bear and a lizard. The Fla'mma-infused blade slices through it like a knife through air. Then I dance to the side, ducking under a swipe from a reptilian dark fiend. Coming up, I sever its hamstrings before plunging my sword into its back a few times.

I leap over the huge, scaled corpse with a sword raised above my head, and bring the sword down on the head of a wolflike fiend.

All around me, my people are locked in a desperate battle. Clashes of swords, predatory roars, and screams of the wounded blend into a nightmarish music. The air is infused with the coppery scent of blood and the repulsive, rotting stink emanating from the dark fiends.

I straighten, then wipe my forehead with bloody hands.

We are surrounded. The other groups' fights aren't going any better. The runners bring more dire news from them each time. It's a matter of time now.

Without any warning, I am shoved to the side. Out of the way of a huge, towering fiend's sledgehammer-like fist. I have not seen this type before. It is straight from the ancient legends of winged dra'agons, ten feet tall and with leathery wings.

Edan's sword cuts off one of its wings and its right arm in one slice. The dark fiend topples to the side, unmoving.

"Thank you," I say, winded. I am not as young as I used to be. "I didn't see it coming."

"At your service, ma'am," Edan says and bows in a mock salute. How he can still find energy and spirit to joke is beyond me.

At the sight of him, love fills my soul, pushing desperation and the tragedy of our circumstance to the side. For a moment, all is right. So long as he is by my side.

"Where is Keelan?" I ask, searching for him.

Edan straightens from his bow. "He is over there," he says, and gestures toward our son, who is cutting his way toward us like a berserker.

Then Edan grunts, and his expression turns shocked. He looks down.

A sharp black bone spike burst through his chest, covered in blood.

Keelan's agonized wail rends the air, along with my scream.

I cut off the tail of the winged fiend I thought Edan killed, and slam my sword into its throat, finishing it off.

Edan, with blood dripping from his mouth, collapses to his knees, his face ashen.

"Healer!" I shout with tears running down my face as I drop by Edan's side. I gather him to me, holding him and looking into his pain-filled eyes. "Please stay with me!" I beg. "Please!"

"I . . . love . . . you," he says with a gasp; then that spirited light fades from his dark brown eyes.

I throw my head back, bellowing, "Gigi! Help us!"

CHAPTER 59

LILLA

"This should last for a while," I say, lifting two large bags made from tyger leaf with water sloshing in them.

After our clothes went missing, we agreed that we needed new ones. It was Rhona's suggestion to look for tyger leaves. She recognized these trees among the evergreen ones. They are long and oval-shaped, with light gray stripes that appear when the sunlight hits their smooth surface. They are durable and easy to manipulate—perfect for crafting new clothes.

It didn't take long to encounter another grove. Finding the tyger trees was a bit more time-consuming. We broke into pairs to search. I didn't like the idea of separating but the arguing kept going on and on, using too much time, until I gave in. I ended up paired with Rhona.

We also found a spring with a narrow waterfall and filled four bags, also made of tyger leaves, with spring water. We each carry two large ones, heading back to the others.

Rhona smiles at me, and her smile is a kind one. "We did a great job together," she states.

I lift an elbow to my ear, sloshing water in the leaf pouch, pretending to check on my hearing.

Rhona snorts. "You heard that right! Now keep going and don't spill too much water."

We step over knotted roots and stoop under low-hanging moss-covered branches in companionable silence. We listen to the music of nature—chirps, squeaks, and screeches, though that clicking-purring sound that indicates an incoming attack from the dangerous bear-wolves cannot be heard. Green vegetation invades the ground and the trees, striving for what little sunshine manages to get through the thick tree canopies. The sunlight paints the air in a fog-like twilight.

"I would go as far as to say that I like our new outfits," I say. These simple dresses that we made by cutting holes for our head, then folding the leaves over our body, and tying it with strands from the trees' trunks, worked out well.

Rhona nods. "They are much more comfortable than one would think—"

The ground gives out under Rhona's feet.

She drops her water sacks and tumbles back with arms flailing. She grabs onto the closest branch, but it snaps under her weight.

With a cry, I release the leaf pouches and lunge forward. I grab her by the hand and yank her toward me with such force that we both land on our sides on the moss-covered forest floor.

Sitting up, we lean over to see a deep canyon peeking through the tear in the thick moss carpet that hid it, until Rhona stepped on it. A perfect trap made by nature or on purpose. I glance around but no one jumps out of the thicket.

"Why did you save me?" she asks but doesn't look at me.

What kind of question is that? "Because it was the right thing to do," I say and get to my feet and gather the four water bags that somehow managed to stay intact.

Rhona takes two of them out of my hands. "I was mean to you. You had the tactical advantage. You could have gotten rid of me."

I snort. "How would I explain that to Callum? Sorry, I killed your little sister out of tactical advantage?" Shaking my head, I resume the trek. "Besides, you would have done the same for me, right?"

Rhona raises an eyebrow. "Maybe."

Not quite the answer I was expecting. "If I admit that you are the better general out of the two of us, will you make peace with me?"

Rhona exhales and then nods. "As long as we both know it. Now let's go back before night comes, trapping us in the forest."

CHAPTER 60

DAY 5

"Intruders!" Ivy shrieks, jolting me awake after a few hours of dreamless sleep, in the middle of the night.

A dark shape of a burly man stands over me, with a wave-bladed dagger in his hand, raised to strike.

I gape at the man, with my heart beating in my throat, frozen and unable to react.

From my right, Belthair jumps up and tackles the attacker. They stumble a few feet back and the man kicks Belthair away.

Belthair shouts. He punches the attacker, alternating between jabs and crosses with his six fists.

The man ducks and sidesteps each hit, fast and graceful in his movements, like a warrior.

My friends get to their feet, confused. I scramble to stand up too and notice another man, locked in a fight with Arrov.

A glinting object flies by me, thrown by the second attacker. It lands in Belthair's right shoulder. He tumbles backward, knocked to the ground from the force, with the dagger embedded. His attacker sprints away free.

The other dark shape turns to escape but Arrov lunges and swipes across his hamstrings. With a muffled shout of pain, the assailant disappears, limping into the woods.

Arrov lets out a blood-curdling roar and chases after the invader.

I drop by Belthair, who thrashes in pain, leaving behind a spreading red pool of blood on the ground. "Are you okay?" I ask and curse under my breath. Foolish question! Obviously he is not okay! "What can I do?" I ask Glenna when she kneels by Belthair.

"Distract him," she says and tries to channel her magic for a second. Then with a frustrated yelp she gives up.

I hold Belthair's top left hand and smile down at him. "You shouldn't have come with me! You would have been safer back on Uhna!"

Belthair, looking pale, laughs. "Don't worry about me, Lia," he says, using the nickname he gave me long ago. "This is nothing. Besides, who would look after you if not me?"

He closes his eyes and bites off a groan.

"Do you have anything for his pain?" I ask Glenna.

Glenna nods and rummages in her tyger leaf purse, turning away. Belthair rips the dagger out of his shoulder with his middle right hand.

Glenna drops the plants. "No! Why would you do that?" She claps a hand over the gushing wound and says, "Put pressure here!"

I release Belthair's hand and put mine over the bleeding wound. Glenna pushes down on my hand to show the pressure needed. "Don't let go until I tell you so!"

I nod and focus on my task. There is so much blood! The coppery scent of it permeates the cold night air.

I close my eyes and pray to The Lady, *Please don't let Belthair die!*

Glenna picks out a few plants and shoves them into her mouth. As she chews, she tears off sections of her tyger leaf dress.

Ivy kneels by Belthair, too. "Will he live?"

"That's so rude!" Isa says and Bella adds, "Don't you think?"

"It's the Marauders' way," Ivy explains and shrugs a slender shoulder, though her expression is compassionate for once. "When someone gets injured on my home world, we only heal them if we know that they'll live. It's not smart to waste precious resources on the soon-to-be-dead." Then she smiles and pats Belthair's injured shoulder.

Belthair winces but grasps her delicate hand in his top left one. "I shall do my best to live. For you, m'lady."

"A simple thank you for being such a great night watch would suffice," Ivy says, self-conscious. "After all, I did save all of your lives."

Rhona picks up a sharp dagger with a long, thin blade from the ground. "Glenna, may I assist you?" she asks.

Glenna lifts part of the string that ties her dress around her waist. "Can you cut it here?"

Rhona obliges her. Glenna spits the plant mush on the square of tyger leaf she tore off her dress and makes quick work of replacing my hand with the newly made dressing.

I get out of Glenna's way and Ivy takes my place, cooing to Belthair. With a flush of color on his pale cheeks that may not have anything to do with his wound, he hangs on her words.

I turn to Rhona, ready to make a funny comment, when I notice her intently studying the dagger. "What is it?" I ask her.

"It's nothing," she says, but her troubled expression belies her words. With lips pressed tightly, she wipes the dagger clean on her leaf dress and cuts a piece from the hem. She wraps the dagger in it and shoves it behind the string belt on her waist, next to her compact sword.

I could have sworn she recognized that dagger. But how? Arrov, with an exasperated growl, lumbers out of the woods. "I couldn't catch those speedy bas—"

A thunderstorm lights up the night sky with loud rumbles. Heavy rain pours down, soaking us in seconds.

CHAPTER 61

"How did you know where to find this cave?" I ask Rhona, sitting by the fire along with my friends, except Belthair, who is out, lying on the other side of the fire with Glenna tending to him.

After the rain started, we hurried to a nearby hillside overgrown with trees. Rhona led us straight into this well-hidden cave as if she's known the location all her life. By the time we settled down and made a fire, we were in our lowest mood.

Rhona shrugs. "I didn't. Well, I didn't exactly *know*. More like an instinct guided me. This area reminds me of where Callum and I used to play as kids and hide from Sawney and Sachary, in a cave very much like this one. My older brothers hated the fact that they could never find us. They would rush by the cave, clueless that we were so close, dying of laughter." She stares into the fire, tracking the minuscule sparkles with her gaze as they fly up brightly before burning out.

The cave entrance hangs low, forcing adults to scoot to enter, but it would have been perfect for two kids. Except this couldn't be the same cave Rhona and Callum played in, could it?

"We will be safe here for the rest of night," Rhona says. "We should get some sleep."

Arrov, sitting cross-legged, leans against the cave wall. "I'm not tired."

Me neither.

I hug my knees to my chest. "When I close my eyes, I see that goon with a dagger, ready to kill me." I shiver and look around at the others. "If Belthair didn't react so fast, I would be dead. If anything happens to him, I will regret it for the rest of my life." My voice buckles. Isa and Bella hug me in consolation.

Could this have been the doing of the enigmatic attackers we encountered twice before?

My instincts tell me this was different from those attacks. This felt personal. Aimed at *me*.

Arrov scribbles on the cave floor with a rock the size of a petite dog. "I regret being stuck in this A'ice giant form, even if it might be awe-inspiring with those superpowers. I left A'ice seeking adventures, knowing there was nothing for me there as the seventh son of the queen. I didn't mind. I had the whole Seven Galaxies to discover. I just never thought I would be stuck looking like *this*."

"I too have regrets. As a battle mage, I've done quite a few things . . ." Ragnald trails off and pauses for a second, collecting his thoughts. "I've spent so many years shutting others out, never trusting anyone. I worried that they would come to fear my magic. Look at me now, with no magic! Oh, the irony!" Glenna puts a hand on Ragnald's arm and smiles at the mage with kindness. He stares at her for a moment before smiling back.

"I regret joking when I should have been more serious," Isa says with a solemn expression, "always searching for fun and entertainment. I did not appreciate the rebellion or being a princess. I did not try to fit in among the other scientists. I judged them harshly because they were scientists, never standing out from the crowd and researching the same old boring subjects. I took offense when they commented on our new tech. Or when our parents or older siblings made remarks about us getting a 'real job' in research, as they did." Bella adds, "We never said good-bye to our family before we, uh, accessed those credits—our inheritance. Now we may never see them ever again."

Ivy gazes at the shadows and light from the fire dancing on the cave ceiling. "I regret how I behaved. I was so mean! You must think I am the worst person to be stuck with on a hopeless quest. That I am useless. Spoiled."

We say no, but Ivy waves away our feeble protests with a shaky smile. "It's the truth. I am the sole heir to the Marauders' Syndicate, and my spoiled uselessness is the main reason I am still alive."

"That can't be true," I say with my eyebrows raised.

Ivy counts off her fingers as she explains, "I didn't get thrown to the canines, like my oldest sister—pushed by our second-older sister. Or flung into a snake pit, like my two older brothers—pushed by our oldest sister. Or poisoned like my three middle siblings poisoned each other. Or killed in my sleep, like the two younger brothers by the then-consort, not biological father.

The dowager queen, my mother, threw him out of the airlock. She didn't like anyone interfering with family issues."

"My gods!" Glenna exclaims, shaking her head. "You were living in constant trauma and stress, fighting for your survival. That's not a normal childhood!"

"That might be so," Ivy continues, "and besides—"

We complete her statement in unison, "—it's the Marauders' way."

Ivy nods. "I became good at playing the dumb blonde until I became her. How is that for irony?"

Isa pats her arm. "There, there." Bella adds, "It's not your fault. This happened to you because your mother allowed it. It was her job to provide you with a safe haven instead of creating a revolving door of terror."

"She wasn't the main reason for my stress," Ivy says, "but a major contributor. Marrying Callum was my best option to escape from her grasp. But now I'll die here, and the dowager queen will win—I'll never be free of her and her plan for my life. I'll always be her pawn."

I touch the sharp fangs at the end of my leather necklace, conjuring Callum's face. I wish I could talk to him. Or hug him. I wish this would be over and we could be together. I love him unconditionally. Not out of royal obligation or as a means to escape from a horrible life.

I glance at Ivy and feel sorry for her. She suffered so much growing up, fearing for her life. Never safe. She had to learn to become superficial and look out for herself. She thought that the way to escape such torture was to marry.

"We can't keep going like this," I say to the others, "looking over our shoulders, worrying about the next attack. We will never have time to complete the quest of finding the Heart Amulet until we deal with them."

"You are right," Rhona says and throws a stick into the fire.

"It's time we do something about it!" I say.

CHAPTER 62

"Why do I have to be the bait?" Ivy whines in the morning as she fidgets in her lacy underwear in a narrow dead end formed by a landslide between two hills.

I lean over a large, flat, gray rock that juts out of the hill on Ivy's right and say, "Because you are the prettiest among us." Next to me, Rhona rolls her eyes, sitting with her back against a rock that looks like an upward-pointing finger.

The twins cover their snickers, hiding behind an elongated rock that reminds me of an angled arrowhead.

We came up with a plan to set a trap and voted Ivy to be the bait since she won't have to do anything other than stand around. The rest of us—with the exception of Glenna, Ragnald, and Belthair, who stayed behind by the cave—will do the hard work of fighting and capturing the assailants once they show up.

I inhale the scents of grass and dirt, closing my eyes for a second. Gods, I hope this works! We desperately need answers.

"They won't be able to resist you," Arrow says to Ivy in a reassuring voice. He lays behind an oversized evergreen shrub with widespread branches, half of its brown jumble of roots hanging over the dead end like a canopy on Ivy's left side. Under him, the hill looks like someone had scooped a big chunk out of it, making the dirt wall look almost like a vertical crescent with dried stems sticking out.

"Oh," Ivy says and swipes her long, blond hair off her shoulder, looking enticing. "Maybe I should be naked so that they—"

"No!" Rhona and I yell just as Arrov says, "Sure!"

Rhona glares at Arrov. "Stop encouraging her!"

I look at Rhona. "Let's hope that this works because I am out of ideas."

Ivy glances up with a hand in front of her eyes against the bright sun in the cloudless sky. "What did you say?"

"I said you are doing great, and this will be over quickly!" I say and then wave at the others to get to their hiding places. "Here they come!"

171

CHAPTER 63

We quiet down and take our places just as three figures come into view, reaching the bright green hilltop of a lower hill, across from our dead end. Forest green capes cover their faces, helping them blend into their environment. Under their capes, bottle green shirts tucked into brown pants are visible as they crouch low in the high grass. They wear longbows over their shoulders with green leather quivers, full of arrows, hanging by their sides. They have strange gloves, made of animal hide, covered in long, dark fur with claws still attached.

They glimpse Ivy, and the lankiest one signals the others to drop down on their bellies. They search the area, with their heads turning from side to side. The lanky one, their leader, lifts his head, sniffing the air.

Come on! Go investigate!

After a moment, the leader pats the shoulders of his stocky companions. They get to their feet, staying low to the ground, and approach Ivy. Before reaching her, the leader points left for the burly one and right for the stocky one. The two separate in silence, dashing up on each end of the elongated hill where we're hiding.

I nod at Rhona, then at the twins, to be ready.

When the leader is a few steps from Ivy, Arrov springs to his feet and leaps over the shrub, landing on him with an inhuman growl.

Isa and Bella throw rocks at the burly man, while I use my energy manipulation trick and push the other man off the hill before he gets close to Rhona and me.

The leader lifts his head off the ground and shouts something in a language that sounds a lot like Rhona's when she sang for the twig bug. The two other men scurry away without a backward glance.

Arrov roars at the leader, then straightens to his full nine-foot height. The man tries to jump to his feet, but Arrov stomps a large foot on his back, knocking him out.

Arrov leans down, baring huge fangs. "Got you!"

CHAPTER 64

"Aha!" Arrov says as he tears the hood of the cape off the head of our prisoner.

After carrying our caped captive back to our cave, Arrov tied him to a tree just outside of the entrance with strands we collected from the tyger tree. Glenna and Ragnald joined us, congratulating us on an operation well executed.

A dark gray wolfish face with a black lyon's mane stares up at us. The prisoner bares his white fangs and narrows his dark green eyes with catlike pupils. What I thought was a strange fur-covered glove with claws attached to it was actually the prisoner's own hand!

I gasp as I stare at the captive, who looks like a thinner version of Callum's battle form—the one I saw when he fought the dark servants back on Fye Island.

I exchange a look with my friends, and they nod. They, too, must remember seeing glimpses of Callum's and Teague's battle forms during our last fight with DLD. Ivy gapes at the prisoner, shocked. I'm glad she had no idea of that side of Callum.

I turn to Rhona to ask her opinion but stop when I see her face. She doesn't look the least surprised or shocked.

The prisoner, tied to the tree, studies us unfazed. A wide sash with metal clasps runs across his green and long-sleeved shirt. Thick, leather gauntlets with metal plates cover his arms that end in strong, furry hands and sharp claws. His wooden longbow, which Arrov holds with one finger, has a sturdy look to it, handmade and well used.

"Who are you?" I ask. "Why are you attacking us? Who sent you?"

"We should interrogate him," Glenna says and scowls down at the man with an almost frantic expression. "He deserves it after what he put us through! He will be lucky to be alive after I'm done with him! I have some tools in my arsenal that would be perfect for such a task! I could make a . . ."

Her voice trails off when she realizes we are staring at her in consternation.

Glenna covers her mouth with a hand. "I . . . uh . . ." She whirls on her heels and runs to the cave's entrance, where Belthair rests on the ground. She drops on her knees by him and checks Belthair's forehead for sign of a fever, while wiping at her eyes.

Arrov scratches his chin and pulls a couple of burrs out of his beard. "I agree with Glenna. We *should* interrogate him."

"I know where to cut to get answers fast," Ivy offers.

I raise a hand. "Hold your ships right there! There will be no cutting!"

Ivy pouts. "Don't act superior, Lilla. It's the Marauders' way, and very effective, I might add."

"It's a good thing we are not Marauders," I say.

Isa and Bella sashay around the prisoner, smiling. "No need to cut this poor soul," Isa says, and Bella adds, "We could get *anything* out of him." They trail their hands over his shoulders, earning a dismayed look from the captive man.

Rhona snorts. "I think he would rather prefer the healer's method over the two of you."

The twins sniff in response.

Arrov narrows his eyes on the captive man. "I could use my claws and peel a layer off—"

"No!" I snap. "No peeling either!"

Arrov looks taken aback. "No need to yell. I was trying to be helpful."

I close my eyes for a moment, forcing patience. "Thank you, Arrov, for your—uh —participation. I've got it from here."

I lean my hands on my knees to look the calm prisoner in the eyes, trying to read him but getting nothing. "We mean you no harm—"

Belthair laughs. "Very funny, Lilla! We are not trying to initiate contact with new life here."

I straighten and look at Belthair. "How do you know that he's seen, um, others before us?"

Belthair points at the smirking prisoner. "Because it's written all over his smug face."

CHAPTER 65

DAY 6

I toss and turn on the cold, hard ground of the cave, but sleep does not come. My mind keeps busy, replaying the events of the past five days. Events that have nothing to do with my quest. Only two days left of the seven.

The prisoner was not much help. We spent long hours in a futile effort to get any information out of him. We had to give up because night fell in its usual sudden manner—from one blink to the next. We retreated inside the cave, exhausted, leaving the prisoner outside, still tied to the tree.

Rustling sounds and I get up, then duck out through the low entrance.

Outside, I search for the source of the noise and my gaze lands on Arrov, who is supposed to be on watch but instead stands neck deep in the surrounding thicket of undergrowth. His eyes reflect the two moons' weak light. Half of a k'squirrel's body sticks out of his mouth. Then he disappears from my view.

I turn to the prisoner, who watches me, probably wondering what new ordeal I am to present to him.

I exhale. I regret setting that trap in the first place. Kidnapping someone and holding them against their will was not my intention. I focused too much on getting answers. I permitted my anger to dictate my actions, and now another person's life is in my hands. It's time to right a wrong.

I pull a sharp, oval-shaped rock from my tyger leaf bag and squat by the prisoner, reaching out.

He lifts his head and glances at me. "Are you going to kill me?" he asks in a deep, low voice. There is no fear in his expression.

I sit back on my heels. "You can talk? I mean, I can understand you!"

He laughs. "Congratulations on your feat!"

"I meant that you were speaking a different language before." One that sounded a lot like what Callum and Rhona use.

"It's this place that lets you understand me."

"What place exactly?"

He chuckles. "You'll learn about it soon." He glances at the stone in my hand and adds, "Now be done with it quick."

Shaking my head, I cut through the tyger tree strands that connect his bound hands to the tree. "What's your name?"

Surprise shines in his slitted eyes. "Marcas."

"I'm sure meeting in a different circumstance would have been better, but it is what it is," I say and cut the bindings around his feet.

"What are you doing?"

"Marcas, you seem like a person who has honor. Well, I do too." I reach for his bound hands, and he lifts them up. "All I ask of you is to tell whoever sent you that we mean no harm. We just want to complete our quest and go home."

Once I cut the last tie, he springs to his feet, shaking his hands out. "I will."

Before he goes, I ask, "There is a way out of here, right?"

Marcas's shoulders shake in silent laughter as he lopes away.

CHAPTER 66

"Where's the prisoner?" Ragnald asks in the morning as we exit the cave.

Ivy points at the yawning Arrov. "It's his fault! I saw him wander off to catch some k'squirrels!"

"No, it's not!" Arrov says with a growl. "I only left for a few minutes to get some snacks!"

I turn to the group. "It wasn't Arrov's fault. I let the prisoner go free."

Belthair waves all six of his hands in the air, though he winces from pain soon after. "How could you do this?"

"Sweetie, why didn't you discuss it with us first?" Isa asks and Bella nods, looking disappointed.

Rhona pokes me. "What is wrong with you?!"

"I could ask the same!" I push back. "Kidnapping? Interrogating people? Torture? What is wrong with *you*?!"

Rhona recoils. "It was your idea! I just wanted to help—"

"By offering tormenting techniques?" I ask.

Ivy taps Rhona's forearm. "Uh, guys?"

Rhona shrugs it off. "Do you even hear yourself?" she asks. "You admitted that I am the better general, but you still won't listen to me! You are ungrateful—"

Arrov steps up to us. "Uh, Lilla?"

I raise a hand to him. "In a moment," I say, my eyes still locked on Rhona. "I am ungrateful?! You are domineering and controlling and—"

Belthair whistles from behind us.

Rhona and I turn to look at him. "What?!"

The others, including Belthair supported by Ragnald, back into Rhona and me, huddling close. Away from the twenty men wearing forest green capes with arrows trained on us.

I gulp. "Oh, that."

177

CHAPTER 67

"Great idea," Rhona says in a low voice, marching next to me, "giving ourselves up without a fight! Now we'll find out who is behind these attacks. Except once we do, we will not live to tell that tale!"

Since we were captured, we've been marching up and down hills, and through a forest for most of the day without any rest. They didn't bind our hands, which is a relief, and they supplied us with water and food to keep us going. How considerate.

"What would you have done in my place?" I ask, glancing around at the caped men escorting us in pairs. "Fight, so we can die together?"

Rhona glares at me. "It might have been the more honorable option than getting captured, don't you think?"

"No, I obviously *don't* think that!" I say and cross my arms, though it makes hiking through high grass more difficult.

"Aren't you glad you released that prisoner?" Ivy asks from behind me. "He sure returned your favor in kind."

I clench my teeth. I don't want to admit it, but she might be right.

Rhona adds, "Don't forget the attempt on your life."

It's not that easy to forget! "It doesn't make sense why they would try to kill me, or any one of us, in the middle of the night, when they have attacked us in broad daylight and out in the open before. They had plenty of chances to take us out, yet they didn't. Explain that."

"I agree with Lilla," Ragnald says. "I have not seen such a drastic change in tactics when the enemy had the advantage. It does not make sense to me either."

Isa smiles. "Now things are getting exciting!" And Bella adds, "This will be fun!"

"I, for one, am skeptical about having any *fun*," Rhona says, "unless you enjoy torture and interrogation."

"You are being a Warrioress of Negativity again," I say, though I do agree with Rhona. I don't want to imagine what waits for us. Instead, I focus my attention on stepping over a twisted and dry root, trying to come up with an escape plan.

Rhona swipes a long branch out of her way. I look up just as the branch recoils and slaps me across the face. I disentangle myself and glare at her. She smiles and says, "It seems you need a bit of help with your reflexes. Or lack thereof."

Hilarious! I spit out a piece of leaf that got stuck in my teeth.

Glenna snaps from the back of the line, "Arrov! Lift Belthair up higher, will you? You are dragging his head in the dirt again!"

I glance back. Arrov carries Belthair in one arm around the unconscious man's waist, letting Belthair's head drag in the dirt behind him.

"I am doing this lazy . . . uh, him, a favor since he chose to faint to avoid walking."

"Ow!" Arrov exclaims. "Glenna, don't hit me!"

"You know full well Belthair didn't 'choose' to faint," Glenna says. "His fever spiked, and he lost consciousness!" We quiet down at that. Belthair's life is in danger.

As we approach the foot of the hill, water glints like crystal shards in the sunlight.

The River of Death.

CHAPTER 68

"If I were you," I say to the hooded men and point at the River of Death, "I would not wade into that death trap."

I shiver recalling our encounter with that k'alligator.

Our escorts, the twenty men in forest green capes, don't react. They keep marching us toward the water.

"They are going to throw us to the k'alligators!" Ivy exclaims. "Alive!"

"There is no point throwing us to the k'alligators dead," Rhona says.

"Stop scaring people!" Glenna snaps just as Arrov says with a roar, "I will not swim with k'alligators again!" I turn to console him, but Arrov flails his arms, Belthair almost slipping off his shoulder, with a wild look in his dark blue eyes, knocking a few of our guards out.

This is our chance to get away!

"Run!" I shout.

We burst into a sprint, heading away from the river. We make a few yards when a heavy rope net lands on us, knocking us off our feet.

"Ow!" Ivy and the twins exclaim.

One of our escorts strides up to us, leans forward, and pushes back the hood of his green cape. Marcas, with a wide grin on his wolfish face, framed by lyon's mane, studies us.

"Marcas?" I ask. "Are you here to kill us?"

He laughs. "I will not kill any of you or throw you to the k'alligators. Dead or alive," he adds before Ivy could ask for any more clarification. He gestures to the other men to remove the ropes from over us.

The others get to their feet, grumbling.

Ivy glares up at Marcas, who towers over her by a head and a half. "Are you going to let us go now?"

He shakes his head. "I'm afraid I cannot do that. I have my orders."

Ivy turns to me. "See? No good endeavor ever goes without a levy! I could have told you that. It's the Marauders' way!"

Marcas snorts and extends a hand toward me. "These Marauders seem to have an interesting approach to life," he says.

I take it and let him pull me to my feet. "You don't even know the half of it."

Arrov picks up Belthair and throws the unconscious man over his left shoulder this time.

"Besides," Marcas says, "we are almost at my village, where food and help await you." He points to the right, where curling smoke drifts in the sky, inviting.

I cross my arms. "We will not go into that river!" Not again!

Marcas laughs and turns me to the left to face a simple wooden bridge. "You don't have to go into the river. I promise."

"Oh," I mutter.

CHAPTER 69

We cross a weathered wooden bridge over the river and head down a green knoll. In front of us runs a wide and winding cobblestone street, with quaint log houses nestled on either side of it. The homes are pressed so close together that they share walls on either side. Their peaked shingled roofs form a descending stairway.

Curious faces, some more tyger, others more lyon or bear, pop up in the windows framed with white curtains but no one comes out to greet us.

Once we reach the foot of the street, a panoramic view of a green plain with forests takes our breath away. On the right side of the plain, an imposing-looking mountain full of evergreen trees curves. On the left side of the plain, a faint image of a majestic city shimmers, with light gray buildings that reach upward into the sky like twisting ribbons.

The moss-covered cobblestone street continues, branching out, flowing among houses, now spread far from each other, with large gardens. A few dirt paths twist and turn toward log houses, with a substantial area fenced in to allow for farming or herding animals. At the farthest end of the street is the largest log house, with a high and slanted red roof. From its chimney the curling smoke twists in the air.

I smile. "We found it!" The source of the smoke we followed on our journey.

"Why are you so happy?" Rhona asks as she glances at me. "They can still kill us later."

CHAPTER 70

"Put him down over there," a petite woman with a saurian face covered in dark gray scales directs Arrov. Her smart, brown eyes spark with impatience as she points to an oval wooden table outside by a small log hut.

Arrov deposits the unconscious Belthair on the polished surface of the tabletop and steps back.

Glenna pushes forward from our group. "Who are you? Why have you brought us here under duress?" she demands and gestures to our escorts. Except the twenty men in green capes have melted away without any of us the wiser.

Rhona crosses her arms. "I'd like to know the answer to those questions, too."

The petite woman ignores us. Her long red forked tongue flickers into Belthair's ear for a second. "High temperature," she mutters, then leans over him with her right ear tilted toward his chest. "Rapid heartbeat. That can't be good." She glances at Glenna, who nods in affirmation.

"I am Daryhna," the reptilian woman says and pushes long black hair out of her face. A thin tail swishes behind her, rattling until Glenna steps back, then disappearing again. "I am the herbalist of this village. Now give me some space."

Glenna sputters, "I will not . . . I mean, I need to examine Belthair . . ." she says but her voice trails off when the herbalist glares at her.

Daryhna, unfazed, rummages in a deep pocket of an apron she wears over a simple woven black dress that reaches to her clawed feet in leather sandals.

Ragnald steps up to Glenna and hugs her shoulders. "Daryhna needs to focus on her work."

I look around and blink in surprise. The villagers who hid in their houses are out now, observing us from a respectful distance. Many look like Callum's battle form with their wolfish face and lyon mane, while others are reptilian like Daryhna, and come to think of it, like Teague's battle form. Some remind me of the dangerous blue bears of A'ice with their large maws and robust size. Dozens of kids, a mix of three types, dart around us, getting closer, until they reach Arrov, who leans on a tree with a shoulder.

Ivy taps Arrov's arm. "This place is full of strange creatures like you!" Arrov stares at her, and Ivy adds, "No offense, but feel free to take some."

"Aren't you hot wearing that long fur coat?" one of the younger kids asks him.

Arrov sighs. "It's not a fur coat, and yes, I am a little hot."

The children giggle, then dash away when a few older villagers, with wrinkled faces and gray hair or mane, approach our group while carrying folded fabrics.

Daryhna, without looking up, gestures toward the elders. "You should go and freshen up after your grueling journey before our esteemed queen meets with you. These elders will provide you with a change of clothes, food, and drink. I recommend that you take advantage of our hospitality. You look half starved."

Hunger pangs rumble in my belly.

Isa says, "We could eat and rest a little bit." Bella adds, "Just until we get our strength back."

"That would be great—" I agree but Rhona interrupts and points at Daryhna, "Why would we do that? Just trust what you say, right away?"

"No need to be so unfriendly," I say to Rhona.

"I am not unfriendly!" Rhona says and crosses her arms. "I am cautious."

Daryhna locks her gaze on Rhona. "Yes, you should trust what I say, and not only because your tyger leaf dresses fail to cover your important body parts, but also because you don't have any other choice."

With that, Daryhna turns her back, dismissing us.

CHAPTER 71

An hour later, I step out of a one-room log hut, complete with a bed, table, and chair, perfect for one person. I ate a few bites and drank the refreshing and cool spring water. My exhaustion evaporated. My nerves over my quest made me head out.

"I'm glad you had chance to freshen up," a female voice says behind me.

With a hand over my throat, I turn to face the speaker. "Thank you. It was, um, wonderful." I smooth the beige dress I wear, its material soft to the touch. The black leather slippers they gave me beat the leaf ones I had on before.

The villagers are so nice, and I can't help but wonder why, given the fact that we were escorted here under orders from the mysterious queen whom Daryhna mentioned. "Who are you?"

She smiles and tiny scales glint in a wolfish face framed by a black lyon mane. She stands at six and a half feet, with a body type of a giant A'ice bear, though hers is a lean and athletic one. Her red dress is cut like mine and hugs her curves in a flattering way. Lyon-like paws in leather sandals peek from under the dress.

"I am Moira," she says with a wide smile, showing off white fangs. "Would you like a tour?"

Would she bite my head off if I say no? "We're supposed to meet with the 'esteemed' queen of this, uh, place."

Moira waves a clawed hand. "Don't worry. You'll meet her at lunch."

A tour won't hurt. Maybe I can get some information out of her. "Where are we, by the way?"

Moira heads down the cobblestone street, toward a dirt path that runs by large, one-story houses with blooming gardens and farms. "You are here, in the Village of Ha'rmony, of course."

That was not very informative.

I double my steps to keep up with her long ones. "I would like to know if we are prisoners."

Moira glances at me and I have the urge to duck my head for asking such a stupid question. "Do you feel imprisoned?" she asks.

I've not seen Marcas, or the others who escorted us here. "Well, no. But that doesn't mean this queen would just allow us to sail away." Heat burns my cheeks at showing my pirate roots, like some backwater girl. "She did go to considerable efforts to get us here."

Remembering those attacks makes me wonder what the point was. Intimidation? Power play?

"It does seem she did," Moira says.

She points toward the small hill behind us and changes the subject. "We are near the Bl'oming Steppes, which means Lava River Plain. Next to it is the Le'aning Ridge, which can be translated to Crushing Cliffs. Over there is the River of De'ath, meaning River of the Fallen Warriors." She points in front of her, toward the humongous mountain range. "That's Bl'ud Mountain, which means Red Rocks, and then the Mountain of Paa'ina, meaning the Cliffs of Wisdom; both can be found on the Sun'set Mountain Range, earning its name from its orange hue."

"If you squint," Moira says, pointing across the sweeping plain, "just above the tree lines on the left, you can see the Sea of S'orrow, meaning the Sea of Blessing."

If I didn't know better, I would think that these are the exact landscape the Teryns showed us. Except the Teryns didn't have any knolls or thick evergreen forests. But there is no denying the eerie similarities.

I turn to Moira. "Have you heard of a Heart Rock?

Moira snorts. "You mean the Heart Amulet?"

"Yes! You know of it?" I ask.

"I do," Moira says. I wait, but she doesn't add anything to it.

I open my mouth to ask again, but we pass by a stocky farmer among neat rows of green, leafy vegetables, who waves at us in greeting.

"How is your daughter, Duff?" Moira asks him. Clever green eyes look up at us from a wolfish face with a kind expression. He's shorter than I am at five feet, with a bearish body type. He removes a straw hat from his bald head. He wipes his other hand on his woven brown shirt.

The farmer nods in respect, then puts his straw hat back on. "The same."

Then Moira and the farmer burst into knee-slapping laughter until they wipe tears from the corners of their eyes.

I gape at the two of them. That's a bit of a strange reaction.

"Who is your friend, Moira?" the farmer asks with unhidden curiosity. He leans on his shovel with his thick forearms crossed on top of the wooden handle. "She doesn't look like the others."

"Someone new," she says and threads an arm into mine, dragging me away from the farmer before I could ask anything.

After following the dirt path back to the cobblestone street, we pass by another, an older reptilian woman, dressed in a woven gray shirt and pants. She herds large animals with six legs and long, flat horns, with the help of a leather whip.

Moira nods at the woman. "Don't forget to corral the k'cows. This afternoon will be rainy."

They laugh again, shaking their heads and saying in unison, "Isn't that the truth!" The older woman adds, "Like clockwork!"

I look up at the mostly clear sky, with only a few whisps of clouds in sight. How do they know it will rain later today?

At the back of the woman's ranch, a lake glints, reflecting the shape of the sun, showing two halves becoming one.

I trip on my own feet as I remember what the fable said: *you can find the Heart Amulet beyond the river, over the last hill, where the two halves of the sun join.*

It seems I have found the Heart Amulet's location.

CHAPTER 72

"Lunch is served at the Gathering Hall," says a young reptilian woman with blond hair, leading our group through open double doors into the largest building, with a slanted red roof.

We tread down a long and narrow corridor until we reach another set of double doors.

The young woman pushes the doors open and gestures for us to enter. "Here we are."

In the middle of the Gathering Hall, a massive and rectangular stone table covered with trays of food piled high dominates the room.

Two long wooden benches run along either side of the table, seating about fifty people, including Marcas. There are eight empty spots near its right end, next to Daryhna, who smiles in welcome. A square pillow the size of a mattress awaits Arrov by our bench.

At the far end, by Daryhna, sits a young wolfish man who looks a lot like Moira. At the head of the table Moira waits, perched on a low-back, wooden chair.

"I should have known you are the queen," I say as I take a seat, "but the tour was still quite enjoyable."

"I am glad you liked it," Moira says, and gestures to her right. "Welcome to my court! May I introduce my son, Keelan? He will play for us on his fiddle after our meal." Then she takes a roasted leg off the tray in front of her. That seems to be the signal to start eating.

We put some sliced meat and root vegetables on our wooden plates.

Rhona bumps her elbow into mine just as I reach for a roll. "Look at that! Arrov got a whole k'boar!"

Sure enough, in Arrov's lap is a large, oval tray boasting the biggest roasted k'boar. He tears a leg off and bites into it with gusto, moaning in pleasure as he chews.

For a few minutes, the wooden trays being pushed on the stone table and plates clanking join the low hum of conversation.

Finished with my meal, I ask Moira, "Why did you attack us?"

Silence descends in the hall and all eyes turn to us, including Marcas's.

"I sent my honor guards twice with the intent to repel you or capture you if you proved to be more than a nuisance."

Twice? "Then who were those two assassins trying to kill me in my sleep?"

Ragnald thumps his wooden cup on the table. "Repel us? It's not like we have a choice to get out of here!"

Moira studies my friends and me with a curious expression. "Those who came before you, sent by Gigi, never had trouble leaving. Granted, they left without their goal accomplished."

The table bursts into laughter.

"Who is Gigi?" I ask.

Moira scowls. "Don't act like you don't know her!"

"I have no idea what you are talking about," I say with forced patience, "and I *will* complete my quest."

Moira looks at me. "You are too stubborn for your own good, aren't you?"

I shrug my shoulders. "I just know what I want."

Moira nods. "You have no idea how many journeyed into my queendom following that inane fable's directions to the Heart Amulet."

She quotes it in a mocking voice, "Beyond the river—the one you crossed over; over the last hill—the one with the main street; and the—"

"The lake where two halves of the sun join—the reflection of the sun in the lake behind that farm," I finish. "This is the place the fable describes! So where is it?"

Moira's subjects burst into loud argument but she silences them. "Quiet!"

Glenna leans forward. "When can I see Belthair?" she asks.

Daryhna wipes her hand with delicate claws in a fabric napkin. "Once I judge him stable, you may visit him."

"We don't have much time to waste," Rhona says.

I turn to Moira. "I must find that Heart Amulet!"

"I can't give you the amulet," she says and clasps her hands on top of the table, "but I can give you something better—a map that leads to its secret location."

CHAPTER 73

"We have less than a day to complete this quest," I say, holding up the map, though it's hard to keep track of time in this place. "We cannot waste a single moment."

"It's going to be dark soon," Rhona says and frowns at the sprinkling rain, "but if we pick up the pace, we can reach the Forest of H'ope and make camp before nightfall."

The group acknowledges. They wait, ready to depart.

Lunch wrapped up fast after Moira gave me the map. I was too impatient to stay a moment longer—bad manners, but I couldn't help it. To my relief, Moira had no qualms with us departing from her queendom right away. We packed provisions—Moira's generous donations, along with the leather knapsacks to carry them. If I didn't know better, I'd say she was keen to get rid of us.

"I can't wait to get out of here!" I say and wipe raindrops from my face. I can't wait to see Callum and finish this quest so I can finally complete my mission.

Belthair picks up his satchel. "I won't hold the group back, I promise. I am much better now, thanks to Daryhna's herbs."

"That's great, Bel—" I say, but I'm cut off by Glenna, shouting from behind me.

"Arrov!" Glenna snaps. "Put Isa and Bella down right this minute!"

The twins giggle as Arrov lifts them off his shoulders, one at a time, and lowers them to the ground. "I could have carried them, you know," he mumbles, and his voice sounds like a snarl.

Isa and Bella pout. "Glennie, you are no fun!"

When the twins look to me for help, I shrug. "Glenna has a point. Arrov needs to conserve his strength for later."

Keelan strides by us, wearing a brown shirt with matching pants on his bearlike body. "You are leaving so soon? I never had the chance to play my

190

music for you," he says, lifting up his black pearl fiddle, and then winks at Ivy, who blushes.

Rhona stares at Keelan. "I swear you look familiar. Did we meet before? It feels like we did."

Keelan studies Rhona and his eyes go wide. "Yes, uh, you look familiar to me too. But I, uh, don't know you. Maybe it was a dream," he says, then cringes.

Keelan shakes his head with a forlorn expression. "May I see the map?" he asks.

"Sure." I hand it to him, wondering why he wants to see it.

Keelan traces the route with his finger, then throws his head back, laughing. "She sent you on a wild-k'goose chase, didn't she?"

"What do you mean?" I ask, holding my temper back. The longer this quest drags on, the less patience I manage to preserve.

Keelan hands the map back to me. "You should ask my mother yourself. It's snack time anyway."

CHAPTER 74

I shove open the double doors leading to the Gathering Hall using my energy manipulation technique. The doors half fly off their hinges and embed in the wooden wall with a loud bang.

Ivy raises an eyebrow on my left. "Now, that's an entrance worthy of a Marauder!"

Glenna steps up to my right, while the others enter the hall. "You have to calm down, Lilla! You should not make decisions while you're angry!"

Great advice—too bad it's too late. All I see is red.

People jump up from the benches, but Moira waves them to stand down.

I march up to her and slam the map on the tabletop, causing the half-empty wooden trays to clatter. "Care to explain why you gave us a fake map?"

Moira glances at the map then looks at me, her expression nonchalant. "I owe you no explanation. You are an intruder in my village."

I pick up the map and show it to the others at the table. "Did you know that this was a false map?"

No one returns my gaze. Even Marcas looks away.

Keelan strides in from an open side corridor behind Moira and says, "She will not explain anything to you. Just as she didn't explain her decision about forcing us to leave this realm."

But where? Realization hits. "You were going after the Heart Amulet yourself!"

They laugh, though why, I am not sure.

Moira gets to her feet. "My son, we have agreed that—"

"I never agreed!" Keelan shouts. "Nor did the others!" Many nod in affirmation but not all. "You made this decision, just like when you trapped us here!"

"I have no idea what's going on," I say to Moira, "but I know this: you had no intention of helping us!"

Moira sits back into her chair with a grimace. "No, I did not."

"Why did you lie to me?" I ask.

"Because there is no way you can get the Heart Amulet," she says.

CHAPTER 75

"The queen lies again!" Keelan says with a snarl. "There *is* a way to get the Heart Amulet."

"Is that true?" I ask, but Moira, irritated, just looks at me.

Daryhna approaches Keelan. "Keelan, my son-in-honor, this is not the right time to discuss these sensitive matters. Not in front of the, uh, guests." She sends a nervous smile in our direction.

It seems that I stepped into a long-standing argument. One that seems to divide the court.

Keelan shakes Daryhna's hand off his shoulder. "If she uses the Extraction—"

"That will not happen!" Moira snaps. "Not as long as I am alive!"

"But you are not!" Keelan says and leans on the table with his hands.

"Why am I not surprised that you choose to save your selfish hide again?" Keelan continues. "Because of you, so many died, and now you will add more to that! I guess it wasn't enough that you killed Dad and condemned us—"

Moira slaps her son, her expression furious.

Arguments break out in the hall. Everyone gets to their feet, shouting at each other across the table.

"What on Uhna is going on?" I ask, glancing at Rhona, who studies the scene with narrowed eyes.

Keelan holds his cheek, his dark brown eyes glint with resentment. "Violence was and still is your solution!"

Daryhna steps back from the table, her expression full of grief. When she looks at Moira, anger that borders on fury flashes across her eyes.

Isa and Bella huddle close to Belthair, who hugs their shoulders with his top arms. "Maybe we should slip away," the twins say together.

Moira stands up. "Arrest them!" she orders the guards, gesturing to my friends and me.

I gape at Moira. "Now you won't let us go, either?"

Moira shakes her head. "Where would you even go? Besides, now I have something I can use to get what *I* want."

"Why are you doing this?" I ask, lunging at Moira, but Rhona pulls me back. "Not now," she says. "We need to regroup and evaluate our options."

Arrov growls. "I have an option in mind. I could break—"

"No," I say to Arrov. "Rhona is right."

The guards, led by Marcas, surround us but instead of grabbing us, Marcas gestures toward the exit. "After you."

Keeping my anger in check takes an effort, but I must know. "What do you want?" I ask Moira.

"What else?" she asks. "Freedom."

CHAPTER 76

Marcas shuts the metal door of the last cell in the basement prison. The windowless brick-walled room under the Gathering Hall houses six more cells, empty and clean with benches and cots in them.

At least it's not a dungeon.

"I am sorry," Marcas says, hesitating, but changes his mind and heads back upstairs. The shadows of the torches flicker on the stone walls. Sounds of locking a door drift to us.

I sigh and turn toward the group, crammed into the cell, which is barely large enough for all of us to fit. Arrov stands hunched, to avoid brushing his head against the low ceiling.

"Now what?" Ivy asks.

Isa and Bella take the cot and pull their feet up. "This went from bad to worse faster than any of our stunts ever have. What are we going to do now?"

Glenna runs to the metal cell door and grabs its bars, shaking them with both hands. "Let us out of here! You hear? Or I will burn this place down!"

"Glenna?" I say but she doesn't seem to hear me, lost to her rage.

Rhona approaches Glenna. "With what? You don't have magic," she jokes.

The others chuckle, but Glenna, swinging her fists, whirls on Rhona.

"Whoa!" Rhona says, recoiling with her hands up. "I don't want to fight you, healer!"

Ragnald grabs Glenna from behind, closing his arms over hers, preventing her from doing anything crazy. "We'll be just over there and . . ." He lifts Glenna off her feet and carries her to the corner, where a stone bench runs half the perimeter of the cell.

Glenna's face pales. "It happened again, didn't it?" she asks Ragnald.

"It wasn't that bad," the mage says, but Glenna covers her face with her hands, stifling sobs. Ragnald rubs her back in comfort, but it's clear he is lost.

Buckets of fishguts! "We can't stay here!"

Belthair steps up to Rhona and me. "I agree. We should break out. If only there was someone strong enough to tear the door off its hinges."

The three of us look at Arrov.

Arrov grins, showing off his fangs. "Gladly."

We get out of the giant's way as he grabs the bars of the metal door in his huge hands and braces himself.

Loud creaking sounds as the metal bars fight back from the pressure Arrov exerts with his muscles straining.

"That won't be necessary," Daryhna says, appearing in front of our cell door and startling us. She dangles a bunch of keys. "This will be easier, wouldn't you say?"

CHAPTER 77

"What are you doing here?" I ask Daryhna.

"I'm here to help because I disagree with the queen," Daryhna says as she opens the cell door. "Follow me." She leads us out of the prison, then turns right, hurrying down one windowless underground passage after another.

"I shouldn't have trusted Moira," I say, trying to make sense of what happened. Moira must be amused at my gullibility! She effortlessly misled my friends and me, almost costing us this quest.

Daryhna glances at me. "No, you shouldn't have trusted her," she says and removes a torch from the wall. "I made that mistake once, too. I thought she was my friend, my family-by-choice. It cost me everything."

Daryhna hands me the torch and points ahead. "This tunnel will lead you to the other side of the river. Escape now before the queen realizes you're gone. Hurry!"

I take the torch and dash into the descending tunnel, leading the way for my friends. I am excited to get out of here, yet a tiny nagging voice insists running away is not the right thing to do.

The badgering little voice becomes louder with each of my steps until it's deafening. I come to a halt just as Rhona stops running too.

The others barrel into our backs.

"Why did you stop?" Ivy whines, panting.

I look at Rhona. "Why did *you* stop?" Maybe I am not alone with this pestering sense of wrongness.

Rhona raises an eyebrow. "I think for the same reason you did. Something is not right."

Arrov pushes forward. "What are you two talking about? What's not right?"

"Lilla, let's go!" Glenna urges, wringing her hands. Ragnald pats her shoulder and adds, "Let's not waste any more time."

"Sweetie," Isa says, "having doubts now is not the best idea." Bella adds,

"Let's hurry before the guards realize we escaped."

I hesitate. It doesn't make sense to me either, but I cannot make myself take another step.

"Go where?" I ask the group, but no one has an answer.

Belthair studies my face. "You know something."

"Not precisely," I say and shake my head. "We should turn back."

Rhona nods. "I concur."

"It's time we found out what's going on," I say.

CHAPTER 78

W e trek the inclining corridors on our way back, careful not to make any noise. When we reach an intersection, I hesitate. I don't know which way to go—Daryhna took too many turns, and I didn't pay attention the way we were heading.

Arrov raises his head and sniffs the air. "This way," he says and points to the left.

We follow after Arrov, stopping when he does to avoid guards, until we reach an open arched doorway leading back into the Gathering Hall.

Muffled voices in heated debate drift from the hall.

We line up on each side of the doorway in two groups, keeping out of sight.

"What's going on?" Ivy whispers from the end of the line, behind Arrov, Rhona, and me.

Rhona shushes Ivy. "We can't hear anything with your constant chirping!"

I peek into the hall.

The long stone table is empty. There isn't anyone in the hall except for Moira and Keelan. They stand facing each other, arguing, far enough from our hiding place that they don't catch sight of us.

"I recognized Rhona," Keelan says. "You know how? I was supposed to meld with her, but you prevented it at the last second!"

Meld? I frown at Rhona, whose expression is puzzled.

"Of course I yanked you back!" Moira snaps. "Or did you forget what happened to Mihail? He—"

"—faded into nothing after he returned from his meld journey and experienced too many deaths. Yes, I know! You've told me hundreds of times!" Keelan snaps. "You had no right to keep me from the meld because you judged the risks too high! This is my life, whatever is left of it, and not yours!"

"I had every right, my son! I watched Mihail, and many others, come back more shattered each time until they couldn't hold it together anymore. I will not stand by and watch my child fade into nothing!"

"It was my choice to make!" Keelan shouts and pulls out a hand-size and wooden stick encased in metal two thirds of the way. Runes etched into the metal glint with power and give off a repulsive aura.

"How did you get that, my son? Gigi proposed the use of the Extraction Wand only a couple of days ago. She somehow acquired the wand infused with Acerbus. I was adamant that it's too dangerous to use—"

"It doesn't matter how I got it," Keelan interjects and raises the wand.

"What are you doing?" Moira swipes at Keelan but he presses on square-shaped runes and zaps her with green-black-colored lightning.

The lightning encases Moira like a thorny magical web from the neck down, paralyzing her.

"What I asked him to do," Daryhna says as she enters the room from the other doorway, unaware of us witnessing the unfolding atrocity.

"You?" Moira asks. "We've been friends since childhood and now you betray me, using my own son against me?"

Daryhna examines Moira wrapped in the green-black lightning as she paces around her, stopping with her back toward us. She extends her hand and Keelan gives her the wand.

"I would say this is not personal, but that would be a lie," Daryhna says. "Because of your indecision, both of my daughters are dead, vivisected in the last Era War! The Archgod of Chaos and Destruction killed them in search of our magical immunity while you stood by and did nothing!"

"You know well that—"

"Now you are going to force us to move into the Lume," Daryhna says, "but we don't deserve it! All those dead, killed because I stood by and let you do nothing. It's a tragedy I won't let you repeat ever again. Now I know what the right choice is—we stay. We fight in this Era War. We die and fade away if we must. That's what we deserve. That is our lot in this illusion of life that you forced us into. You trapped us here, and now, when we could make a difference, you want us to move on? How dare you!" Daryhna screams the last words into Moira's face, spittle flying off her forked tongue.

"Are you going to force me into the wand and coerce me to meld as punishment?" Moira asks with a sad resolve. "Do you think that will bring back the others?"

Daryhna shakes her head. "No. I have something else in mind."

"That's not what you promised me!" Keelan shouts and leaps toward Daryhna. "You said we will let her out once she cooled down and sanctioned us to stay!"

Daryhna takes out a handful of herbs from her pocket and throws them into Keelan's face. He goes down, unconscious.

"My dear honor child," Daryhna says as she pokes at Keelan with her foot, "all you had to do was trap your mother and give me back the wand. Not ask questions."

Keelan just lays there, immobile.

"Do not involve my son in this! I'll do anything you want!"

"Too late for that, my friend," Daryhna says, smiling without any compassion. "With this wand I can take your soul, your power, and break them down to their very essence, allowing me to infuse myself with them. Then I will be the queen, leading us in the Era War. Just as Guardian Goddess Laoise wants us to do."

"I should have known Gigi was behind this!"

"You should have known a lot of things, but you didn't." Daryhna points the wand at Moira and presses a group of runes that have curly legs.

Purple-colored smoke, like tentacles, slams into Moira. She throws her head back in a silent scream, her outline shimmering. She is breaking down.

A flash of memory of DLD's syphoning my magic sends shivers down my spine, raising goose bumps on my arms. I won't let anyone else suffer like that!

I rush toward Daryhna.

She snarls in surprise and points the wand in my direction. The purple tentacles slam back into the wand and Moira's outline stop shimmering.

The wand does nothing. Daryhna yells in frustration, pressing on the runes in desperation.

I almost reach Daryhna. She punches with a cross at my face.

I twist my body out of the way and grab her arm. Using her own momentum, I shove her down by my side and I trip her front leg.

Daryhna lands with an oomph on her back, with both of her arms by her head.

I drop down and grab her hand with the wand. I twist her hand and press at the soft pad under her thumb. Daryhna cries out in pain and releases the wand.

"Move and I'll break your arm," I say, snarling at her.

CHAPTER 79

The honor guards rush into the Gathering Hall. Marcas takes in the scene, frowning at us since we're supposed to be in our prison cell.

Marcas yanks Daryhna to her feet and nods respectfully toward me. Another guard lifts Keelan and throws the unconscious young man over his shoulder.

"Take them away and lock them up in separate cells," Moira orders, still covered in that green-black thorny magical web. Marcas opens his mouth to argue, but she cuts his words off with a sharp glare.

"You fool!" Daryhna screams as Marcas drags her away. "You ruined the Teryns' future!"

Daryhna's words cut deeply, and my face turns cold. What if she is right?

The guards drag the thrashing and screaming herbalist out of the Gathering Hall along with the unconscious Keelan.

Belthair pats my back. "I'm glad you remembered the takedown I taught you."

I glance at Belthair. "Are you now?"

Isa and Bella step up on the bench and sit down on the stone tabletop. "Did you just claim credit for what Lilla did?"

Belthair raises his six hands. "You know I'm right. Without my teachings, Lilla wouldn't have been able to—"

Arrov, on silent feet, steps behind him and covers Belthair's face with one huge hand. "Ah, quiet."

Belthair quits flailing his arms, and Arrov takes his hand off his face.

"No need to get your fur in a bunch," Belthair says, dazed. "I was just, um, joking."

Moira clears her throat to get our attention. "A little help here?"

Ragnald and I pace around Moira, studying the thorny magical web. "I have never seen anything like this in my two hundred years."

Ragnald inches a finger toward the web. A thin green-black bolt of lightning whips out and shocks him. He stumbles backward, dropping on his bottom, stupefied.

Rhona hands me the Extraction Wand. "I won't even know where to start. You are the best person to figure this out."

"Said the crew of the pirate ship before they sailed into shallow waters," I mutter as I take the wand.

"Hurry!" Moira says. "It's not easy standing suspended in air like this! I can't get out of this snare on my own! My magical immunity doesn't always protect me from magical traps."

I study the Extraction Wand, holding it between two fingers, resisting the urge to throw it far away from me. The repulsiveness of Acerbus makes the hair on my arm stand up. It takes a lot of effort to think past it.

I turn the wand to reflect the torches' light. "There are three columns of distinctive runes etched into the wand," I say and point them out on the metal section without touching them. "I remember Keelan touched the square ones in the first column, and it sent out the web to paralyze you."

Moira's eye twitches in impatience or in irritation; it's hard to tell. "I can't say whether you are right or wrong," she says. "I wasn't paying much attention to that cursed thing!"

"We saw," Isa and Bella say together. "That's correct."

I point at the third column. "These runes with curly legs were the ones Daryhna pressed when she tried to siphon your soul into the wand."

"Best not to touch them again," Moira says. "I do not care to repeat the experience."

"I wasn't planning to," I say. She sure doesn't trust me, does she? "Only the middle row is left, with triangular runes." Half of them have an open circle around them, while the others have a line crossing over them.

"Try not to kill the queen," Ivy says as she peers over my shoulder.

"Ivy is right," Isa says. "It's possible that some of the runes can kill." Bella adds, "I would include it in my version of an Extraction Wand."

"Are you saying that there is a good chance I could kill Moira?" I ask as my hand trembles.

Isa nods. "A very good chance," Bella says. "You also have a very good chance of freeing her."

Ivy rubs her hands. "Oooh! A game of luck! How Marauder!"

"That is still not a compliment," I say. How will I make the right choice?

Ragnald shakes off his daze and gets to his feet with the help of Glenna. "I'd try the circular ones. I have seen them in scrolls before, though I cannot say I understand their meaning. I also happen to like their shape." Belthair, the twins, and Glenna also vote for that rune.

Arrov rubs his chin. "What if they were in those scrolls as a warning? I'd rather try the crossed-out ones." Ivy and Rhona also give their support.

They both raise good points, but none of them helps.

I take a deep breath and let my instincts guide my finger. I press down on the crossed-out runes on an exhale just as the others shout, "Don't do it!"

The green-black magical web shatters around Moira and retracts back into the wand.

Moira steps forward and shakes her bearlike body. "Took you long enough."

I hand the Extraction Wand to Ragnald. "Now will you tell us what's going on?"

CHAPTER 80

"Please sit," Moira says and takes a seat at the head of the stone table in the Gathering Hall.

My friends and I settle around her.

Moira glances at the wand on the tabletop in front of Ragnald. "My own son and my best friend, conspiring behind my back. Planning to betray me. How did I not see it? How was I so oblivious? I wanted the best for my people."

I have no answers. I touch her arm for a moment in comfort.

Moira looks up. "At least you are not showering me with platitudes."

"That wouldn't help, now would it?" I ask. If I were in Moira's place, I wouldn't want anyone's pity or judgment either.

Moira sighs. "Then let me start at the beginning. *I* am the Heart Amulet."

I blink at her. "You? How is that possible?"

"To understand why I am the Heart Amulet, you have to know more about this realm," Moira explains, "and how it shouldn't exist. You can call it an alternative realm or spirit realm—"

"Or green Teryn?" I suggest.

Moira nods. "The point is that it shouldn't be. *We* spirits shouldn't exist either." She swipes with her right arm to encompass her whole queendom.

"When I learned about the consequences of long-term melding, I started to fight back against it. Forbidding my people. In turn, Gigi turned me into a fable, an *item* to be acquired in a quest to solve her problem when the number of melds decreased. Thus desperate Teryns, who wanted to redeem their honor, flooded my realm to achieve the impossible. No one ever got as close as you did."

"Is this realm the reason why Glenna, Lilla, and I can't feel our elemental magic?" Ragnald asks.

"Yes," Moira answers. "Your body isn't here, only your soul."

Just like Callum said when he contacted me via the hologram. "How was I able to use my energy manipulation technique?" I wonder.

"Oh, the famous Saage-women technique. As you know, it's not magic"—Moira gestures upward with both of her hands—"and everything is made out of energy, even our souls."

Then the floodgate of questions opens.

Rhona asks, "Then why do I have my compact sword with me?" I add, "Or my necklace?"

"If our bodies are not here," Belthair asks and crosses his six arms, "then why did we, uh, get so sick after eating those wild berries?"

Isa asks, "Or almost killed by those bear-wolves?" Bella adds, "Or by the k'alligator?"

Arrov frowns. "Why did the forest part on its own?"

"How can we feel hunger or thirst? Bleed when injured?" Glenna asks.

"Let me see," Moira says, thinking over our questions. "Injury, hunger, and death can happen because, my dears, you still have a body, while I don't. Should your spirit die here, your body will die out there. This realm is nothing but a repetition of six beautiful days, two of them rainy for variety's sake."

That is why that farmer knew that rain was coming when there were barely any clouds in the sky!

"We have what we need," Moira says, "crops and animals that never run out and always reset at the end of six days. Not that we need them, but it gives us work and the illusion of accomplishment and routine many crave over being idle. There is no disease. No war. What you see—the houses, the furniture, weapons—never get damaged or lost. Even the doors you broke are back to new, Lilla." We turn to see, and it's true. "The lone visitors we ever had were the new Teryns. Then you came along, my dear, with your friends."

That would explain why the first farmer thought Moira's question so funny and his sudden interest in my presence. But to live out the same six days, no matter how perfect they are, in perpetuity, must be a nightmare and not an idyl.

"About the forest, wildlife, and wild berries?" Moira asks. "That was me having a bit of fun with you. As to how I could manipulate this realm? Let's just say there is a reason I was the queen of the Teryns then, just as I am the queen of the Teryns now."

Moira pauses for a second, then continues, "If only I could have the power to free my people to move on, then there would be no more Teryns as they know it. Daryhna is right about one thing—it would crush the new Teryns' future, whoever they are, or wherever they came from. I would not be surprised if Laoise had to dig them out from under a rock just to have her precious Teryn lineage carry on and not die out with my people's destruction. They are compatible to hold a spirit."

Callum's people are not the original Teryns? That is a lot to take in!

"When I asked Gigi for her help I did not realize what I agreed to—a forced existence. How could I have known that many would chose to fade away instead of going on another miserable day or experiencing another death? When I confronted Gigi, she didn't listen or care about our suffering. She wanted me to adhere to the bargain, no matter what. I have been struggling with Gigi for centuries—fighting for my people's freedom to move on while she pressures me to stay. You, my dear savior, are caught in the middle of this struggle."

"It wasn't intentional," I say and make a face. "How am I supposed to get Gigi's—I mean Laoise's—blessing now if I can't bring her the Heart Amulet?"

"Before I answer your questions," Moira says, "let me ask you this: who are you? You are not a Teryn, that much is clear."

"I am Sybil Lilla," I say.

Moira rubs her eyes. "This is a lot more elaborate than I thought. How did you end up in my realm in the first place?"

"A strange wind sucked my friends and me into a column of air," I say, "when I visited the Wise Women to petition for Laoise's blessing."

Moira looks at me with a mirthless smile. "My dear, you were set up for failure not once but twice."

CHAPTER 81

"I must have heard it wrong," I say. "I thought you said that 'I was set up for failure twice.'"

"You heard right, my dear," Moira confirms. "Gigi's blessing is the meld with one of my spirit warriors."

"Is that why Callum had a battle form?" I ask.

"Correct," Moira says. "It's impossible for outsiders to *become* a Teryn. A person must be compatible with my spirits, and so far, only the new Teryns were able to survive a meld. Goodness knows, Gigi tried it with many other races until she found the new Teryns. Not all are worthy, of course; that is why the new Teryns send their young ones at age fifteen into my realm on their 'trial' to prove their worth and earn the respect of one of the spirits. The new Teryns don't remember their trial in detail—it is more like a dream for them. Once the selection is made, I give my permission to the spirit and Gigi infuses the new Teryn with the spirit of the old Teryn, thus giving her 'blessing.'"

Rhona clears her throat. "Was I not worthy of a spirit warrior?"

Moira reaches over and pats Rhona's hand. "My dear, you were more than worthy! I forbade my son to meld with you. It is my fault and not yours that you don't have a battle form."

Rhona pulls her hand away and presses her lips tightly. "You have ruined more than just your son's meld."

"Why is this meld so important?" I ask. Was Callum not good enough the way he was before the meld?

"The new Teryns are strong fighters. They are relentless, fearless, and can go berserk on their own merit. But without my spirit warriors, they would miss out on added strength, speed, and superior senses, and also wouldn't have the much-coveted magical immunity. The spirits, in turn, get to live through the warriors but without the ability to take control. The new Teryns often refer to the spirits as their conscience or instinct—that is the extent to which a spirit can influence the new Teryn. Not much of an existence, if you ask me. One reason I have never participated in a meld before. Of course, there are other reasons, but let's not veer off the topic."

"This explains a lot," I mutter, remembering the strange things Callum said and did when I first met him on Uhna. How he was faster than others, or how he could withstand my magic when I lost control and it burst out of me.

"Now you are in peril. You have discovered the secret of what it means to be a true Teryn. A secret that has been protected by generations of new Teryns."

This is the treason Caderyn referred to when he argued with Callum!

"Back to you, Lilla, I believe there is a much bigger agenda at hand, and you are the catalyst. I can't decide whether for a disaster or success."

"Thanks," I say with a grimace.

Moira laughs. "I did not mean to give you a backhanded compliment, but think about the fact that you are here, in my realm, discovering the biggest secrets the new Teryns harbor, and that you are the last of your kind."

"What would Laoise gain with me out of the way?" I ask, thinking out loud.

Moira clasps her hands. "That is the question, isn't it?"

My stomach sinks. "Laoise is setting up the new Teryns to become the new Lumenians! But just because she wants them to be the new fighting race in the Era War, they still won't have the Lume magic to eradicate fully corrupted dark servants!" Callum tried to defeat them on that beach, back on Uhna, but they kept regenerating until my Lume magic eliminated the Acerbus corrupting the dark servants, killing them in the process.

"That's right, my dear!"

"Without Lume magic to counteract Acerbus and corruption, the Era War will be lost!" I exclaim. Whether Laoise likes it or not, I am the only one who can defeat the fully corrupted.

"Gigi set her eyes on the prize," Moira says. "She does not care the cost the Seven Galaxies would pay for her mistake, when the Archgod of Chaos and Destruction wins the Era War, because you won't be there to stop Him and His armies. It seems to me that to finish your quest, you have to go through Gigi first."

CHAPTER 82

"Are you sure this will work?" I ask as I kneel by Moira, who lies on her back in the middle of a grassy plain. Among the long grass, her spirit warriors gather, surrounding the two of us. They pretend we are in the middle of a battle and I'm winning. My friends are positioned among the spirit warriors, acting like they are part of the pretend battle too.

Moira lowers her hand and pushes the Extraction Wand out of her face. "Yes, I am. This will get Gigi to enter the realm; then we can force her to open a gateway for you. Once you and your friends are out, Marcas volunteered to meld with you in the Wise Women's cave, thus helping you to become a Teryn. Simple."

"I meant to say that it sounds too easy, don't you think?" I ask, worried. Moira and I came up with this plan mere minutes ago—to convince Laoise that she has no choice but to let my friends and me go, and to bestow her blessing on me or risk losing Moira's soul.

"The best plans *are* easy," Moira says. "Don't worry, Marcas won't change his mind. You impressed him with your sense of honor."

I look up and Marcas waves from the right, grinning.

"Don't think about how strange melding with Marcas will be," I mutter under my breath.

Moira chuckles. "You just blushed!"

I clear my throat. "Are you sure Laoise will hear me? What if she won't appear? You did say you never tried anything like this before." Sending a message out to Laoise requires Moira to thin the border of the spirit realm so the guardian goddess can receive my message.

"Yes, I'm sure," Moira says. "Now enough with the questions. We have a role to play. Everyone, get ready."

I raise the Extraction Wand again, directing it at Moira, careful not to press on any runes while making a threatening face.

Moira rolls her eyes. "Is that the best you can do?"

Before I can answer, Moira closes her eyes, concentrating, then says, "Now!"

CHAPTER 83

"GUARDIAN GODDESS LAOISE!" I bellow. "Come here or I will steal your precious queen's power!"

I whisper down to Moira, "Was it convincing?"

Moira winks. "I believed you."

For a long moment nothing happens. A soft rustling of the long grass stalks can be heard as they bend in the warm wind.

Then above us, to the right, part of the sky turns into swirling, dark shadows, much like the portal produced by Belthair's Umbrae travel gauntlet.

A thin woman steps through it, descending until her feet in brown sandals touch the ground. Black hair frames a pale grayish-toned face that hovers on the border of beautiful and handsome. Her boxy brown dress doesn't help to tilt the scale toward beautiful—it lends her a shapeless, unassuming look. Her dark brown gaze, bursting with banked power, examines the scene.

"Bestow your blessing for my meld with Marcas and then open a gateway for us."

"Why would I do that?" Laoise asks in a beautiful, melodious voice. She tilts her head to the side in an unnatural way, narrowing her eyes on me and the Extraction Wand I'm grasping in my trembling hand.

"Because if you don't let us go, I will steal the queen's power!"

Laoise clasps her thin and boney hands in front of her. "Again, why would that matter to me?"

If I didn't see greed flashing in the goddess's eyes, I might believe her nonchalant reaction.

"Gigi, be reasonable," Moira says with a convincing quaver in her voice. "I don't want to disappear into nothing! I understand now that you need my people's help to win the Era War. I can see reason!"

Laoise reaches into her pocket. "Can you now?" she asks and pulls out a wand made of wood and meal that's a lot like the one I have in my hand but with fewer runes on it. "I find it suspicious how you seem to have changed your mind, my old friend. Not to mention, I was expecting Daryhna and not you."

"Daryhna was reckless to think she could defeat me!" Moira says. "Though we both underestimated Lilla!"

"I would be a *fool* to believe a word you say, Moira." Laoise points the wand at my friends and presses on a group of runes.

A torrent of pure, black Acerbus explodes out of the wand, heading straight at the group.

Time stops.

Nic, with a bloody slash across his throat appears in my mind. I know without a doubt that I cannot stand by and watch my friends die. Never again!

I jump to my feet and throw myself in the line of Acerbus.

CHAPTER 84

I take the torrent of Acerbus stream into my chest.

Pain lights up my nerve endings. All-encompassing agony crashes down on me. White-hot agony tears inhuman shrieks from my throat.

The Acerbus explodes in my body, wreaking havoc. Blood vessels burst. Blood drips from my eyes, mouth, and ears.

I am burning in the cold fire of Acerbus!

CHAPTER 85

M y heart thumps sluggishly in my chest, each beat an effort.

"I can't heal you!" Glenna screams, kneeling by my side. "I . . . I don't know what to do!"

I turn my head toward her, blinking blood out of my eyes.

Warm hands close over mine, and a wail sounds from Glenna. Isa and Bella, crying, hug Glenna's shoulders.

"Gigi, please heal her!" Moira says and kneels on one leg, begging the guardian goddess.

"What are you waiting for?" Belthair demands.

The warriors drop to one knee in the green grass, with their hands outstretched in a silent plea to their goddess.

"Why should I help her?" Laoise asks Moira. "She is not even a good Sybil! She was ready to sacrifice herself for her *friends*, forgetting about her role as the Protector of the Seven Galaxies. My children, melded with your spirit warriors, would be a much better choice. All I have to do is get rid of the Sybil. Then my Teryns will be the legendary warriors. There is nothing the Archgoddess of the Eternal Light and Order can do now! She allowed Her Sybil to walk into my ambush. I planted that useful tidbit about the Bride's Choice in one of my Teryns' ear. I had just enough of the sight to know this would set into motion a series of events that would lead the Sybil to Teryn and then into this realm. It all worked out as I knew it would, though I was expecting my assassins to take you out sooner."

It was Laoise, not Moira, who sent those assassins!

"What kind of guardian goddess are you?" Arrov says with a growl, his eyes flashing red.

Laoise sneers. "You have no idea what I had to sacrifice for my Teryns!" She glances at the Extraction Wand in Arrov's furry hands and adds, "I will consider saving the Sybil if Moira gives up her spirit essence to me."

CHAPTER 86

For a moment nothing but my loud wheezing can be heard on the grassy plain.

"Don't give up . . . your freedom . . . to Laoise . . . not for me," I stutter. "This . . . is . . . a trap!" Laoise's way to advance her Teryns and steal Moira's power!

"Conserve your energy for healing," Glenna says and wipes the tears off her cheeks.

"The depth of your depravity disgusts me!" Moira shouts, her expression furious. "I don't recognize you anymore! You destroyed my beloved Gigi, forgetting about what it means to be a guardian goddess!"

Moira spits in the air at Laoise, then turns to me.

"There might be a way to save you," Moira says, "but I cannot guarantee the outcome, as I have never tried anything like this before."

My eyes close for a second, my lungs heavy in my chest. Blackness descends. When I come to, Moira hovers over me. "Lilla, wake up!" she yells. "Do you accept my help?"

"Your . . . help?" I ask. I can't think past the pain. My back bows as I struggle for air.

"I don't—" I manage to say, but Rhona cuts in, putting her hand on my arm. "Please just this once, stop being so stubborn and let someone help you!" Rhona turns her head in frustration and wipes tears from the corners of her eyes.

I look at Moira through a curtain of blood. "I . . . accept."

Moira's lean and bearlike body turns into a beautiful rainbow-colored shimmer from one second to the next.

A shimmer that I've seen around Callum when he transfigured into his battle form.

"NO!" Laoise screeches. "I forbid you!"

The floating shimmer dives into my body, sinking under my skin.

216

CHAPTER 87

I was wrong! This meld is nothing like what I saw happen to Callum! The rainbow-colored shimmer bursts with barely contained power. Power that's not magical in nature. Something more. Something ancient.

The meld lifts me off the ground. I hover in the air in a vertical position, a few feet from the grass, suspended in a cocoon of power.

Healing warmth spreads through my body—a dozen times stronger than Glenna's A'ris magic. A hundred times better than the Sybil talisman was ever able to produce.

Blood vessels, cells, and organs heal. The internal injuries vanish, repaired by the meld.

See? I told you I can help, Moira says in my mind.

How is it that I can still hear you? I think to Moira as the shimmer dissipates and I float back to the ground. *Didn't you say the spirits give up their freedom and are oppressed after they meld?*

Lilla, don't worry. I doubt either of us will lose herself to the other. We are equals. Moira smiles. *Nice magical tattoo, by the way.*

How do I know you're smiling?!

I told you, my dear, that there is a reason why I am the queen.

I snort. *In other words, you have no idea why.*

None whatsoever.

I wipe dirt off my dress and look up, into Laoise's shocked eyes. "We are leaving now!"

CHAPTER 88

"Y ou are wrong!" Laoise shouts. Dark gray ribbons of magic swirl around her. She seems to become larger. She levitates six feet off the ground, with her arms spread wide like a divine sculpture. Her shapeless brown dress, plastered to her body, billows from an imperceptible wind. Her black hair floats around her pale face.

A weblike structure comes to life around me, reflecting the light of Laoise's magic—visible in the sky, on the ground, in the very air we breathe. From this web, a transparent tube no wider than my palm connects to Laoise like a magical umbilical cord.

"Why would I ever let you go?" Laoise asks and narrows her gaze on me, on *us*, her dark brown eyes glowing teal with unbanked power. A faint male face twisted in a pained expression flashes over Laoise's face, then vanishes.

"You are nothing," Laoise continues. "You can't even transfigure. You will never be a true Teryn!"

More expressions flicker interposed over Laoise's face. Each one is different, male or female, but all frozen in grotesque masks of pain.

Can we meld? I think to Moira. *Or transfigure?*

Moira sighs. *Probably. We have to meld first, before we can transfigure. But I need more time to, uh, settle.*

Dark gray magical swirls gather in both of Laoise's palms, crackling with electric lightning. She raises her hands and lobs her magic at us.

CHAPTER 89

Settle faster! Before Laoise kills us both!

Moira/I dodge the two dark magical orbs. They hit the ground where we stood moments before, exploding grass and dirt. The ground shakes with increasing tremors as the magic sinks deeply.

The warrior spirits look around unsure, while my friends back away from the hole.

Cracks materialize, running outward at a blinding speed, spreading wider in the grassy plain, opening up like canyons. Then mountain peaks, full of cliffs and sharp ridges, burst from the ground.

I look at Ragnald for help. "This is terra-builder magic," he says, "from the T'erra element. Mostly harmless to me—" Screams and shouts interrupt Ragnald from the left. A new mountain explodes upward, from under the feet of a group of spirit warriors, carrying them until they lose their hold and slide down the jagged slope, disappearing in the deep crater at the bottom.

Ragnald gulps and says, "—unless I happen to get caught without my T'erra magic to dispel it."

Then there is no more time to talk. We scatter and burst into a run. We leap over cracks or backpedal from mountain peaks shooting up in front of us.

I reach for my Lume magic, desperate for it to work. For the first time since the magical poisoning, something pulses deep inside. Sluggish and acting overtired, but the aftereffects of that magical poisoning seem to be lessening.

Moira rolls her eyes. *Great, now we have sore magical muscles!*

Moira, focus! Can we meld now?

Not yet!

Laoise shakes the dark gray magic out of her hands. A flicker of a new and tortured expression flashes by on the goddess's face. Straw yellow orbs of swirling A'nima, bursting with fiery sparks, appear in her palms. She puts her hands together, mixing the two orbs of magic. Then pulls her palms apart, shaping the swirling magic into a flat, mirrorlike circle. Then she throws it toward us.

The magical disc flies away from Laoise; then it stops and hovers in mid-air like a vertical gateway.

How can Laoise have so many powers? From what I know, guardian gods have one element they are assigned to, just as they guard one world.

Moira clenches her fangs. I was wondering the same! Now stop bothering me!

Hundreds of huge, shrieking creatures fly out of the magic gateway, flapping their two pairs of sixteen-foot-long featherless wings, with claws at their ends. Patches of black feathers cover their eight-foot-long gray, wrinkled, and thin bodies. Sharp incisors glint in their long beaks, dripping saliva. Two pairs of beady eyes track our movements.

"Uh-oh," Ragnald says. "That's a summoning magic, from A'nima. It wouldn't be a problem in any other day—"

"—but neither you nor I have our elemental magic available," I finish Ragnald's sentence.

More creatures dive at their target, picking up warriors and trying to gulp them down. The warriors slash at the birds' heads until they drop them.

A swoosh of air makes me glance up to find a creature plunging right at us. "Duck!" I shout to Ragnald.

A tremendous bird glides above us, missing the mage and me by a few inches.

Laoise laughs and conjures swirling, red Fla'mma spheres into her palms. She throws them on the mountain peaks until each has a red magical cover.

"What now?!" I say with a groan, then dive to the side to avoid piercing-sharp claws of another plummeting bird-monster.

"I used to love animals," Glenna mutters next to me as she drops to the ground, "but I despise these with the burning heat of two suns!"

Ivy lands on her stomach by Glenna, barely escaping the reaching claws of another creature. "You are not alone!"

The mountains shake, absorbing the Fla'mma magic that covered them. Then boiling hot lava erupts, raining down the mountainsides.

I crouch low and Ragnald squats by me. "That's lava-conjuring magic, from Fla'mma. I, uh, have nothing to advise other than to avoid them."

I glance at Ragnald. "Good plan." Though how long we can evade Laoise's never-ending attacks is another question. I must find a way to fight back!

Moira!

Almost there. Patience!

"I am out of patience," I mutter and leap over a widening canyon that formed right under my feet.

"Down!" Arrov shouts. When I comply, he bats a bloodthirsty bird-monster away from me with a thick tree branch.

Belthair lobs rocks from each of his six hands at the circling winged predators. Rocks that the twins and Glenna hand to him from the scree at the bottom of the mountain on our left. Rhona watches, yelling directions where to move or when to dodge.

Laoise throws her head back and laughs. "You will never win against me!" Light and dark blue-hued, transparent ribbons of A'qua and A'ris circle her arms.

Moira's people freeze, paralyzed, while my friends and I remain unaffected.

Now would be a perfect time to blast Laoise out of the sky with my magic. I reach for Lume again. It feels like wading through thick and unrelenting molasses to reach the faint-looking orb. Just how long does Lume need to replenish?!

"What is Laoise preparing to unleash?" I ask Ragnald as he gets to his feet on my right.

Ragnald shakes his head. "I have no clue, but I am afraid we will find out sooner than I'd like."

Laoise lifts her hands up, covered in the multihued magic. The frozen spirits rise too, high into the sky, above the lava-spewing mountains, above the screeching bird creatures, lining up in a half circle along the edge of the spirit realm.

Laoise cups her hands. When she opens her palms, A'qua and A'ris magic, combined into a transparent orb, hovers over her hands. Placing her right hand above it and her left hand under it, she proceeds to pull the orb apart.

The spirits in the sky bow their chests and howl in pain. The boundaries of their bodies begin to shimmer, breaking apart into particles.

No! Moira screams in my mind.

"How is this magical variety show possible?" I ask Ragnald. He shakes his head, lost for words.

I must wonder, Moira thinks to me, *what happened to the guardian goddess of the new Teryns? All that power that would have dissipated without having any charges to guard. After she relocated that tribe, I did notice she was more powerful than before. Coincidence?*

Are you telling me that Laoise had somehow "cannibalized" another guardian god's power?

Moira shrugs. *More like multiple guardian gods' if I'm to judge by the impressive assortment of magic Gigi just displayed.*

"I have read about it, but never seen the rare soul obliteration magic," Ragnald says in shocked awe. "It combines A'qua and A'ris magic. I have no idea how to defeat Laoise. She is too formidable."

Buckets of fishguts!

I am not ready yet, Moira says with a growl in my mind before I even prompt her.

I rub my face in frustration. I can't reach Laoise! I can't use my Lumenian magic! What *can* I do to end her games?

An idea pops in my head.

I lock on Laoise, who hovers in midair a few hundred yards in front of me. Raising my leg, bent at the knee, I extend my arms in front of me. Stepping forward, I open my arms in a shoving motion, propelling energy outward.

The force of the energy cuts off the peaks of a few mountains, sends dozens of winged beasts careening into the lava rivers, and slams into Laoise.

Laoise flies backward a hundred yards, propelled by the Saage women's energy manipulation trick. The spirit obliteration gets interrupted, though Moira's people still hover in the sky, suspended.

I stare at my hands in wonder.

Your Saage women's trick got quite a power boost from our meld, my dear. You can thank me later.

"That was impressive!" the others cheer, surrounding me.

Laoise straightens, angrier than before. "You will pay for this!"

CHAPTER 90

Laoise flies forward, stopping a short distance from me and floating in mid-air. "I will make you suffer!" she shouts and holds her left hand to her chest.

"You already made us suffer!" Moira/I say in a distorted voice.

"I am disappointed in you, Moira," Laoise says. "Time and again you refused my offer to help you, until it was too late. When you accepted my aid, I saved you and your people without any hesitation. I made you this realm, a paradise, safe and full of resources you need." Laoise releases her aching hand to gesture in a sweeping motion around her, encompassing the realm, including the weblike magical architecture connected to her via a transparent, magical umbilical cord.

"I never asked for this forced existence!" Moira/I say. "I never asked for servitude! You have abandoned us, the old Teryns, for the sake of your new Terns!"

The pain that Moira hid from her people envelops my soul. Tears spring to my eyes. She suffered so long from guilt, feeling lonely and struggling under the burden of responsibility.

"I have sacrificed everything for you, Moira!" Laoise shouts, her eyes alight with teal flashes of power. "I searched the whole Seven Galaxies for compatible people to meld with! I found a primitive tribe at the last minute. I had to rush to save them before a black hole could pulverize their planet. Then I transported them to Teryn and ensured their spiritual compliance for the meld. I did all this so you can live on, happily! Enjoying the life you should have had, but the Archgod of Chaos and Destruction robbed you!"

Hearing the history of Callum's people from Laoise is a confirmation of what Moira alleged. This is the reason why the new Teryns never fought in any Era War! They are too young compared to Moira's people.

"What you did was a sick definition of help!" Moira/I yell and raise my hands in fists. "You interfered with the Balance when you saved us and that poor tribe! Acting like *you* were the Omnipower. You trapped my people in this realm! You didn't let us move on to the Lume, as we should have done, after our death! What you did was the most despicable act toward your very own people you were supposed to protect!"

Teal-colored power explodes upward from Laoise in a mist before dissipating. "I warned you that the archgod was coming, didn't I? You were too stubborn and dismissed my warnings. *You* decided to stay and fight, decimating your people by the millions. Risking not just their lives but mine too. A guardian goddess cannot exist without her charges! I would have died along with you!"

"I should have known it was about saving your own self!" Moira/I shout.

Laoise laughs without any shame. "I did what was best for all of us," she says and points at me. "Just as I am still doing now! Getting rid of her is what's best for the whole Seven Galaxies! She cannot alone persevere in the Era War! My children are numerous and strong! They are the ones who should lead, not that pathetic creature!"

I shake my head. "You forget one important issue—how would your precious Teryns defeat the fully corrupted?"

Laoise raises her chin. "It's only a minor issue. I will solve it in time."

Just not before trillions of innocents die or get corrupted into dark servants.

"Where did you get that wand that shoots Acerbus?" I ask. "Who gave it to you?" Who did she ally herself with?

Laoise shows the wand that discharged Acerbus at my friends. "It was an unexpected gift. Too bad it was useless." She tosses the wand into a nearby lava flow. It melts down to nothing in seconds, destroying any evidence that Laoise ever had it.

Ragnald, wearing a shocked expression, shakes his head. "I have never heard anyone who is on the side of the Archgoddess of the Eternal Light and Order to willingly cooperate with a minion of the Archgod of Chaos and Destruction."

Gigi crossed a line this time, Moira thinks to me, and I agree.

"You have betrayed the Archgoddess of the Eternal Light and Order," I say. "As Her Sybil, I order you to stop!"

Teal-colored power ribbons coalesce into a whirling column around Laoise. "You cannot order me to do anything!" Laoise shrieks and directs the torrent of whirling magic at us.

CHAPTER 91

The torrent of teal-colored magic barrels toward my friends and me.

We jump away, but not quickly enough. The ground breaks open under my friends' feet, and they plummet into a deep canyon.

"NO!" I shout. "You killed them!"

"Good riddance!" Laoise says. "What will you do about that, *Sybil*? Cry over it?" Laoise laughs, throwing her head back.

A red curtain descends over my vision. Fury like I've felt once before, when Nic died, burns through my veins. It clears a path to my magical orb, scorching up the last remnant of the magical poisoning.

"You are an aberration!" Moira/I shout in a distorted voice.

"You are wrong!" Laoise shouts and gathers more magic to her. "I am the future!"

A light-blue fur-covered hand slams on the ledge of the canyon. Arrov holds Belthair's top right hand with his left, while Isa and Bella grasp Belthair's two left hands. Ragnald, Glenna, and Rhona grip onto Belthair's right three hands. Ivy has her arms around Arrov's neck, dangling from his back. Arrov roars, struggling to pull himself over the edge with the added weight.

Laoise waves a hand toward the suspended spirits still paralyzed in the sky. They cry out as their bodies shimmer harder, with more particles separating from them.

I burst into a run toward Arrov but after a few steps I jerk to a stop.

No! Moira cries. *Help my spirits!* Moira's will intensifies over my body as she wants to head toward her people.

My friends first! I struggle to regain control, but Moira won't let up. We stay rooted to the spot.

Teal-colored magic slams into my chest, propelling me up. I slam to the ground, landing hard on my back. The air escapes from me and I struggle to breathe. Laoise's magic tries to sink under my skin. Moira's magical resistance kicks in and repels it.

I try to sit up but collapse back. *Moira! Meld now!*

Laoise flies over, the transparent and magical umbilical cord following her. She lands next to me and stomps down on my chest with one foot. "Look at you, crawling in the dirt like a serpent!"

I can't! I haven't settled yet! Use your magic to buy us time!

"Why are you so quiet?" Laoise says, sneering. She steps on my chest and leans down, saying, "Are you having trouble with your pitiful meld? It's not so simple, isn't it? You have to be *compatible*. Sadly, you'll never find out whether it could have worked or not." She puts pressure on my chest until bones pop.

I cry out in pain and shove against her foot but cannot budge her off me. Blindly, I reach for Lume. The feeling of molasses is gone. I grab a thick thread of Lume, shaping it into a dagger, and let it fly at the magical umbilical cord that floats above me.

CHAPTER 92

The Lume dagger cuts through the magical umbilical cord that connects Laoise to the spirit realm.

The realm and the magical architecture shudder.

Don't let the realm implode! Moira shouts in my mind.

Laoise screams and stumbles back, away from me. "What have you done?!"

I get to my feet and engage my magic. Hot-and-cold-and-hot-again feelings burst over my body, my skin glowing golden.

Time stops.

I erase the volcanoes and make the bird creatures disappear with multiple ribbons of Lume.

With a Lume rope, I lift Arrov and my friends out of the canyon.

With a thick thread of Lume, I re-form the ground back to normal, until the green and grassy meadow is restored to its natural beauty, undamaged.

Shaping Lume into a blanket, I catch the plummeting spirit people and set them down safely.

I thread thick Lume ribbons into the magical architecture of the realm, saturating it, until all the spirits are covered, sparkling bright white. The realm stabilizes.

"You have no idea of the consequences!" Laoise screams, her face a grotesque mask. She tries to leave through the border of the realm.

With a thought, I tighten the realm's Lume architecture, preventing it. "There will be no escape for you!" Moira/I say.

I know without a doubt that I can never let Laoise leave, not after what she did to the spirits, to Callum's people, and to the other guardian gods. I have no desire to kill the goddess. I would be no different than she is.

Then an idea forms in my head.

CHAPTER 93

After what feels like hours, but only a few minutes, I step back and study my creation.

A thirty-foot-tall tree made of transparent Lume, complete with a lush crown, stands in front of me. Its branches spread wide, vines running up its thick trunk. Its roots sink deep into the realm, reenforcing it. In the middle of the tree Laoise screams, anchored and bound by Lume. To our relief, the sound cut off after I completed the tree's canopy.

"This is how your Saage tattoo would have looked," Ragnald says, "had you finished your purification process."

I shake my hands out. "This Lume tree should be strong enough to hold Laoise in place, trapped, but harmless to others. Until The Lady decides Laoise's fate." I'm glad I don't have to make that decision.

It did turn out better than I thought it would.

I nod in thanks.

Belthair kicks at the tree, then winces. "It's solid, but how can we see your magic?"

"It must be because the realm is now infused with Lume," I say, and Moira nods in my head in confirmation, "and now I have control over the realm. Much like when Moira parted the forest."

I tie the umbilical cord to the roots, letting go of the realm. For a second I feel a temptation to take that cord back, to keep that power for myself. But I refuse to let it corrupt me, as it did to Laoise. "Now we can get back to my quest."

"I think it's been more than seven days," Ivy says. "Lilla, you failed."

I take a step back from her. "It can't be, can it?"

Let me think, my dear.

"How could I have failed?" I ask. "I have the, uh, Heart Amulet in the form of Moira; I melded, which is what Laoise's blessing is in a seashell. Thus I *have* completed Caderyn's quest!"

Rhona places a hand on my shoulder, her expression compassionate. "Even if you did all of this, you must follow the praelor's condition to the letter—finish it in seven days *and* prove it to him."

"But—" I manage to say when Moira interrupts, speaking through me, "It hasn't been seven days yet. We still have an hour left to finish the quest. Time flows differently in my realm."

Relief floods through me. I still have time to prove myself to Caderyn.

"Then what are we waiting for?" I ask and open a doorway out of the realm, parting the Lume in front of me just wide enough for us to step through.

CHAPTER 94

"I feel kicked in the head," I mutter, sitting up in the Wise Women's cave, struggling to keep my eyes open. My muscles ache after being stationary for so long. Lukewarm healing trickles from the Sybil talisman. I touch my necklace with k'alligator fangs on it; luckily, it survived the trip back.

How do you think I feel? Moira says with a groan in my head. *I've never left my realm.*

"Lilla!" Callum shouts from the entrance of the cave. "You're back!" He embraces me, lifting me off my feet and kissing my face. "Gods, I love you!"

I kiss him back, breathless. Pouring my love into that kiss.

He is more handsome than I thought, based on your memories, my dear.

I frown and pull back. *You can see my memories?*

Moira nods. *Until the meld settles, our memories are wide open to one another. See for yourself.*

I close my eyes and concentrate. Flashes of memories float by of Keelan being born; of so much love with Edan; of DLD's arrival; of battles and death; and of so much suffering. *I should not be privy to your private memories.*

Moira sighs. *You are right. From now on, I promise I won't peek.*

Ragnald conjures fireballs onto his palms. "My elemental magic is back!"

Glenna slaps his shoulder. "Put those things away before you burn someone's eyes out!"

Arrov gets to his feet, staring at his light-blue-toned hands, which are no longer covered in fur. Nor does his muscular body have a fur cover anymore. "I'm back!" he shouts and shoves dark blue hair out of his angular face. "I have no idea how, but I'm back to myself again!"

Ivy sits up and wiggles her eyebrows at Arrov. "I've noticed, handsome!"

"See? You were not cursed!" I say, keeping my eyes strictly on his face.

"Yes, he is cursed," Callum says with a growl, "with ignorance."

Arrov takes the jacket with six sleeves that Belthair hands to him and then drapes it over his wide shoulders. The jacket reaches the top of his muscular thighs, just long enough to cover what needs to be covered.

Isa helps Ivy to her feet while Rhona glances around. "Where are the Wise Women?"

I search the empty cave. There are no signs of the Wise Women or their skeletal attendants. When I glance up, I gape. "Why is the sky visible?" I ask. The cave's ceiling and most of its far-left wall are missing, showing the view to the red canyon below.

Callum crosses his arms. "It's an improvement."

"What Callum is trying to say," Teague says as he enters the cave, "is that in his frustration he did some redecoration. With his bare hands. He also refused to leave your side."

I turn to look at Callum, who does look a bit gaunt. "You did that?" Callum just grins.

"The praelor is waiting," Teague says with a grimace.

I head toward the cave opening. "Then let us not keep him waiting any longer."

CHAPTER 95

Callum and I step outside, followed by my friends. We trek back to the City of Honor, which is not too far from the cave. We find a large crowd gathering at the edge of the city. The mass parts enough for us to get to the center of the cobblestone street, where Caderyn, his family, and the three Wise Women wait. We stop in front of the praelor.

The crowd closes, surging forward like a clamp.

My claustrophobia clamors at me to *flee!* and I stumble, breaking out in a cold sweat.

Moira shudders. *I don't care for that strange feeling!*

Me neither. I take deep breaths to keep my panic in check. I cannot fail now!

The gathered Teryns shout and jostle, forming an incoherent throng. Callum pushes many of them backward to make room around me.

Caderyn raises an arm, and his subjects go silent. "Your time is up, Lilla," he says.

"I have completed the quest for the Heart Amulet," I say, "and earned the Guardian Goddess Laoise's blessing." Well, sort of, in a roundabout way, but let's not focus on that.

"Guardian Goddess Laoise did not give this *liar* Her blessing!" the Wise Women say in an eerie unison.

The Teryns shout in anger, but Caderyn silences them again. "Is that true?" he asks.

"She didn't *personally* bestow her blessing, but I have melded with the Heart Amulet. I can prove it in, uh, an honorable way."

Caderyn scoffs. "Am I to believe that you, who is inexperienced and never fought in an Era War—"

"Nor did you," I point out.

"—somehow managed to meld with the fabled Heart Amulet?" Caderyn finishes.

"Don't forget the part where I said, 'I can prove it.'"

"Now that you know our secret," Caderyn says, "you and your friends must die."

"Unless you can prove your claims with honor by fighting the Executioner and winning."

The crowd cheers even louder, chanting, "Fight with honor!"

Callum turns to me. "Lilla, don't do it!"

"I won't let my friends die because they made the mistake of accompanying me on this outlandish mission," I say to Callum, then turn to Caderyn and ask, "What happens if I win?"

The praelor laughs. "Then you did the impossible—became a Teryn, in an honorable way. *If* you survive, then you can recruit my army."

"Then I accept the fight with the Executioner."

CHAPTER 96

"No!" Callum shouts, but it's too late.

Cries of outrage sound from the crowd as Teryns get shoved to the side by someone large heading straight at us.

"Melded form is permissible," Caderyn says, "but *any* use of magic will earn you and your friends a death sentence on the spot."

A huge, half-naked, and bald man with protruding muscles pushes through the crowd, stomping his way toward us. He towers over me by two heads. A greasy sheen covers his pockmarked and square face. He sneers down at me, his expression ruthless. The Executioner.

My muscles freeze as I stare at the Executioner.

What is it? Why are you so scared? He is just a man. Granted, a callous one.

At Caderyn's request, a skinny warrior sets up a fight circle with three vertical rows of lasers around it.

"Until one is standing!" Caderyn says and the Teryns shout.

"Celebration fights are always till first blood!" Callum shouts. "You would sanction the Sybil to get killed?"

Caderyn opens his arms wide. "Ground Rule number seven grants the option of killing as the fighter or fightee sees fit. Subsection ten, addendum hundred and one states that fights like these can happen when matters of Teryn-related issues are in question. Or are you disputing the Ground Rules? Would you prefer a swift execution instead?"

Callum grinds his teeth.

"That's what I thought," Caderyn says. "May the better and more honorable fighter win!"

Shaking, I follow the Executioner and step over the laser border of the fight circle, then head to the center of it.

The Executioner leers with a blood-chilling expression. Ruthless menace glints in his dark eyes. "This fight will be short," the Executioner boasts, and the onlookers laugh. "I will teach this fraud what it means to be a true Teryn!"

I know he will kill me this time.

I stand rooted to the spot, paralyzed with a cold fear that shreds all my courage.

What are you waiting for? Moira shouts in my mind. *Fight him!*

I can't!

The Executioner lunges and grabs my shirt, bunching it in his meaty hand just as he did the last time.

He throws me to the side. I almost stumble into the laser border of the circle.

"Lilla!" Callum roars, his voice pained, struggling against Teague and five other warriors restraining him.

The Executioner watches me with a smirk.

Fight! Moira shouts again, trying to take control of my muscles but to no avail.

I hear the Executioner's voice in my mind as he recounts the Ground Rules until I have to cover my ears to drown them out.

I can't! Not without my magic!

Phantom pain lights into my right shoulder, the one the Executioner broke. Blind from the memory pain, I don't see the jab until it's headed straight at me.

CHAPTER 97

The Executioner's jab flies at my head. I turn and raise my left shoulder to take the brunt of the hit.

I cry out, preparing for the white-hot agony from a broken bone. Pain floods my body, but the bones stay intact.

Lilla, you are not alone in this fight!

"I'll kill you!" Callum bellows. "You hear me? I don't care if it's against the Ground Rules! If you hurt her, I will tear you apart!"

The Executioner laughs, looking at Callum. "You couldn't defeat me the last time. What makes you think you'll *ever* win against me?"

"Because I will help him!" Arrov growls, his voice sounding like the A'ice giant he was. My friends step up to the fight circle in support.

The Executioner laughs. "You are weak! You have no honor in my eyes!"

Don't listen to him, Lilla!

I can't pay attention to Moira. I am saturated with so much fear that I can't push past it.

The Executioner fakes another jab. I lean back to dodge it. He kicks me in the stomach with a fast front kick.

Air escapes from me in a burst. I gasp, unable to breathe.

Why won't you fight back?!

Air fills up my lungs and I back away from the Executioner. Then I lunge at him, jumping up to kick him in the head.

He anticipates my move and grabs my leg, deflecting the kick.

"You still haven't learned your lesson," he says, chortling with a vile expression. He twists my legs.

I scream, with tears blinding me. I can imagine hearing my knee pop, ligaments tearing.

Stop this, Lilla! Your knee is not torn!

The Executioner lifts my leg up high and shoves me away. "Beg for my mercy and I might not kill you."

I land on the ground, with my left hand out. I scream as imagined pain from a broken wrist envelops me, but the bones won't break this time.

Get up! You are fine!

I can't win against the Executioner! I am not strong enough without my magic!

I roll to the side, scrambling to my feet, and hold my injured left hand.

Your hand is fine! Bruised, but not broken! See for yourself!

"Lilla!" Rhona shouts. "What are you doing?!"

Before I can move, the Executioner kicks the back of my right thigh with a low roundhouse kick.

My legs buckle. I topple onto my hands and knees, scraping them bloody. Hopelessness saps my energy.

Fight back!

The Executioner kicks into my stomach, lifting me off the ground. I land on my back, once again the air knocked out of me.

CHAPTER 98

I *CAN'T FIGHT BACK!* I cry.

How can you give up? Are you willing to let your friends, let us *die without trying?*

He is too strong! I cannot win! I have nothing left in me.

"Lilla!" Glenna screams. "Snap out of this!"

Get up! Stop feeling sorry for yourself!

I roll to my side, gasping. The Sybil talisman sends trickles of healing magic through my body. I sit up, then slowly get to my feet, facing the sneering Executioner.

You never gave up when I sent my spirit warriors after you! You kept going, no matter what! Stop giving this man so much power over you!

The Executioner paces around the perimeter of the fight circle, cracking his neck and rubbing his hands. "I will do a favor for the Seven Galaxies by taking you out!"

The Executioner attacks with a hook.

I backpedal from him, getting too close to the border, the lasers singing into my left calf. I pivot away, bleeding.

"Are you trying to forgo this fight?" he asks and rams into me with his head bent. He grabs me by my waist, then throws me over his head.

I crash to the ground, all air knocked out of my lungs, for the third time. The Sybil talisman sputters, trying to send healing waves, but it cannot send air.

Lilla, you didn't use real magic in that last fight! Remember? You outsmarted him without it!

"Lilla!" Callum roars. "Don't leave me! Fight!" There is so much pain and angst in his voice that they cut deeply into my heart.

CHAPTER 99

It's because of you, Lilla, that we can't meld! You are resisting me! You need my help! If we don't finish the meld soon, you will prove the praelor right! Innocents will pay the price!

I glance at my friends. I wanted them to believe that I am capable. That I am worthy. I tried to hide any weakness from them, lying that my magic wasn't gone. I shouldn't have done that. They never cared about my magic.

Moira is right. I am strong even without my magic. It does not define me.

I glare at the Executioner. I don't have to fight him alone. As Rhona taught me, a good general knows when to use her people for her own advantage.

I get to my feet and face the Executioner.

"You should have stayed down!" he says, stalking toward me.

I sprint away from him, giving into the meld and dissolving any reservations I had.

The Executioner changes direction and intercepts me.

Can we transfigure now, Moira?

He head-butts me. Pain explodes on my forehead and blood gushes into my eyes.

He grabs my right forearm and lifts his right fist up.

Moira bares her fangs. *I thought you'd never ask!*

239

CHAPTER 100

From one step to the next, a rainbow-colored shimmer washes over me, gone by the time I blink.

Dra'agon legs support a strong bearlike body, covered in black scales that shine with multicolor hues. Powerful lyon arms ending in finger-long black claws throb with strength. A thick black mane frames a wolfish head with dark brown eyes. Black feathers cover a deadly eagle head with clear blue eyes and a black beak. The same multihued black scales cover a dra'agon head with dark violet and slitted eyes. A red forked tongue flicks out from its elongated maw full of fangs.

"Behold, the Cymmerion battle form!" we roar from three mouths, our voice thundering. "The true Teryn!"

The crowd goes silent. Then a warrior hits his chest with his right fist, without stopping. Another warrior joins him, and another. Until the whole crowd applauds.

Caderyn gapes at us. "How could this be possible?" he asks. "No one has a battle form like you!"

Callum grins with pride. "Lilla has the Heart Amulet!"

We turn to look at the crowd from our ten-foot height and extend our leathery wings to their full twenty-foot length. Our thick, scale-covered tail, ending in a scorpion stinger, rises into view.

Moira, please tell me we don't have three heads.

We narrow three pairs of eyes on the Executioner, towering over him. He struggles to transfigure but can't turn into his battle form.

Moira shrugs. *Fine, my dear, I won't tell you that we have three heads.*

The Executioner pales, still clutching our forearm while he stares up, unable to figure out which pair of eyes to look at.

We lean down and say with a snarl, "Run!"

CHAPTER 101

The Executioner drops our arm and dashes away on shaking legs.

How. . .? I mean in the spirit realm you had one head!

This is the reason why I am the queen of all Teryns—I can choose my form out of three. I am a Cymmerion. No other spirit can do this. It was inherent in my family's line.

We lumber after the Executioner, in no hurry to catch him. When we get close to him, we fly over him and whirl to face him.

"Please!" the Executioner says.

It didn't take long for him to beg for his life, Moira says.

Our tail with the stinger slams into the Executioner's chest, sending him to the ground. A paralyzing agent injects into his body before we pull our tail back, propping him on his feet in the process.

Don't worry, I've given him just enough to temporarily petrify him. He deserves to feel helpless, wouldn't you say?

The man stares up at us in horror, muffled screams locked in his throat.

I'd rather not sink to his level, Moira. I don't ever want to be anything like him.

We grab him by the throat with one hand and spit into his face.

That should counteract the numbing agent. Though it does cut into the fun I was having.

The frozen muscles on his face and body regain their function. We let him run away, but when he tries to jump over the laser border, we slam our tail into him again.

"Are you trying to leave this fight circle?" we ask him.

CHAPTER 102

The Executioner recoils, hearing his own words thrown back at him. He dashes to the left.

"Who is weak and pathetic now?" we ask him and lunge into his way. With our right wing, we punch him.

The Executioner yelps. His left eye swells up and blackens, shutting closed.

"What did you say to us? 'Beg for my mercy and I might not kill you'?" we ask and lean down from three heads.

The Executioner takes a few steps back. "I, uh, didn't mean it!"

"We don't appreciate your sense of humor," we say and spit a fireball at his feet.

He screams in pain and tries to kick us with a hook kick.

We deflect his weak attempt and knock him down with our tail.

The Executioner scrambles to his feet to face us.

We smile. "You should have stayed down."

The Executioner pales.

We study him. We find a tired and miserable spirit huddling in the man's mind. We hurt from the spirit's suffering and howl to the sky in frustration.

The Executioner screams and backpedals from us, but we follow him. He punches with jabs, crosses, and hooks, but we repel his hits without any trouble.

He tries to kick us in the wolf head.

We grasp his leg before his kick can land. Our right hand snaps out, and we grab him by the throat. "We will do the Seven Galaxies a favor by getting rid of scum like you!" we roar into his face.

We flap our wings, once, twice, three times, until we are seven feet off the ground, dangling the man from our extended right arm.

Moira growls. *I saw your fight with him in your memory.*

We dive and slam the man to the ground, sinking him a few inches deep.

I saw him beat you without mercy.

We spread our wings and step onto the man's chest, with the sharp stinger pointing into his sweaty face. He urinates himself.

We lean forward, snarling from three heads, and put pressure onto the man's chest.

Moira, you'll kill him if you don't stop!

We throw our heads back, bellowing in anger and frustration.

I saw him brutalize you because he enjoyed inflicting pain! I could avenge your beating! I could avenge the suffering he caused to his spirit! He deserves it!

I thought we agreed on not peeking into the other's memory.

Moira raises an eyebrow. *This was an exception, my dear.*

I look down on the immobilized and whimpering man, with a pee stain running down his pants. He is not formidable or scary anymore. Whatever dominance he held over me is gone. He will never drown me in fear or in panic. He will never haunt my dreams.

Please don't kill him, Moira. Do not add his death to his spirit's suffering, staining our conscience.

"It's time you learn your lesson!" we growl from three heads. "Ground Rule number eleven: fight us at your own peril!"

CHAPTER 103

"You've won!" Callum shouts. At a gesture from Caderyn, he disengages the laser border of the fight circle. He comes to a stop before us.

The Teryns keep staring at our Cymmerion form, open-mouthed, though keeping their distance from us.

Don't worry, my dear, Callum does not look the least bit afraid of us, Moira says, reading my mind before I can realize my own thoughts.

We turn our three heads and stare at Caderyn.

The praelor narrows his eyes but does not look away.

He is a strong one, my dear. Better watch out for this one.

"You have brought back the Heart Amulet," Caderyn says, "and somehow managed to meld with someone—"

"—with the Queen of All Teryns!" we boom. *All Teryns?* I think to Moira, and she laughs. *Best to remind him of that fact.*

He grinds his teeth before adding, "with the queen. How were you able to do it without Guardian Goddess Laoise's help?"

We grin at Caderyn, showing off all our fangs. "It's our secret that we'll kill to protect."

Caderyn crosses his arms. "You are the true Teryn, aren't you?"

We just glower at him from three pairs of ravening eyes.

Caderyn sighs. "I give my permission to recruit my armada."

"And?" we ask.

A muscle jumps in Caderyn's jaw. "And I won't kill your friends."

"And?"

He says with a growl, "And we can discuss your Bride's Choice. Later!"

A discussion is not an outright no. I take it.

My friends cheer from the sideline. Glenna waves as she says, "I'm so proud of you!"

You can let go of the man now, Moira. It's over.

Moira snarls in my mind in answer, but we retract our stinger and move our tail back.

We growl down at the Executioner when he tries to get up.

I am not finished with him.

Moira, you promised you won't kill him!

Moira doesn't answer; instead she engages a thin thread of Lume. We lean down and kiss the greasy forehead of the Executioner with the eagle's beak.

The Executioner's body, like a wooden plank, rises, staying flat and horizontal, floating. An iridescent light bursts out of his body, guided by the magic thread.

The light lingers for a moment in front of us, in thanks. Then we guide it toward Lume, letting instinct take over.

"We are made of Lume. When we die, we return to Lume," we whisper from three heads as the spirit completes its final journey.

Moira smiles. *You didn't mind, did you?*

It's a bit late to ask, isn't it? I laugh. *But no, I didn't mind. I could feel that spirit's suffering, too. It was the right thing to do. If you or any of your people would like to move on as well, now is the time.*

Moira blinks. *You would let me go when you have my power in your control?*

I am not Laoise. I will not hold you or your people hostage. If I learned one thing from Caderyn on how to be a good leader, it is this—you cannot rule with an iron fist, forcing your will on others while ignoring their desires. You want to right your mistake? Now is your chance.

Moira ponders my words, then nods. *I will stay until this Era War is over. Can you help me talk to my people in the Spirit Realm?*

I grab another Lume thread, letting it connect with the Spirit Realm, which is suffused with my magic now. A gong resonates inside the realm, and I can feel all the spirits, shining with Lume magic, turn their attention toward the sky.

You may speak now, Moira.

Moira takes a deep breath and says, "I have ignored your pleas for a long time because I was drowning in my own guilt. I thought that the best way to correct my mistake. was to pressure you to move on. I see now that there are other resolutions. Any of you who wants to stay, I will not hold it against you. Those who wish to move on can do it now—just raise your arm."

A few hundreds of the million spirits raise an arm, most of them villagers I have not met.

I separate more Lume threads, weaving them into the Spirit Realm, connecting it to those who raised their arms.

From one blink to the next they turn into shimmering lights. I guide them through the border of the Spirit Realm, to Lume.

"We are made of Lume. When we die, we return to Lume," we say along with the spirits who stayed behind.

EPILOGUE

Sunlight breaks over the Savage Mountain Range the next morning, painting the bottom of the still-dark sky in a pinkish hue on the Teryn home world.

Many have gathered down at the Beware Hills to watch the presentation of the Teryn armada.

Dressed in black military uniforms, thousands and thousands of warriors line up, in neat and arranged squares, as far as I can see. A soft breeze picks up coral-red sand, twirling it around the warriors who stand, like well-armed statues, in the rising heat of the day.

"This is only those who are stationed on Teryn," Caderyn says proudly and leans on the railing of the raised wooden platform where we stand. "There are twelve hundred generals leading armadas like this, all over Galaxy Six. I did not recall them, so you just have to trust my word, little . . . uh, Sybil."

Sorcha smiles at Caderyn in approval. "I am sure the Sybil is impressed with your army."

"I am," I say. "It is beyond anything I could have imagined." I turn to Callum, who squeezes my hand, and then look at my grinning friends behind the praelor's family. We did it.

The Archgoddess of the Eternal Light and Order now has Her first army recruited for the Era War.

Mission accomplished.

ACKNOWLEDGEMENTS

I'm so excited to continue the journey of Lilla and show you, dear readers, what's next in store for her.

A lot of teamwork goes into creating a book. I would like to thank these wonderful individuals who helped bring this book to life:

Thank you, Matt, for the keeping up with the valiant effort of combating my bad eating habits. I always find new ways to challenge you.

Thank you, Leslie, for brainstorming and for your encouragement.

Thank you, Julie and William, for the amazing editing you both provided.

Thank you, Dan and Natasha, from NY Book Editors—it is such a pleasure to keep working with you.

Thank you, Ed and Don, the best PR guys in the whole Galaxy One.

Thank you, Melissa, the best office manager, and friend in the whole Galaxy Two.

Thank you, Clif, the best map illustrator in the whole Galaxy Three.

Thank you, Tim, the best cover artist extraordinaire in the whole Galaxy Four.

Thank you, Lukas, the best illustrator in the whole Galaxy Five.

Thank you, Ray and Abigail, the best web design wizards in the whole Galaxy Six.

Thank you, dear readers, for being the BEST READERS in the whole Seven Galaxies. It is not an easy job, but you are more than up for it. Congrats to you all!

Last but not least, thank you, God, for giving me the opportunity to live my dream.

Family—see the dedication page. (I love you but no need to be attention hogs.)

GLOSSARY

A

A'nima element
Nature magic.

Ankhar
Right hand, avatar, and general to the Archgod of Chaos and Destruction.

A'qua element
Water magic.

Archgoddess of the Eternal Light and Order
One of the ruling archgods. She is ageless and fights on the side of Light and Order in the Era War. Lilla is her Sybil. She is the mother of all Lumenians. Her acolyte is Aisla.

A'ris element
Air magic.

Arrov, Prince
Seventh son of Queen Amra. He is from A'ice. A great pilot. Very handsome, though at the moment he is experiencing some technical difficulties that involve lots and lots of light-blue fur.

B

Belthair
Six-armed ex-rebel who once was Lilla's boyfriend. Now he is an opinionated, I mean valuable ally.

Bride's Choice
An ancient Teryn tradition where a woman can claim a man as her intended, which Lilla did. On Callum.

C

Caderyn a'ruun
An imposing and large but fit older warrior who is the emperor of the Teryn empire. Callum's and Rhona's father. He has a well-established beard.

Callum a'ruun
Second general in the Teryn army. His clear blue eyes tend to glint with intellect in his tanned face. He always looks sharp and confident in his black, military-style uniform that emphasizes his muscular body. Lilla loves him.

compact travel sword, Teryn
Rhona's portable sword that fits into a black and rectangular box. Very handy.

consuasor, Teryn
A Teryn title meaning senator.

Cosmic-Web Propulsion, aka CWP
A Teryn technology that uses the cosmic-web like space highways for faster space travel. With the help of the beaked salamanders, the Teryns collect space particles, then filter them down to hydrogen atoms to slingshot to their destination, cutting down travel time to a few weeks as opposed to a few lifetimes. One side effect: it tends to push space debris ahead of them.

D

dark fiends
They are creations of the Archgod of Chaos and Destruction. They tend to be monstrous.

dark servants
They are creations of the Archgod of Chaos and Destruction. They don't like Lumenians or anything alive, to be honest.

Daryhna, herbalist
She is a hospitable healer.

devotee, Pada
Devotee is the second-highest rank among the Pada monks.

disciples, Pada
Lowest rank among the pada. They are not allowed to speak.

DLD
Shortened version of the Dark Lord of Destruction, a nickname the Archgod of Chaos and Destruction prefers to use. It does drive the point home, if I may say so.

E

elements, chaos
There are six chaos elements that are the domain of the Archgod of Chaos and Destruction—Murky A'qua, Black T'erra, Shadowy Fla'mma, Dusky A'ris, Rabid A'nima, and Acerbus.

elements, light
There are six light elements that are the domain of the Archgoddess of the Eternal Light and Order—A'ris, T'erra, A'qua, Fla'mma, A'nima, and Lume.

Era War
A devastating and recurring galactic war between the two ruling archgods that happens when the imbalance of power between them becomes too great. Like now.

Executioner, Teryn
His job is to execute.

F

Fearghas, battle horse
Lilla's powerful battle horse. He tends to bite or charge at you for no apparent reason.

fight circle, portable
Palm-size, round, and red device that can create a very useful shimmering yet transparent fight circle anywhere. It is highly customizable when it comes to its borders. Examples: three rows of daggers that point inward, five rows of horizontal laser lines, fire, etc.

Fla'mma, element
Fire magic, one of six light elements. Fun fact: can be formed into fireballs!

Fye Island, Uhna
A snow-covered island where once the Crystal Palace stood; half carved into the Piercing Mountains. Then DLD happened.

Fyoon Ocean, Uhna
Beautiful but deadly ocean that surrounds Fye Island.

251

G

Gigi
A benevolent woman.

Glenna, healer
Petite best friend of Lilla. Talented healer. Has beautiful dark crimson hair with white strands and dark crimson eyes.

Ground Rules, Teryn
Ten rules with fifty subrules and hundreds of addenda that are very important to the Teryn warriors.

H

honor, ideology
The Teryns always keep honor at the forefront.

***Hundred Fables of the Frail*, collection of stories**
Teryn literature at its best.

I

I loved writing this story. I hope you'll enjoy reading it! ☺

J

jokes, plenty
There are even more jokes in book 2!

K

k'bird
A manta ray-like bird that has a flat and round body covered in fur and a pair of feather-covered wings that are barely an arm length. Multiple forward-facing horns protrude from its narrow head. Eight spider legs are usually tucked under its belly when it's flying. They are great at flying and catching, especially in the Valleyball game.

k'bug, communicator
Teryn technology. It is a yellow, button-size insect that attaches to the back of the ear. The thin, long hairs on its leg resonate when pressed on its back, creating sound waves that can reach another bug "device" at far distances.

Keelan, artist
An artistic young man. He is great with the fiddle.

k'hawk
Wild, predatory bird that likes to eat twig-like insects.

k'hounds
Black-and-white colt-size Teryn dogs that have six legs and are good-natured.

k'mountain lion, elevator
A large Teryn animal with six powerful legs that are double jointed. They have two thin arms that end in a paw with seven long fingers. The Teryns attach wooden chairs-like contraptions to their backs so they can carry nonwarrior people up steep mountainsides.

k'tree, scrap food disposal
A huge and shabby-looking tree that is a disturbing cross between a tropical palm tree and a giant spider. They eat *everything*.

k'zoombug, cleaner
A small, round, and purple bug that scatters around the room, cleaning it like a vacuum.

L

Lady, The
It is the favored nickname of the Archgoddess of the Eternal Light and Order.

Laoise, Guardian Goddess
She is the Teryn guardian goddess. She speaks through the three Wise Women.

Lume, element
Powerful magic of light and energy.

Lumenians, legendary
A legendary race that the Archgoddess of the Eternal Light and Order created. There is only one left now: Lilla.

M

Marcas
He is a loyal man.

Moira
A powerful woman.

N

Nasty Beast
Fearghas's nickname.

O

Omnipower
An unknown power that governs the Seven Galaxies with balance in focus.

P

Pada, Galaxy Six
It is the name of the lush, green world and of the monk-like people who reside there. They are mysterious and highly magical. They are also the first world the Teryn Praelium conquered. Without a fight, I might add.

Praelia, Teryn
Title, meaning empress.

Praelium, Teryn
Name of the Teryn empire.

praelor, Teryn
Title, meaning emperor.

Q

Queen
There is one in the story. That's all I can say without spoiling anything. Sorry!

R

Ragnald, Elementalist Mage
A loyal friend of and ally to Lila. He is a two-hundred-year-old handsome mage who is expert in magic. He has triple elemental affinity in T'erra, Fla'mma, and A'qua elements. On occasion he is known to build stairs for himself out of rubble by using his T'erra magic.

Rhona a'ruun
She is a Teryn warrior woman who wants to be a general. She is also Callum's sister.

River of Death, Teryn
A wide river that flows lazily.

S

Senatus, Teryn
Teryn senators as a group.

Seven Galaxies
Where this story plays out. It has (you guessed it!) seven galaxies in it.

skeletal men, Teryn
They are emaciated, bald, and skeletal-looking men with light corral-red skin who are the attendants of the Wise Women.

Sorcha a'ruun
She is a Teryn warrior woman and empress. Mother of Callum and Rhona. She is a great hostess.

Steaphan, Consuasor
A young, handsome, and tanned Teryn man who is a senator.

Swordplay, game
A Teryn game wherein the players gather in an open stone-tiled area. It has two wooden frames at each end. Rushing through the open frame is the goal, but often the game breaks down into a brutal sword fight. The team with more players standing at the end is the winner.

Sybil
Right hand, avatar, and general to the Archgoddess of Eternal Light and Order. Lilla holds the honor of being the current one.

T

talisman, Sybil
A talisman that is finger-long, oval, and transparent. It is lodged into Lilla's spine with intricate gold filaments that are coming from a pair of crab-like claws at each end of the talisman.

Teague, Colonel
A Teryn colonel who has streaks of scarlet, white, and blond in his black hair that frames his tanned face. He constantly munches on something, while mischief glints in his dark brown eyes.

T'erra, element
Ground magic.

Teryn, Galaxy Six
Name of the planet and its people.

Turned mages
A corrupted magic user who is bent on destroying everyone and everything in their way. Blood-thirsty and ruthless.

Twins, Isa and Bella
Isa and Bella are twin princesses from Barabal. They are great hackers and friends of Lilla.

tyger leaves
Long and oval-shaped with light stripes on them, visible as the sunlight shines on them. They are easy to manipulate and shape into items or even into clothing.

U

Uhna, Galaxy Five
The oceanic home world of Lilla. Name of the planet and its people.

Umbrea portal
It is a shadow portal that can be opened via an ancient-looking leather gauntlet. Belthair has one such gauntlet.

V

Valleyball, Teryn game

A game of strategy and tactics the Teryn warriors play. The goal is to knock off more players from their flying k'bird into the gaping valley below. Hence the name Valleyball.

W

warship, Teryn

A tremendous black and rectangular ship. Its size is so massive it could easily double for a small city. Its jagged surface is covered with world-erasing cannons, space missiles, and energy-shield piercing arrays. In other words, very dangerous.

"Weak, Wimp, and the Wuss" anecdote

An anecdote from *Hundred Fables of the Frail*, a cautionary tale of redemption and trying to earn oneself honor.

Wise Women, Teryn

Three black-haired and young women who are the vessels for the Teryn Guardian Goddess Laoise.

X

Ex, like ex-rebel or ex-girlfriend/boyfriend. Both can be found in this book.

Y

A letter in the ABC. Also, short for why.

Z

Zimon, Devotee

Dark-haired Pada monk, dressed in a red robe with A'nima yellow and A'ris blue sashes on its front.

Zorion, Devotee

He is the leader pada monk with rune-like tattoos on his right cheek. He wears a dark blue ceremonial robe with a silver ruffled cape. He has two sashes that run down in the front of his chest; one is A'ris blue the other is Fl'amma red.

AWARDS

2020 New York Book Festival
Winner: Romance
Honorable Mention: Science Fiction
http://www.newyorkbookfestival.com/

2020 San Francisco Book Festival
Winner: Science Fiction
http://www.sanfranciscobookfestival.com/winners_2020.htm

2020 Annual Best Book Awards
Winner: Best Cover for Fiction
http://www.americanbookfest.com/2020bbapressrelease.html

2020 New England Book Festival
Winner: Science Fiction
Honorable Mention: General Fiction
http://www.newenglandbookfestivals.com

2021 Independent Press Award
Distinguished Favorite: Fantasy
https://www.independentpressaward.com/
2021distinguishedfavorites

2021 Independent Author Network
Finalist: First Novel, Fiction: Science Fiction
https://www.independentauthornetwork.com/
2021-botya-winners.html

2021 eLit Awards
Winner: Science Fiction/Fantasy
Winner: Romance
Winner: Book website for fiction
https://www.elitawards.com/2021_results.php

2021 Eric Hoffer Award - First Horizon Award
Finalist
http://www.hofferaward.com/First-Horizon-Award-finalists.
html#.YIxlnmZKheg

2021 Eric Hoffer Award - Da Vinci Eye Award
Finalist
http://www.hofferaward.com/da-Vinci-Eye-finalists.html#.
YIxl5GZKheg

2021 Eric Hoffer Award - Grand Prize
Short List
http://www.hofferaward.com/Eric-Hoffer-Award-grand-prize-
short-list.html#.YKRCAH1KgeY

2021 Eric Hoffer Award
Honorable mention: Science Fiction/Fantasy
http://www.hofferaward.com/Eric-Hoffer-Award-winners.
html#sci-fi

2021 Speak Up Radio Firebird Award
Winner: Cover Design for fiction
https://www.speakuptalkradio.com/july-2021-winners/
https://www.speakuptalkradio.com/author-s-g-blaise/

2021 Readers Favorite Book Award
Romance - Fantasy/Sci-fi
https://bookawards.com/book-award/the-last-lumenian

2021 Los Angeles Book Festival
Runner-Up: Romance and
Honorable Mention: Science Fiction
http://losangelesbookfestival.com

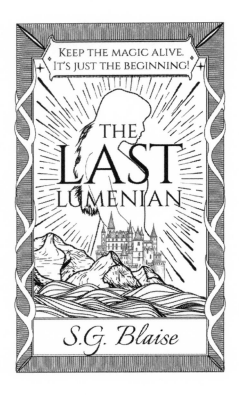

🐦 @SGBlaiseAuthor
f /thelastlumenian
📷 sgblaiseofficial

www.sgblaise.com

Made in United States
Orlando, FL
11 April 2022

16697459R00159